The Ancestor
Virginia L. Lewis

Library Cat

Also by Virginia L. Lewis

Future Titles

Romance at the Fiber Guild Series
II L'enfant terrible
III The Way Forward
IV The Spinning Wheel Maker
V Universal Design
VI Knitting While Blind
VII No Room for Grief
VIII The Mentor

Past Title

Schön Kästnerisch verfahren

Visit VirginiaLLewisAuthor.com

Library Cat Publishing, Aberdeen SD 57401

For rights and permissions, please contact:

Virginia L. Lewis
librarycat@midco.net

Cover design by Rhonda May

Contents

For my children, without whose inspiration it would be impossible for me to write the fiction I do.

1

The Newcomer

IT WAS A COOL October afternoon in Prairie Plains, when a youthful stranger made his way out of the dust-driving wind and into the cozy yarn shop, pushing the door shut with his brawny shoulder. Tabitha Howell almost dropped a stitch in the shawl she was knitting, while the flaxen-haired woman seated beside her, fellow fiber guild member Fran Zumbaum, abruptly stopped talking about her latest finished object, and looked up from her Saxony-style spinning wheel as if the scarecrow adorning the stoop outside had suddenly come to life. And Ms. Dee, elder statesman of the guild and one of its founding partners, stared dumbfounded at the rugged youth through her pink-framed trifocals, betraying her very advanced age.

Who is that guy, Dr. Howell asked herself, *and what is he doing at our monthly Flatlands Fiber Guild meeting?*

Whoever he was, allowing their surprise to override the exigencies of common courtesy was hardly acceptable. Shoving a few stray beaded box braids back over her shoulder, Tabitha broke the curious spell that had fallen on this matronly coven, and moved to greet the newcomer as someone who—potentially, at least—might belong there. He certainly seemed to think he was in the right place, even if his heritage boots and raw denim jeans suggested otherwise: he scanned the cubbies and baskets overflowing with yarn, and smiled as though he were in his happy place.

But the moment Tabitha opened her mouth, he beat her to the punch, even addressing her by name: "Dr. Howell! Oh my gosh!"

Dr. Howell did not know this kid, who looked like a castaway swept in from somewhere off the grid, from Adam. But it frankly didn't surprise her that *he* recognized *her*. After all, she was the only Black professor at the local university, having been snatched up by the otherwise all-white-male history department, thanks to an anonymous endowment that was so generous, she would have been an idiot to turn it down. As of three-plus years ago, American history was being taught at Great Plains University from something besides a firmly white male perspective. Could this collegiate whelp have been in her class?

"Do we know each other, son?"

"Sorry, Professor. I'm Jeff." He approached the group with tentative steps, his eyes grazing many a colorful skein of wool along the way. "Jeff Nietmann. My roommate took your class. He told me a lot about it."

I bet he did, the cynic inside Tabitha interjected silently. "All good, of course?"

Jeff smiled broadly. "Most of it."

Tabitha suppressed her urge to follow up with a snarky retort as she asked herself what this rugged male could possibly want in the midst of their estrogen-laden séance of spinning, knitting, and tea-drinking, this rare refuge from the trials of her home life. As she took in his nervous gaze and fidgety hands, she acknowledged that the kid looked lonely. He was by himself, after all, and may well be in need of companionship. *Urgent* need—otherwise, why would a twenty-year-old man be here in this room full of middle-aged yarnies?

She exhaled with relief when her colleague and best friend, Norwegian fiber goddess Astrid Karlsen, whose natural locks were as blonde as her own were black, piped up with a cheerful invitation for the newcomer to join them. That drew a gasp from Fran, her inability to embrace the arrival of this denim-clad dude in their wooly coven written on her wrinkled brow.

"Thanks. I hope I'm not intruding." The newcomer continued inspecting the warm-hued, wool-filled space, known outwardly as "Dee's Yarn & Fiber Emporium," and bursting with an array of yarn, fiber, handmade goods, crafting accessories, spinning wheels, and books, with a charismatic smile. At the very least, the whelp had donned a most appropriate beanie, worked with skillful colorwork technique, in spite of the garish neon colors used.

As Jeff made his way to the table, Valerie Dittendorf, Ms. Dee's granddaughter and co-owner of the shop where they were gathered, leaned in toward Tabitha, peering over her half-frame reading glasses, and whispered: "There's no way he knitted that."

"Why don't you ask him?" Tabitha whispered back.

The youngest woman among them proved the strongest magnet for the unlikely visitor. Known in her own words as "Nurse Brenda" by day and "MOM!!!" by night, Brenda Wurth had just learned how to spin, and sat proudly in her western-style blouse, honing her skills on the thousand-dollar wheel she'd recently purchased. "Come have a seat." She beckoned the athletic-looking crasher, noisily patting the empty chair beside her.

Jeff set a felted bag on the table and followed Brenda's cue. "Thanks. My marketing professor told me about this group. He thought I might enjoy it."

Half a dozen eyebrows were raised in contemplation of this notion, while Tabitha, the idea of the lonesome student's fitting in here growing on her, said: "Of course, Dannie. Professor Novak's wife, right?"

"Right." Jeff's shoulders relaxed as the ice began to break.

"Yes, Daniela's a regular here. I think they're at a conference this weekend."

"That's right. Dr. Novak said you only meet once a month. So if I was interested, I should strike while the iron is hot." His broad smile lit up the room.

"So, tell us about yourself—Jeff, is it?" Fran addressed him in her gentle librarian's voice. She resumed her work, rhythmically spinning the blend of wool and alpaca she'd snapped up at the fiber festival in August.

"OK, well, I'm Jeff." He chuckled nervously. "And I like to knit!"

But why? Tabitha asked herself, as though this David of the college set were intruding on their womanly territory of knitting and crocheting. Then she recalled the previous man who'd been a member of the group, and wondered what had become of him. "I find myself reminded of Manuel. Do you all remember him?"

"Of course," Valerie said. "He's up in Fargo now."

Fran glanced Valerie's way. "Isn't he the one who had a baby?"

"Right. It was in the paper and everything."

"The first male to give birth in Prairie Plains!" Brenda exclaimed.

Jeff knit his brow. "Is he trans or something?"

"That's right." Thanks to her experience with trans youth at the high school, Brenda had cultivated a useful appreciation of the challenges they often faced, something Tabitha appreciated about her. "Apparently, he didn't transition all the way."

"I think we're trying to determine whether you're the first male who's been a part of our group or not," Fran explained.

Astrid flashed a playful smile. "Let's just agree to say 'no,' but with a little room for doubt."

"Did you knit your hat?" Finally, Valerie took up Tabitha's hint.

Jeff nodded as his green eyes roamed to Valerie's own work in progress, a Fair Isle cowl in muted colors: olives, grays, and burgundies—a far cry from the neon green, orange, and turquoise of his own cap.

Well, that was a start. But Tabitha knew Valerie well enough to be certain that, when she smelled a potential customer, she would pursue every angle to market her wares. Of course, she did: "What pattern did you use? It's so...so flamboyant!"

Astrid nodded in agreement.

"Oh, thanks. I just made it up as I went along." Jeff opened his felted bag and reached inside, unearthing a work-in-progress to knit on during his unanticipated visit.

Astrid's brilliant blue eyes focused on him like lasers, while Valerie studied his knitting with interest.

"Tell us about your process," Tabitha invited him.

"Oh. Well, it's all about the math, right?" Jeff shifted nervously in his chair. "And of course about the color. I mean, you start with a DK or a worsted or whatever you want, and just do the math—eighty stitches in the round, say, two-by-two rib for a couple of inches, then just pick out some colorwork motifs, and there ya go!"

Fran's jaw dropped. It was perfectly understandable—Tabitha was convinced not a single one of them had ever heard a man, a twenty-something dressed in cuffed jeans and leather boots no less, talk so confidently about knitting a colorwork piece. "Amazing!"

"I dunno," Brenda piped up. "Sounds pretty straightforward to me."

"Yeah," Jeff agreed, flashing those sparkling, white teeth at them again. He doffed his cap, offering to share it with anyone who cared to admire it more closely, and exposed a well-mannered mop of wavy brown hair that gave his eyes an olive tinge.

"God, he's cute," Fran mouthed, causing Tabitha to make a face—he must be less than half her age.

As the newcomer settled back in his chair, he unrolled the half-made sock he'd retrieved from his project bag, its vibrant colors similar to those of the beanie he'd handed to Brenda for her to inspect.

Tabitha observed him as the WIP's shape became evident. "Is that intended to go with your hat?"

A non-committal nod prefaced his response. "More or less. I guess I kinda do like the bright colors." His inviting smile served as a reminder that this abrupt intrusion of testosterone into their matriarchal midst had surprised them into a lapse in their usual hospitality.

Valerie stepped into the breach. "Would you like some tea, Jeff?"

But why in the heck would a young man who was more suited to energy drinks and espresso shots be remotely interested in a cup of hot tea? "Don't we have any Monster on hand?" Tabitha asked tongue-in-cheek.

Jeff released a chuckle. "Tea's fine."

Brenda offered to get it for him. She looped the silky yarn she was spinning around her wheel's orifice hook, and got up with a show of eagerness to serve their visitor, whose handknit cap was well on its way around the circle.

"Thanks, Brenda."

"Black, green, herbal?"

"Uh, maybe green. It's healthy." He quirked a lopsided smile.

"Green it is."

"So Jeff, what do you study at the university?" Astrid asked, breaking the silence that had attended her remarkably intent observation of the visitor. Tabitha couldn't help wondering whether she was assessing his suitability as someone she ought to introduce to her nineteen-year-old daughter. She knew Sigrun was still unattached. Her own daughter was as well—at least, she assumed so. Tabitha hadn't spoken to Laurel in a good two years.

"Business," he replied.

"I see. And do you enjoy it?"

He shrugged his shoulders. "Well enough, I guess." He aligned the double-pointed needles attached to his colorful sock and started knitting.

"Dpn's," Astrid remarked. "A traditionalist."

Jeff smiled. "It's what I learned on."

Tabitha was impressed. This youthful adonis really knew what he was doing as a knitter. She decided to test his knowledge further: "What kind of heel are you going to make?"

"Actually, I'm trying an afterthought heel."

She smiled in amazement. Next thing you knew, this fuzz-faced dish would be talking like a granny about gussets, moss stitch, and Turkish cast-on. In what world did afterthought heels mesh with heritage boots that rightfully belonged in a forest full of antlered bucks?

"So, we were just doing our show-and-tell, Jeff," Valerie explained.

"No kidding. Sorry I was late—I took a wrong turn on my way here. What'd I miss?" He glanced around, and his face lit up as his eyes fell on so much luxurious wool being transformed into this or that object around the room. Ms. Dee was chain-plying some natural gray fiber gathered from one of her own sheep. Tabitha admired how Bonnie still raised a few Gotlands at her farm, in spite of her age. And Astrid was knitting yet another sock for someone in her family—not a single Karlsen ever donned a store-bought sock.

And what was Tabitha knitting? A shawl, of course. Just like her mother and grandmother had knit before her. This one challenged her with its intricate lace pattern in deep orange alpaca blended with cashmere.

Jeff eyed her work with arched brow. "Are you knitting that for yourself, Professor?"

"That's a good question, Jeff. I'm not sure there are enough days in the year for me to wear all the shawls I've knit. So let's just say, I'm knitting it for my *collection*." She conveyed her contentment with a smile, hoping the business student would look beyond her reputation for academic rigor and stubborn refusal to cut second-rate students any slack, and embrace her as a fellow knitter.

"Watching you reminds me of watching my grand-mother knit. You do beautiful work."

"Why thank you, young man. That's very kind."

Astrid interrupted their exchange. "Well, never mind about us. What about you? We'd love to know more about the projects you're working on." Her blue-eyed gaze seemed to challenge their guest to conjure up something more worthy than a colorwork hat of their big-league fiber show and tell.

"Me?" Jeff returned the expectant looks aimed at him from around the table. "Well..." He set down his knitting and grabbed at the waist of the sweater he wore, pulling it straight so the women could better appreciate it. "How about this?"

Brenda was in the best position to get a good look at the cabled pullover. "You made *that*?" she asked, her mouth agape.

Well, why not? This *child* was clearly some kind of knitting genius, Tabitha realized. There was little point in ignoring his obvious prowess as a crafter of woolen garments.

Jeff nodded assertively.

"That's crazy!" Brenda exclaimed. "Valerie, isn't that crazy?"

Valerie lowered her reading glasses and stared wide-eyed at Jeff's black sweater. They all knew how hard it was to knit anything black, much less something with all those beautifully executed cables. "Must've taken you a good while to finish!"

Jeff resumed work stitching his sock. "I started it when I was fourteen. Knitting such a dark color is no walk in the park—it's almost impossible to distinguish the stitches from their shadows. But I just had to make it. I finally finished it my senior year in high school. Won a purple ribbon at the county fair!"

"I bet it did!"

"Now, ladies, this isn't such a rare miracle," Astrid told the group, her accent peeking through her words. "In Norway, lots of boys learn how to knit. My own son is a very capable knitter. You don't need to embarrass poor Jeff here."

He aimed a smile at her. "It's no problem, Professor Karlsen. I'm used to it. I'm just glad not to have to knit all by myself for once. My roommate thinks I'm a little weird." He chuckled.

"What about your girlfriend?" The instant Brenda asked that, several pairs of eyes zoomed in on her. It seemed the one question on everyone's mind: was Jeff *really* that rare instance of a straight male knitter that was about as common as a four-leaf clover in the desert?

"Don't have one."

He didn't have one. Fine. But that didn't mean he wasn't *looking* for one. Tabitha thought of her own estranged daughter, and came dangerously close to suggesting that knitting would be a great way to win over a girl, when she realized she was just as clueless regarding Jeff Nietmann's sexual orientation as everyone else. She wasn't about to burden him with her uninformed assumptions. Instead, she reassured him: "Knitting is hardly restricted to the fairer sex. Just tell your roommate Ryan Gosling knits with the best of them. That should shut him up for a bit."

"Believe me, I did. It helped...a little." That irresistible smile returned. Tabitha had to admit, whoever was lucky enough to enjoy Jeff's smile day in and day out, be they female, male, or whatever, would truly be favored by the fortune of romance.

"Well, I for one would love to know more about how you managed to knit that handsome sweater," Valerie prodded him. "Where did you get the pattern? And what about the yarn you chose?"

Jeff's eyes lit up. "It's a wool-cashmere blend. My parents bought the yarn for my fourteenth birthday—it cost a pretty penny. I found the pattern in a magazine my grandma had. She's the one who taught me to knit."

"That's so sweet!" Brenda gushed. "She must be so proud of you!"

Jeff nodded. "She is, actually. We're very close. She's an amazing knitter. She taught me how to make the cables and everything."

Valerie's smile was huge. "I love that!"

Astrid agreed. "It really is impressive. So Brenda, what about you? Something to show and tell?"

"Not after that!"

"Don't let him steal your thunder," Valerie pronounced. It was she who'd taught Brenda to spin over the summer—their lessons together had been fodder for more than a few conversations among the guild members. "It looks like you're making great progress there."

"Well, maybe." Brenda reached into her bag and pulled out a bobbin of handspun. She passed it to Jeff, who studied it at length.

"My grandma wants me to learn to spin. But what with all my studies and everything, I don't have time."

"That's because you're too busy knitting, Jeff." Tabitha wasn't a spinner either—there were only so many hours in the day.

Jeff flashed that now familiar smile. "This is spun beautifully, Brenda! I've heard all about the art yarn and such, and this is definitely not art yarn."

"Thanks, Jeff. I appreciate it."

Valerie seconded that. "He's right. You're doing great, Brenda. Jeff, we're really glad you came today."

"I'm glad I did, too." His pink cheeks and fuzzy dimples warmed Tabitha's heart. He passed the bobbin on to Valerie, removed the tea bag from his cup, and took a big swig of unadulterated green tea. "Healthy," he quipped, surveying the matriarchal group of fiber enthusiasts with a smile.

2

The YouTuber

"THIS PROJECT WILL BE worth one hundred points out of a thousand toward your final grade, so I advise you to take it seriously," Dr. Novak told the class of twenty or so advanced marketing students. He surveyed them with a stern gaze, followed by an encouraging smile.

Jeff appreciated the smile. This was one of his more enjoyable classes. He made a habit of sitting in the back of Novak's room. Marketing was an important subject for him, but as a serial knitter, he preferred not to distract his fellow students with his addiction.

He kept several small projects going at a time, choosing whichever best fit the environment where he happened to be knitting. Some were beanies, but most were socks in various stages of development, his "flying under the radar" projects. That's what he was knitting now, a sock. And sticking to muted colors made his suspect activity less obtrusive. As he listened to Novak wrap up his discussion of the "Marketing Improvement Project" he'd assigned, Jeff's eyes were trained on calming blue-and-gray sock yarn.

Admittedly, he could be training them on some cute girl or other. It wasn't like the class was devoid of eye candy—other dudes were finding plenty. And a few were even looking at the professor, making a show of the respect they thought earning a good grade demanded of them. No, Jeff was fine looking at his sock as it grew on the four wooden needles. Just fine. He'd feasted his eyes on a girl back in high school. A real beauty. A Native girl he'd adored. But he'd messed things up, stuck his foot in it, come off as racist and insensitive, when that was the last thing he'd meant to do.

Yarn made Jeff feel secure. It wouldn't walk away because he'd slipped up, dropped a stitch, had to frog a row. Thus his addiction.

Novak pushed his black-rimmed glasses back up on his nose yet again. "Of course if you need anything from me, you know what to do."

Yup! Jeff knew what to do. He knew why he was here. His future lay in wool: he would follow in his grandparents' footsteps and own a yarn business. And he'd have to market that yarn. That's why he'd signed up for this class, and all the other classes he was taking for his entrepreneurship degree. 'Cause that yarn wouldn't sell itself.

He packed up his knitting and his laptop as the students started making their way out of the room.

"Hey, Knitwit!" a classmate called him from a few seats away. "What time are we going?"

Jeff looked over and smiled. Colin Milliman had lived down the hall from him freshman year. He'd decided Jeff's quirky addiction to turning yarn into clothing just made him that much more interesting. And his ideas for turning that addiction into a profitable business served Colin as proof that Jeff was, in words that brought the color to his cheeks, "quite possibly a marketing genius."

Those ideas involved YouTube, and rural outposts, and the surprising entertainment value of knitting that Jeff was quickly capitalizing on, just as a good entrepreneur should.

"Let's shoot for 3 p.m. Does that work?"

That elicited a thumbs up. "Perfect!"

Jeff joined his bushy-haired companion and they made their way toward the front of the room, where Dr. Novak's bespectacled eyes met his own. "How'd you like the guild ladies, Jeff?"

He released a chuckle. "It was awesome. They were really nice. Thanks for suggesting I give 'em a try. I couldn't think of a better social outlet, personally."

"So, do ya think you'll go back?"

"I do. I have yet to meet any knitters I don't like. Oh, and would it be all right for me to do my project on the Humane Society? I was checking out their marketing campaign, and I think I could come up with some good ideas for them to improve it."

"Contact them, copy me, and let me know if they're game. I'm game if the Humane Society is."

"Great, Professor. See you on Wednesday."

"See you then, Jeff."

He met up with Colin at the student dorm parking lot that afternoon, where another college chum, Freeman Brown, joined them.

Colin had followed Jeff's advice and put on some jeans to protect his legs from the brambles they were likely to encounter on their trek. He had his Weimaraner along. "You don't mind if we take him in your truck, do ya, Jeff?"

"That's fine. Come on, Hugo, up ya go!" The sleek young dog jumped into the back seat like it had been reserved just for him.

Jeff cued up Google Maps, and the boys started out for the skeleton of an old prairie house he'd spotted on his way back to campus in August. He figured the dilapidated structure would make the perfect backdrop for his next "Extreme Knitting" video, the third in a series he hoped would popularize the rewarding craft among young men like himself. Jeff harbored no illusions about the uphill climb his mission entailed. But he'd convinced himself there was a huge untapped market of potential knitters out there, "rugged males" active in everything from ice fishing to mountain biking, who might just benefit from knitting their own accessories to support their outdoor lifestyle.

When he'd shared with Colin that he would bill himself as "Knitmann" from his last name, "Nietmann," and film "Extreme Knitting" videos to build his brand, Colin had surprised Jeff by insisting he should be involved.

"Really? Why?"

"Well, I need the experience. And besides, if you can sell dudes on knitting, then you can sell anyone on any-thing. I've gotta see this!"

Plus, Colin had taken a couple film production courses for his communication minor. So they agreed he could do the filming for a modest share of any profits they took in from YouTube.

To Jeff's amazement, the gamble was paying off, per-haps in part because of the risks they were taking, tres-passing on private properties that happened to appear abandoned. "Knitwit," Colin reported with huge eyes as they sat in his truck, "I checked today, and you've already got 5,052 followers just from our first two videos. Way ta go, dude!"

"Marketing genius at work!" Jeff pronounced with a smile.

Freeman Brown released a "Woot! Woot!" and engaged in his own private round of applause. As the energetic sidekick who appeared alongside Jeff as they undertook their less-than-lawful adventures on film, his role in selling their message was key. Not that he had any intention of becoming a knitter, the St. Louis native had made that painfully clear. The day Fik-Shun took up knitting—he happened to be Freeman's role model—was the day he'd reconsider.

But the "rurex" part of their game had him hooked. Exploring those architectural skeletons forsaken by the pioneers who'd built them excited his obsession with history, an obsession he shared with Jeff, and gamboling around the ruins satisfied his hip-hop proclivities. Plus, Freeman was an awesome friend. And as Jeff's parents pointed out on a regular basis, he could stand to cultivate more of those.

After a half-hour drive out of Prairie Plains in Jeff's rust-scarred pickup, they parked on the roadside near a small power station. From there, the trio hiked beneath drifting clouds along a gravel road lined by maples and Siberian elms—these would soon sacrifice their leaves to the cold. The distant calls of red-winged blackbirds sounded from a slough off to the north. Their reedy "Conk-la-rees!" stirred Jeff's soul.

After a good hundred yards, they sighted a small, wood-framed house that looked like it had ceded its

place more than a century ago to the larger residen-
tial structure—they must conceal their trespassing from
whoever lived there—visible across the recently-har-
vested soybean field. It looked just as it had back in August, only the surrounding foliage was now yellow instead of green. Autumn was well underway, and Jeff took
a deep, restorative breath.

"Time ta load'er up?" Freeman asked.

"Yup!"

Colin let Hugo out of the truck and unpacked his camera. He helped Jeff and Freeman with their mics, and Jeff
positioned his project bag over his shoulder. Today's knit
was a ribbed cap, the yarn an alpaca blend of variegated
black and gray. With any luck, it would stand out just
enough against the light browns and grays of the dilapidated house to show up well in the film.

After all, entertainment was key, that's how this kind
of marketing was supposed to work: its effectiveness lay
in how it didn't come across as marketing. It was all
about suggestion. Jeff reasoned he had only to gamify
his knitting, to push it into the realm of competition, in
order to sell viewers on his "rugged knitter" philosophy.
He'd show them how far along he was on his project
when they set out, then knit as much as his fingers could
stand while he and his pals trekked about the object
of their exploration. At the end of the video, he'd show
off his progress, inviting his audience to marvel at how
much he'd accomplished. So far, the trick had worked
well—5,052 subscribers was nothing to sneeze at!

Involving Freeman had been a stroke of genius. When
he'd first thought up the video series idea, Jeff had intended to do like he always did, and fly solo. But he'd

seen Freeman perform in a hip-hop routine during GPU's back-to-campus festivities. How cool would it be, he'd thought to himself, to involve this electric personality, with his corn rows and leather basketball shoes, in his rurex film adventures?

Fortunately for Jeff, Freeman had come back with how cool it would be for him to accompany the quirky male knitter who "rocked those woolly beanies like some kinda Irish fisherman," as he threatened to fall through rotting floors and stumble over broken beams in ruined barns and wrecked outbuildings. For both, the answer had been clear: pretty fucking cool! So yeah, they'd gone and joined forces.

Jeff positioned himself outside the entrance—well, it seemed like the most likely candidate for an entrance, it had a hole about the size of a door, and was framed by jagged shards of presumed boards—to the derelict structure. "OK, guys, let'er rip!"

Colin followed his cue. "Three, two, one, you're on!"

The filming began.

"Hey, fiber fans!" Jeff backed his way across the neglected terrain with Hugo the Weimaraner loping alongside him—perhaps he wanted to keep Jeff from stumbling. "Today, we're checking out a venerable old house that looks a lot like something my three-times great-grandparents could have lived in when they first found themselves plunked onto the Great Plains of North America after leaving the Russian Empire."

Jeff held up the unfinished hat that would accompany him as they explored what he asserted was inches away from being a forgotten pile of rubble he and his pals were rescuing from permanent oblivion by filming this record of its doomed existence. After prompting Colin to zero in on his luxurious alpaca fabric in its natural hues, Jeff led the way inside, as Freeman assured their audience their fearless leader would beat his previous record with regard to how many rows he knit while they scoped out the ramshackle domicile.

Careful not to cause any more damage than had already been done to the house by age and the elements, Jeff knit like a beast while climbing over busted-up floorboards and navigating around cobwebs and defunct wasp nests. They all chipped in with comments regarding who'd most likely lived here when, what their lives had been like, what had happened to the ruin since, and the shards of beauty and wonder still clinging to the dusty wreck. The house was small, barely six hundred square feet; their exploration took well under an hour. But they milked it for all it was worth, drawing viewers' attention to every possible detail of interest—a doorknob here, stone hearth there, even a broken bottle or two, evidence of possible squatters after the house had been abandoned by its owners.

When they were done, Jeff had Colin aim his camera at the beanie he'd been knitting.

"Fourteen rows!" Freeman announced. "Great job, dude!" He fingered the knitting with a broad smile. "This one's for me, right?"

Uhh, no, that's not exactly what Jeff had had in mind. Colin trained his lens on him, documenting his hemming and hawing.

Well, what of it? Freeman was his friend, and Jeff appreciated him. "You bet. My dad can have the next one. I promise, Dad!" Jeff looked into Colin's camera with a grin. "But ya might have to send me a little more yarn."

Colin and Freeman's laughter punctured the air.

"Tune in next time as we explore an old abandoned church on the prairie," Jeff concluded. "Don't forget to like and subscribe, and leave a comment about your own latest extreme knitting adventure."

"Cut!" Freeman hollered into the camera, nearly causing Colin to fall over. They all laughed.

Then they exited the house, looking around to make sure no one had caught onto their illicit activity. They made their way back to Jeff's truck, taking in the pungent autumn air and congratulating themselves on a successful trek, while Hugo aimed his snout at every relic that could provide some clue as to the previous canines who'd staked their claim on this territory.

Editing and cutting the video was Colin's job. The minute they arrived back on campus, he promised he'd get right on it and have the video uploaded before the day ended.

The next morning, Jeff followed Dr. Novak's advice and contacted the Prairie Plains Humane Society. The marketing improvement project he had in mind would give him a nice opportunity to get involved in animal welfare. Pets had always been important in his life. He missed the family cat and his Gordon setter, Fritz.

When Jeff learned the shelter welcomed the chance to work with him, he was on cloud nine. He made an appointment to meet with the staff the following Monday before class. After discovering a group of like-minded people at the Flatlands Fiber Guild, Jeff might just unearth yet more like-minded people at the Humane Society. Combatting his lonely ways and growing his circle of friends could only be a good thing. Who knew what might come of his involvement at the shelter?

3

The Daughter

THE MOMENT JEFF ENTERED the homey yarn shop to attend the November meeting of the Flatlands Fiber Guild, the very motherly Brenda Wurth expressed her approval: "Oh, good! You came back!"

Yes, Jeff did come back. His social outlets were few and far between. These women might not share his youth and love of the outdoors, but they shared his obsession with yarn—he figured that was as good a foundation as any for a useful rapport.

"Oh, Brenda, surely we're not *that* disagreeable." That was Valerie Dittendorf—Jeff recalled her reading glasses and frizzy hair, as well as her speed-demon approach to knitting colorwork.

Brenda eyed Jeff with a smile as he came into the gathering area. "I know. But we're a bunch of women, most of whom could be his mother, or even his grandmother."

Bonnie Dittendorf chuckled. At her advanced age, great-grandmother was more like it. "He strikes me as the kind of boy who gets along with his mother. If he likes her, he'll probably like us." Her sparkling eyes met Jeff's as he looked around for a seat.

"Well, you seem to come from pretty good stock." Finally, someone addressed the object of their gossip directly. "I'm certain you have a very likeable mother. And father, too." Astrid's words seemed intended not so much for Jeff, as for the blonde beside her, whom she quickly introduced as her daughter, Sigrun. "She was a little hesitant to join us today." The comment turned Sigrun's face red. "Something about seeing friends at the park, going for a jog, stopping for ice cream..." She aimed a playful gaze at the girl.

"Oh, Mother..."

"What? I thought you might be interested in meeting a fellow student who just happens to be gifted at knitting."

Sigrun scowled, making for quite the first impression. "Or, I might be interested in getting out of the house while avoiding getting rained on."

"Oh. So coming here had nothing to do with the fact that our boring *women's* guild has been joined by a good-looking college man."

Sigrun grazed Jeff impudently with her piercing blue eyes. "Well, you can never have too many friends, even if it's just a guy with a nerdy infatuation with wool."

Jeff removed his beanie and shook a few raindrops from it. The girl's attitude didn't especially bother him—it wasn't like he was on the prowl, after all.

"Where's your umbrella?" Fran asked him.

He greeted that with a broad smile. "I'm wearing wool. Who needs an umbrella?" Icelandic wool, to be specific—impervious to the elements and satisfyingly durable, thus one of his favorites. "I lucked into this yarn at a thrift store and decided it should be turned into a sweater like the ones they wear when they round up the sheep in Iceland." He hoped the guild members would admire his woolen masterpiece, with its bold, geometric-patterned yoke he'd knit up in royal blue, grass green, pale green, and white lopi.

Sigrun's eyes hovered over his creation just long enough for Jeff to conclude she was impressed, as Astrid looked on with a smile. Not the first time a girl's mother had attempted to interest her in him. But as this girl's mother was someone whose respect Jeff sought to cultivate, he felt the need to tread carefully.

Brenda beckoned him. "We're so glad to have you join us again. I saved you a chair. Should I get you a nice hot cup of green tea?"

Jeff laughed. "Sure, I'd like that. Gotta stay healthy." He was touched by Brenda's care, and grateful for the warm welcome that embraced him in this space, sheltering him from the inhospitable weather outside. As he took his seat, he noticed two guild members who'd missed the October meeting. He recognized his marketing professor's wife, Dannie Novak. And a gray-haired woman in a gingham shirt was crocheting a stuffed animal—a hedgehog, or maybe a porcupine, very cute. "Did I make it in time for show-and-tell?"

"Of course," Valerie assured him. "My grandmother has been weaving some handspun into a table runner for her grandniece. That's just about to make its way around."

As Dr. Howell whisked her way into the circle and settled herself at the table, Ms. Dee took her granddaughter's cue and retrieved a striped runner perfectly suited for display beneath a festive Christmas spread. Snowy-white strips set off the deep greens and saturated reds. Jeff pictured an assortment of pies and cookies emitting enticing aromas of Yuletide as they sat on the exquisite piece. Christmas wasn't so far off—he was look-ing forward to it.

The guild members took turns sharing their projects. Dannie was trying her hand at double-knitting with a floral scarf, and Brenda passed around her first two-ply handspun.

As he knit mechanically on a forest green sweater des-tined for his sister, Jeff noticed Sigrun's baby blues rest-ing on him with uncomfortable frequency as the showing and telling proceeded. And when it came his time to share a project, he grew tingly all over. He'd been raised to respect his elders—clamoring for their attention like a spoiled child was hardly appropriate. But as he contem-plated the girl seated across from him, her self-satisfied face framed by blonde tresses and set upon a neck that would do the loveliest ballerina proud, he realized she was actually quite the looker, and his manly pride started taking over.

Just when his struggle reached fever pitch, Brenda interjected: "What about that hat you were working on in your last YouTube video?"

Jeff's cheeks grew hot. "You saw that?"

"Of course! Did you all know, Jeff here has a knitting channel?" Brenda surveyed the guild with arched brow.

"Really?" Fran asked.

Followed by Dr. Howell: "Do tell!"

Jeff met her inquiring gaze. "Uh, yeah." He cleared his throat. "It's about 'extreme knitting.' Not, like, knitting ginormous things on huge needles, but knitting out-doors—combining knitting and outdoor activities."

"Sounds fascinating!" Astrid invited him to share more. Jeff suddenly questioned his decision to wear Icelandic wool—he hadn't expected to break out into a sweat over the guild's monthly show-and-tell.

Brenda reached inside her purse. "Here. Have a look." She held out her phone with his latest video cued up.

The loner in Jeff felt like crawling under his chair. On the other hand, it seemed his videos were doing so well, even this small-town Prairie Plains audience was finding him on YouTube—definitely something to be proud of, and the true aim of his marketing efforts.

Brenda made sure the people closest to her could glimpse Jeff and Freeman rambling around the ramshackle pioneer house they'd explored a couple weeks back.

Astrid seemed riveted. "I love it! So creative!"

And Sigrun's raised brow suggested his video had likewise piqued *her* fascination.

Well, damn! "I'm sorry I didn't bring that hat. I already gave it to Freeman. I made a new one for my dad, though—same pattern." Jeff shook off his butterflies as he shimmied his phone out of his jeans pocket. "Here. He texted me a photo of him wearing it." He emulated Brenda, holding his phone aloft, then passing it around, as everyone insisted on getting a good look.

Brenda glanced back and forth between Jeff and the photo. "He has your green eyes."

Then it was Valerie's turn. "And your smile, too. What does your father do, Jeff?"

Fortunately, he did the sort of work that was likely to bolster the group's positive opinion. "He owns an outdoor sporting goods store. My mom works there, as well. She manages the accounting and stuff."

Tabitha studied the image when Jeff's phone reached her. "Is that why you're interested in business? Because of your parents' profession?"

"Yeah. Sort of. I mean, I kind of have this ambition of doing something with my love of yarn and wool, to make a business out of it. So I thought it made sense."

"Agreed. But don't rule out studying a little history on the side. You can knit in my classroom anytime." The history professor flashed a smile from beneath the intricate braids crowning her striking face.

Jeff considered Howell's reputation for being a hard-ass, contrasted that with her sunny features as she told him she'd enjoy having him for a student, and wondered if he should give her a chance. "I'll keep that in mind, Dr. Howell."

"You do that."

But the YouTube video wasn't what he'd intended to share at today's fibery show-and-tell. He'd brought some mittens along. He'd knit them over the summer using Fair Isle technique, working them in British four-ply with a lining of alpaca. Because the project had involved a dozen colors, Jeff was sure it would impress the guild members. Who knew, it might even impress the offish Miss Karlsen.

The finished object met with the positive reception he'd anticipated. Fran praised the pleasing rainbow effect of the colorwork, while Brenda gushed over how luxuriously soft the mittens were.

When they found their way to Tabitha's hands, she dug for more details. "This looks like something Marie Wallin or Alice Starmore might have designed. Where did you get your inspiration, Jeff?"

He set down his sweater project. "I like Starmore's designs a lot, but I developed the patterns on my own. I have a book that uses photographs from nature as inspiration for geometrical knitting patterns. The motifs are based on insects from my grandparents' ranch—beetles, shield bugs, and moths."

Brenda gasped. "That's absolutely genius!"

Astrid acknowledged the artistry in his work, prompting a smile of contentment.

When she handed his mittens to Sigrun, she turned them this way and that, then looked him in the eye. "These are really nice." Her smile was just crooked enough to come off as coy.

Jeff blushed as he met her gaze. "Thanks. I had fun knitting them."

The crafters continued their show-and-tell, indulging in tea, coffee, shortbread, and banter as they stitched and spun. All struggle to make a positive impression on the women aside, Jeff welcomed this respite from the stress-inducing lectures and assessments that peppered his week as a college student. But he wasn't the only undergrad at the table—Sigrun attended Great Plains University as well. And when it came her turn to show off her craftwork, Jeff was all ears. No, he really wasn't on the prowl. Or was he? Because his growing desire to know more about the good-looking Norwegian suggested otherwise.

Sigrun had brought a cowl executed with Scandinavian star motifs in maroon and white. Jeff lingered over the piece when it reached him, admiring her precise stitching and the high-quality yarn she'd used. He looked across the table at her. "I'm guessing this is Norwegian yarn?"

"Of course. Only the best."

Jeff smirked. He could easily school her on how there were any number of American mills equally capable of producing yarn that rivaled the best Scandinavian products. Sadly, he was too shy to go that route. Instead, he asked: "Do you knit a lot?"

Her penetrating gaze made him sweat all over again. "It's hard to find time, now that I'm in college."

Jeff shifted in his chair. "Are you taking some hard classes?"

"Not too hard, but the chemistry is sort of time-consuming."

"So you're a science major?"

"Pre-physical therapy. I have to earn good grades—it's very competitive."

"That makes sense."

Jeff couldn't tell if Sigrun was flirting with him. She kept punctuating her responses with those needlelike gazes, as if she would knit *him* up into something. Was she checking him out? Trying to lure him out of his shell? Or challenging him, as though they were rivals? Wow—what an alpha!

Astrid plugged in the ensuing silence by talking about her adventures in spinning some flax she'd bought from a vendor in Fargo. It seemed Sigrun was done talking to Jeff for now. As the meeting unfolded and he immersed himself into the sweater he was knitting as a Christmas present for his sister, he settled into a relaxing rhythm and took his "rival's" presence in stride. He let the sounds of knitting, spinning, conversing, and tea drinking wash over him like a healing mineral bath, expelling from him the stresses of collegiate life.

Brenda asked what he was working on, raising the topic of his family. His 23-year-old sister had never caught the knitting bug, he shared. She'd earned her bachelor's in forestry and was working as a park ranger the next state over.

Sigrun having expressed no interest in Jeff's career goals, Brenda took up her slack. "Tell us about this yarn business idea of yours. It sounds intriguing."

He connected the dots between his entrepreneurship studies and his YouTube goals, and Brenda enveloped him in her encouraging gaze, while Sigrun eyed him with knitted brow, conveying the doubt Jeff knew all too well, that there wasn't a snowball's chance in hell he could inspire a single hunter of ducks or deer to so much as pick up a pair of knitting needles and a ball of wool, much less make a winter-wear accessory with them. Her demeanor was beginning to turn him off—he wished she would stop looking at him.

Instead, she did the opposite. In fact, she went much further: she actually asked Jeff on a date. "Not like a real date or anything, but like, we could go out for coffee or something, you know?"

They were just leaving the yarn shop as she cornered him outside the entrance, the rain now having passed. Astrid stood a few feet away, acting as though she were heading towards her Volkswagen. Jeff suspected she was dilly-dallying so she could listen in on their exchange.

"Sure, sounds nice." He'd rather not come off as apathetic. The positive opinion of all the women in the guild, especially Sigrun's fiber-art-professor mother, mattered to him. "What's the best way to contact you?"

Sigrun shared her phone number with surprising eagerness, insisting on setting a time and place *now*—they might as well, they were right there, talking to each other, why wait? So Jeff had yet another obligation to fulfill during the week: he would meet Sigrun Karlsen at the campus coffee shop Wednesday evening at nine, after his accounting study group. He wondered what the café's selection of non-caffeinated beverages looked like for students who actually prized their sleep, so they could get through the next stressful day without dozing off during class.

When they did get together, Sigrun seemed slightly less snooty than she had on Saturday. She'd watched all three of Jeff's "Extreme Knitting" videos not once, but twice—maybe even more than twice. She inundated him with questions about how long he'd been knitting, what he liked knitting most, what his friends thought about his obsession, where he got his yarn from, whether he'd visited yarn stores in Europe or ventured further into the fiber crafting world over there. She showered him with lore about her family's home country, and how even though she'd spent most her life in the US and become a citizen, she still held dual citizenship and loved going to the land of her birth. She admired the knitting traditions of her ancestors, even if it wasn't necessarily her "passion."

While Jeff definitely savored certain moments of this first one-on-one meeting with the Norwegian looker, whose enviable intelligence and intense energy inspired his respect, he was overwhelmed by her sheer Amazonian force. Did Sigrun actually seek the give-and-take of a companion in life? Or was she more interested in a sounding board for her personal engagement with the world and its challenges? Jeff found himself withdrawing from the words her rose-colored lips spewed forth. Instead, he took in the aroma of her Americano, the aura of her lush, golden locks, the soft texture of the merino floof he was knitting into a beanie, and the uncomprehended hubbub of the conversations around them. That was all just stimulation enough to keep him awake.

"You know what I mean?" That signaled the end to a lengthy paragraph relaying her summer spent with family in Trondheim.

"Yeah, sure." Jeff had little idea what Sigrun had just said. He had a history of being a less-than-attentive listener. But she rambled on as though he were hanging on every word. Yet in spite of his inattention, she was actually growing on him. As she shared more and more bits and pieces of her being, his eyes roamed back and forth hypnotically between her sparkling baby blues and the luxurious hat growing visibly in his hands. It all cast a pleasant spell over him.

"Do you need some more tea?" Sigrun's abrupt realization that she might be ignoring his needs as she gushed about her own concerns caused Jeff to start.

"Oh, sure." Why not? Why not—because now he was sentenced to spending the time required to down another mugful of peppermint tea with this girl who, though really, really hot, and endowed with a fascinating background, was also as needy as she was self-centered. *Maybe those two things go together*, Jeff thought to himself. He struggled to digest the long strings of words she unfurled. Every time he indulged her with a question he thought related to what she was saying, he grimaced inwardly, as it just led to more endless talk on her end.

But he wasn't ready to give up on her. She was only nineteen, after all. And he had no desire to undermine his friendship with her mother by rejecting Sigrun before she even had a chance to prove herself. Plus, it was normal to act weird on the first date. Her self-absorption may simply be the result of nerves. And Jeff had to admit, his love life wasn't exactly humming along like a well-oiled machine, was it? Though spirited and a little stuck on herself, Sigrun Karlsen might prove a devoted partner one day, as good at listening as she was at being listened to.

She glanced at her phone. "Shit. I have an exam in the morning. I need to review for that."

Jeff breathed a sigh of relief as he packed up his knitting. He was ready for a break from this confusing situation. But he agreed to meet Sigrun again. Sticking things out with her might make Astrid happy. And what if the time he invested in this valkyrie evolved into a useful friendship, if not something more? Wouldn't that be better than subsisting in endless bachelorhood?

He offered her a ride to wherever she was headed to do her studying.

"Oh—I drove my mom's car here. I parked in the faculty lot." She said it with a hint of self-importance. It was almost cute.

"I can walk you there if you'd like."

"Sure!"

They returned their mugs to the counter. As Jeff clutched the fancy Harris tweed bag containing his beanie project, he appreciated having this comforting item—a birthday gift from his sister—to occupy his hands as they walked side by side on a dark and breezy November night. He tried to redeem himself by actually listening to her. They talked about her test. Her admission that she had to work much harder in chemistry than in her other courses showed a refreshingly humble side he hadn't been sure existed until now.

They arrived at Astrid's crossover. The overhead lamp illuminated Sigrun's smile. "I enjoyed tonight, Jeff."

The half moon visible just beyond the library roof caught his eye, reinforcing his urge to combat his inner hermit. "Me too. Say, maybe you'd like to come along next time we do a rurex video."

Her face lit up like the lamp above them. "That'd be awesome!"

"OK, then. I'll be in touch."

"Great. Thanks, Jeff!"

"Sure thing. Good night!"

"Good night!"

He left her with a moonlit wave, and asked himself how he should involve Sigrun Karlsen in his next YouTube adventure, without her getting in the way.

4

The Blizzard

IN SPITE OF HIS ambivalence about inviting Sigrun along on his next rurex knitting adventure, Jeff kept his promise and put in a video call to her Thursday night. Her smile told him she was happy to hear from him. But once they got past sharing how they'd enjoyed their time together the previous night, things got awkward.

Jeff had a plan: "We'll leave from the north campus parking lot at 9 a.m."

Sigrun found reason to object: "You do realize there's a blizzard warning for Saturday, Einstein."

Jeff leaned back against the wall as he sat cross-legged on his twin XL dorm bed. "Well, I studied the forecast, and I'm not too worried." They'd been planning the filming for two weeks now—he had no intention of letting a little wind and snow interfere with his next extreme knitting adventure.

"But why take the risk?" Sigrun's puppy dog face tugged on his confidence. "Why not just wait till the weather clears?"

Jeff studied her irksomely attractive image on his phone's screen. *She's trying to tell me what to do. That's not OK.* "What, don't you trust me?"

"It's the weather I don't trust, dingus. Why risk your neck over a knitting video?"

Jeff took a breath. "I feel like you're making the risk out to be greater than it is."

"Maybe. But then again, maybe not."

This opening to push the girl away felt welcome. The risk of involving her in an enterprise that harbored so much personal reward outweighed that of getting stuck in a blizzard. He could let her off the hook, and move forward without her. "You decide, Sigrun. Nine a.m., the parking lot outside my dorm. We'd love to have you along!" It felt safe to add that claim—her likely decision to exclude herself would be hers alone.

"Let's just wait and see what the radar says tomorrow night, OK? Don't take a chance, Jeff. I don't want you to get hurt!"

"You're very sweet, Sigrun. I can handle myself." He smiled into the camera.

She shook her head a little, and wished him luck.

"Thanks."

Jeff glanced over his marketing project notes once more before turning in. He'd visited the Humane Society twice now. In addition to some welcome encouragement, he was gathering great material for a fundraising campaign to benefit the shelter pets. The organization was already leveraging an annual rummage sale to increase their budget, but Jeff thought they should supplement this by auctioning off pet-inspired objects created by local artisans. What if he proposed to consult with the Flatlands Fiber Guild to get such a project off the ground? Including this idea in his assignment for Dr. Novak seemed strategic. At the very least, he wanted to get more involved in helping the dogs and cats whose fate lay in the Humane Society's caring hands.

The next morning, he was distracted from his Saturday filming plans by an ill-timed accounting exam. Fortunately for him, he'd studied just enough to get through the test with his pride intact.

As he left the room, he fended off the alarm bells set off by the wintry blast predicted for the morning, and turned his mind over fully to his video project. His research had dredged up engaging details on the abandoned church they planned to explore. The challenge of demonstrating appropriate reverence for a religious edifice, while satisfying the adventurous leanings of his core target audience, was proving a more interesting intellectual challenge than all the information on the equity method he'd just spewed out.

He was making his way out of the business building beneath the looming clouds that augured the weather to come, when he heard a woman call his name. He turned his head, protected from the raw November air by a colorful chullo he'd knit from Peruvian llama, and noticed Dr. Howell waving to him as she quickened her steps. To see this striking professor, known as much for her research output as she was for challenging her students, to say nothing of the red-hued braids crowning her head, hurry toward him, a college junior who felt like an amateur tightrope walker as he balanced his studies with his aspirations to reap life's rewards—to witness her apparent delight in seeing him acknowledge her greeting—actually gave Jeff goosebumps.

As Dr. Howell reached him, she was beaming. "I see you signed up for my Black Women's History course. I'm so glad you did, Jeff! The more men I have in that course, the better. It tends to be almost all women."

Jeff's palms grew sweaty. "I'm looking forward to it." He noticed the ornate, burnt-orange shawl draped around the professor's shoulders over her camel-hair coat, and wondered if that was the one she'd been working on during their guild meetings. "My advisor said it would fulfill the rest of my history requirement. Plus, it'll give me more upper-division credits."

Dr. Howell snugged her shawl around her neck. "Well, I appreciate it, Jeff. You know how it is—we instructors have to justify the classes we teach to the administration based on how many students sign up. And to be honest, I value having your young white male perspective represented as we discuss the issues I want to cover."

"It's an interesting time to be a young white male," Jeff quipped. "I'm always game for breaking down prejudices. I've experienced how tough it can be to say the right thing no matter how hard you try to avoid offending someone. I dated a Native American girl for a while back in high school. I feel like things didn't work out 'cause I couldn't get my feelings across without putting my foot in my mouth. Maybe your class can help me get in touch with my own faulty assumptions, and avoid sounding insensitive when that's the last thing I want. I appreciate your offering it."

"I'm glad you understand why it's important, Jeff. Hopefully that young woman knows in her heart of hearts you never meant to hurt her."

"I hope so, too. She ended up returning to her reservation and going to a tribal school for college."

"That's good—she's pursuing her education. That's never a bad thing. Oh, and by the way, Astrid tells me you're thinking about venturing out in that storm they're predicting for tomorrow. Do you think that's such a good idea?"

Ah—word had gotten out. Maybe Sigrun had shared her concerns with her mother, who'd shared them with Tabitha. It seemed Jeff was on Sigrun's mind—she was trying to look after him. It was kind of touching, when he thought about it. "That's the plan, Dr. Howell. But please, don't worry about us. If it looks really bad when we're getting ready to go, we'll call it off. The thing is, the channel is about *extreme* knitting. I have to stay true to my brand, you know?"

"Just be careful, Jeff. I'd hate to miss out on having your unique perspective represented in my course next term because you came to harm." She flashed an encouraging smile.

"Understood. No worries. I've driven around in snowstorms before, and I checked my truck's four-wheel drive. It still works fine. Enjoy your weekend, Dr. Howell."

"You do the same. And by the way, Jeff, outside of class, feel free to call me Tabitha. After all, as fellow crafters we're definitely friends, don't you think?"

"Of course." While Jeff acknowledged her sincerity, it would be a while before he could bring himself to call the distinguished professor by her first name. "I really appreciate it."

"Sure thing. I look forward to your video."

Jeff chuckled. "Hopefully, it'll turn out."

Snow was already falling as Jeff downed a couple breakfast bars and a Red Bull that Saturday morning. His roommate snored audibly. Jeff worked quietly as he dressed for the cold, donning a merino base layer, his handknit Icelandic sweater, a cabled scarf he'd stitched from his grandmother's handspun, freshly-conditioned leather boots lined with wool, and the striped merino hat he'd knit on during his meeting with Sigrun. He capped it all off with a brand-new parka his mom had bought him, then made his way to his truck, checking the latest radar images as he took in the mounting layer of frozen fluff on the ground.

There was no doubt about it: this would be a significant snow event. But the wind wasn't due to set in for a few hours. Jeff aimed to use the window of falling snow minus arctic winds to film a video that nailed the elusive sweet spot between daring he could bill as "extreme" and actual threat to life and limb.

Colin Milliman was waiting for him when he reached his pickup, with Hugo at his side.

Jeff greeted him with a nod. "The hat looks nice, dude!" For in addition to his own striped beanie, he'd knit up two just like it—call it a branding attempt. With any luck, the broad yellow and marine-blue stripes would show up against all the white stuff dropping on them today. "Hugo, buddy, I think you need a sweater!" Jeff petted the sleek, short-haired dog, feeling sorry for him on a frigid day like today.

"I think he does," Colin agreed.

"Remind me to make him one. I've never knit a dog sweater before. I'll do a little research—it'd be fun."

"Sounds like a plan."

They'd only waited a minute or two when Freeman showed up, wearing his striped beanie beneath what looked like three hoodies. He happened not to own a parka. "This is crazy! What are we even doing?"

Colin grinned at him. "Having fun!"

The three students jumped into Jeff's truck with Hugo. Once they were all buckled in and the dog lay safely at Colin's feet, Jeff turned the key.

Nothing happened.

He scolded his ageing vehicle. "Come on, turn over! Come on, baby! You can do it!" After a couple more tries, the engine chugged a few times, protesting the cold, then gradually fell into its accustomed purring.

Freeman leaned forward from the back seat. "Sure hope we don't get stuck out there."

"I've got everything we need in case we do. Blankets, food, water, flashlight. But I know this baby—she won't let us down. The battery's got enough cold cranking amps to survive the winters in Fairbanks. It'll be fine."

"It'll be great!" Colin shouted.

"It'll be awesome!"

They made their way out of the parking lot. There was next to no traffic—that favored their success on this risky journey. Jeff kept his speed low along the snow-covered road, getting a feel for the conditions and adjusting his driving accordingly. This was hardly his first winter driving rodeo.

The church they were heading for lay about thirty miles away. The route was taking them half again as long as normal. The snow kept falling, heavily at times, and the road surface was getting slicker by the minute. Jeff's four-wheel drive held steady, and he maintained the traction needed to keep from going in the ditch. Things got dicey when vehicles came from the opposite direction, but the other drivers, few as they were, seemed as keen on avoiding disaster as they were.

After three quarters of an hour, they turned off the highway to reach the abandoned church. All traces of the gravel road had disappeared under the quilt of snow. The students conferred as they proceeded, deciding what trees, bushes, depressions, and signposts indicated where the road surface was. Thanks to Jeff's experience and their observational teamwork, the trio finally spotted the crumbling edifice, using it as a beacon to guide their remaining progress.

Colin sheltered his equipment inside the truck as he got it ready.

Jeff urged him to speed it up. "We'd better film this one as efficiently as we can."

"Ya think?"

Freeman started shivering. "Want me to grab your dog, Colin?"

Colin nodded. "Good idea."

They scrambled to get all their gear together, then headed for the church.

One thing was clear—no one would be around to interrupt the YouTubers' trespassing. The trekkers were keen to respect the objects they explored and presented, and to leave as few traces behind as humanly possible. No one should know they'd ever been here.

Today's knit was a hard-wearing scarf Jeff was making from British wool received as a Christmas gift from his parents. The natural gray fiber from Gotland sheep was dyed in a deep scarlet. It would show up well against the falling snow.

He welcomed his viewers as the camera rolled, asking Colin, who was flanked by his shivering dog, to pan around and share their idyllic surroundings. The trees in the shelter belt beyond the church had shed most their leaves, exposing many a curved and bent form that broke up the murky sky like a Jackson Pollock painting. The harsh form of the wooden church, constructed over a century ago by Norwegian pioneers who'd raised it in dedication to their Lutheran faith, loomed eerily against the foreground of the countless large, white flakes that had begun blowing about nervously with the northerly wind. Once painted white, the church's coating had worn nearly all the way off, revealing the now thoroughly weather-beaten gray siding. The steeple rose starkly against the storm, asserting its decrepit determination to continue existing in abandoned obscurity.

As the trio approached the building, their feet disappearing in the snow, Jeff's unfinished scarf punctuated the flake-ridden air like a scarlet splotch signaling the grief of loss that marked this bereaved church, deserted by its congregation and left to succumb to nature's savagery. Jeff talked into the camera, sharing what he'd learned about the people who'd lived and died here, and built this modest, once-white edifice to worship in. The history attached to this house of prayer was akin to his own history, the history of the German-speaking Russian ancestors on his father's side, who'd given up everything to leave the Russian Empire and start a new life on the rugged prairie of North America. The falling snow put him in exactly the solemn frame of mind he strived for, as he shared their exploration of this sanctuary that fought for its very existence, while winter's wrath unleashed itself overhead.

The explorers entered through one of the boarded-up windows that were inexorably surrendering to wind, dust, and age. Now sheltered from the raging weather, Jeff and his friends enjoyed their short-lived escape from the wind-driven snow that had been pelting their faces, and marveled at what remained of this simple, yet noble structure, their contemplation disturbed by occasional moans raised by the wind as it forced its way in. The wooden interior asserted its musty fragrance in spite of the cold, and the traces left by the altar and pews instilled them with reverence.

Freeman spiced things up with a few humorous remarks, but a softly uttered "Wow!" left his mouth more often than any other word, betraying his appreciation for this architectural gem. Jeff stood quietly knitting as Colin, whose Weimaraner's shivering had subsided since they'd come inside, panned around the space, breaking their silence with occasional orders to look at these expertly hewn beams, or that careworn molding, and his ribbed scarf grew visibly in length, its deep red reminiscent of the blood of Christ drunk here during the Lord's supper many a decade ago.

The trekkers considered the advisability of exploring the crumbling bell tower.

"Looks a little risky," Freeman observed.

Jeff aimed a quizzical look into the camera. "On the other hand, we came out all this way in a storm."

Colin added his two cents as he cradled the camera against his shoulder. "So you're gonna do it?"

Jeff released a breath. "*We're* gonna do it."

"All three of us?"

Jeff grinned. "Whoever's game. But it won't do much good without you taking some pictures."

Colin grinned, too.

A rickety staircase led into the tower. Jeff stowed his knitting as he and Colin made their way gingerly into the tiny space where the bell, long since salvaged, had once hung. Freeman stayed behind, keeping an eye on Hugo and sparing the splintering stairs from the additional burden of one more 160-pound explorer.

Jeff resumed his stitching as he and Colin peered into the storm from the raw opening that had formerly served as a window. The snow draped everything in its white down. Jeff imagined it as carefully carded wool spread across the frozen land like an endless comforter, and invited his audience to share in his woolen vision. The snow-covered landscape enveloped them in its stillness; even the wind had relented in the face of the remorseless blanketing of the earth.

Jeff then took a moment to share his progress, and his scarf's crimson hue stood out like a warrior's wound against the wintery canvas. Something about the tenacity of one insignificant human forming stitch after tiny stitch as this object of his making asserted its becoming struck a chord of awe inside him. The realization that he was the *homo faber*, the "making man" he'd once learned about in philosophy class, filled him with wonder. His breath caught, and Colin trained his camera on the knitter as he waved his half-made scarf over the white landscape, his throat seizing as anguished amazement over the steadfast human struggle to defy life's transience through the act of creation overcame him.

Colin stopped filming and they climbed back down the splintering stairs. Jeff heard a cracking noise as one of the treads gave way beneath his foot. He grabbed onto the stringers and eased his way down to the next step. Relieved when they made it back down to the sanctuary, they resumed their video odyssey with Freeman and Hugo.

They voiced their admiration of the dauntless people who'd built this church, using a minimum of technology and a maximum of hand-crafted know-how to raise a building they could rely on to grant them meaning and inspiration. Then they returned outside, carefully shutting the fragile door behind them.

The snow was deeper now than when they'd arrived. Jeff likened the deepening blanket to the lengthening scarf in his hands, and homilized over mankind's nature-given capacity to make things: warm things, sturdy things, protective things that made life easier and better. Signing off with his renewed reminder to like and subscribe, he signaled to Colin to stop the filming.

The three youths waded hastily through the drifts toward Jeff's snow-capped truck, led by Hugo, who wagged his tail with abandon as Colin opened the door and ushered him inside. Reassured when his engine turned over on the first try, Jeff took comfort in their banter as they discussed this successful rurex adventure. He gripped the steering wheel as he guided his Chevy across the buried country road toward the highway. The snow had begun to drift, and they got stuck some twenty yards away from the approach.

Freeman shot a nervous look at Jeff. "You have a shovel, right?"

"Right." Jeff jumped out, letting the engine run. He sized up the situation, and rushed to remove the snow blocking the wheels on the driver's side. Then he hopped back in, made sure the four-wheel drive was engaged, and eased his way forward.

Ignoring the "no travel" advisory now affecting the area, he made his way onto the highway. If it had been plowed, that had clearly been before another few inches of snow had coated it. It was no surprise that they were the only ones foolhardy enough to be out driving in these conditions. But in spite of a few hiccups, he got them back to Prairie Plains, grateful for all the driving experience that allowed him to conquer what was now a blizzard.

He pulled into the residence hall parking lot a full hour later, clueless as to how to line his vehicle up with the obliterated yellow stripes. The explorers sat there for a few moments, taking in what they'd experienced with deep and calming breaths, and grateful that their lust for adventure had been so richly satisfied. Jeff thought back on his conversation with Sigrun the other night. He was sorry she'd missed out on their adventure. Given her love of winter sports, she would probably have enjoyed it.

And yet the undertaking had been so perfect with just the three of them, accompanied by the eternally happy Hugo. When push came to shove, Jeff wouldn't have changed a thing about their bracing adventure. If anything realized the spirit of "Extreme Knitting" as he conceived of it, this video definitely would.

5

The Dinner

FINAL EXAMS WERE WELL underway, and so was the stress that went with them. But Jeff was determined to attend the Flatlands Fiber Guild's December meeting. He had so few outlets for indulging his knitting obsession with like-minded others. Even though he felt like a fish out of water among those middle-aged women who were bogged down in their professional and family lives, all he needed to feel connected with them was their shared humanity, and their addiction to wool.

Jeff leveraged his experience, cultivated over several past semesters, in tackling the seemingly endless succession of tests and projects during the last week of classes, and carved out the three hours needed to partake in this monthly ritual of sharing his craft. He might not make it when the clock struck one, but he would come close. As he drove along College Ave. to Dee's Yarn & Fiber Emporium, taking in the pristine beauty of the snow-covered lawns from last week's early blizzard, he wondered if he'd see Sigrun there today.

They hadn't connected since she'd opted to stay behind while he and his friends had pursued their latest extreme knitting adventure. Jeff's mind dredged up a few likely scenarios. Sigrun would stay home, put off by Jeff's penchant for risking his neck. Or Sigrun would show up, and they'd stumble through awkward silence. Or she'd be there waiting, anxious to fall all over him with enthusiasm for his latest video. There was no sense expecting any of these things—whatever happened, happened. Jeff was going to enjoy the afternoon regardless. If he wanted to stress out, he could dwell on his organizational communication project. He refused to stress over an afternoon of communal fiber crafting.

It was past one by the time he pulled up in front of the yarn shop. But Jeff wasn't alone. Tabitha Howell had likewise just parked her sedan. When Jeff got out of his truck, he saw the professor leaning over her back seat, juggling the items she wanted to take inside.

"Can I give you a hand, Professor?"

She turned to look at him. "Well hello, Jeff! Yes, actually, you can. Here. Take this. I did a little baking for today." Dr. Howell handed him a covered tray. "I actually made these with you in mind. They're cheese straws. I just love them at this time of year. And young men like you need plenty of calories. I hope you won't hesitate to enjoy them. Eat as many as you want."

Jeff took the tray and cradled it against his Icelandic sweater, one of his favorite winter-worthy garments. "Thank you, Dr. Howell—"

"It's Tabitha, Jeff. Here we're knitters, without status or rank. Just fellow travelers, sharing an avocation that makes us equals."

Jeff returned her smile. "My bad, Tabitha. Thank you. I look forward to trying them."

They made their way over the neatly shoveled walk into the shop, where the guild members were settling behind their spinning wheels, or over their knitting or crochet-ing, or pouring themselves something hot to drink. The aroma of cinnamon filled Jeff's senses.

"Mulled cider," Tabitha remarked as they dodged a rack full of colorful sock yarn. "Bonnie makes it every year for the December gathering."

"Sounds like a nice tradition."

Having abandoned the cold world outside, Jeff delight-ed in the warmth of his surroundings. The shelves lined with skein after skein of wool, cotton, and alpaca were like comforting shields, protecting him from life's uncer-tainties. All differences between him and the other guild members aside, Jeff belonged here. It seemed Sigrun did, too—her face lit up as their eyes met, and her smile inspired Jeff to flash one right back at her.

But as happy as Sigrun seemed to see Jeff here, Brenda Wurth greeted his arrival with the bubbliness of a fresh bottle of champagne, insisting that he sit next to her, offering to pour him some cider, and watching over him like the mother-slash-nurse she was as he settled in at the table.

"Astrid brought Linzertorte today, Jeff. You have *got* to try that! Let me get you a slice."

"Sure. Thanks!"

He reached for the plate of cheese straws Tabitha handed to him and reflected on something he'd learned about Brenda from a chat with Professor Novak. His wife had shared that the high school nurse took peculiar plea-sure in his attendance at the guild meetings. It turned out that, between Brenda's own two boys and the high schoolers who crossed her path on a daily basis, she dealt constantly with youths whose potential to realize their parents' dreams was accompanied by equal potential to fulfill their worst nightmares. In Jeff she saw a reassuring example of a young man who knew his endeavors would lead him where he wanted to be. It was precisely his knitting skills that heartened her: he followed his own star, ignoring the naysayers and staying true to his path. According to Novak, she hoped her own boys would do the same. Knowing all this was as humbling as it was encouraging, and Jeff prized his friendship with the novice spinner.

Brenda settled into her chair and waxed enthusiastic over Jeff's latest video. "That was simply amazing! You actually made me appreciate the beauty of a winter storm. And everyone knows how much I hate winter storms. But the way you transformed a treacherous weather event into a thing of beauty and awe, and how you described the people that built that church, with their grit and determination to fill their hard lives with meaning—oh, Jeff, that was just masterful! Did you guys see his last video?" Brenda surveyed the group with arched brow.

"I did!" Sigrun's response drew Jeff's mouth into a smile. "It really was amazing. I honestly wish I would've come. I just didn't think you guys would make it through all that snow. I was kind of worried."

"No problem. You were definitely missed." Jeff said that because he felt he should. He wasn't sure he believed it. He polished off another cheese straw and opened his project bag.

Brenda's eyes grew wide. "Oh my God! That's the scarf! The red one you were working on in the video!"

Everyone peered at the crimson object he pulled out of his bag.

"That's really beautiful, Jeff."

"Thank you, Fran."

Tabitha released a huff. "OK, so now I have *got* to see this video of yours. You say it's on YouTube?"

Jeff nodded. "I go by Knitmann there." He spelled it for her, as others joined in reaching for their phones.

Dannie set down her spindle. "That's clever. I love it." She started tapping on her phone.

Valerie Dittendorf furrowed her brow. "Wow—you have over eight thousand subscribers? *Eight thousand?* Our yarn shop doesn't have *half* that many!"

Jeff's cheeks grew hot. "It's crazy how many people wanna see you trip over some busted boards while you're knitting a sock."

Laughter filled the space. The guild members indulged their curiosity. How had he come up with the whole rurex idea? Who were his co-conspirators? What about that silver dog—he was so endearing! Was he making a few bucks? Where would he film next? What was his ultimate goal?

Jeff shared his plan to film the next video at his uncle's Christmas tree farm. After that, he wasn't sure. They all chipped in with ideas: there was an abandoned dam south of town; a defunct gold mine a hundred miles away; a tiny ghost town in the next county; the doomed remnants of an old college campus further south.

The real gold mine here was all this information, for which Jeff thanked them profusely. He shared that his channel was booming, which was good, because the savings he'd managed to accumulate over the summer from working at his parents' store were about gone.

Halfway into the gathering, Jeff decided to invest some of his YouTube earnings in a little sock yarn to beef up his supply. As he passed by the selection of chunky yarns intended to satisfy Prairie Plains' hygge-oriented knitters, he realized Sigrun Karlsen was following him. He turned and noticed how her silky blonde hair fell over her lice-patterned sweater in lavender and cream, which she'd paired with white jeans. She was actually quite the catch. If her Insta posts were any indication, she made a point of staying fit, jogging, biking, hiking, even hanging out with a tennis player or two. So why hadn't she been caught?

Jeff met her blue-eyed gaze. "I like your sweater. Did your mom make it?" Somehow he knew all-out sweater knitting wasn't Sigrun's thing. Not yet, at least.

She nodded. "Do you like it?"

"It looks great. I'd love to get the pattern."

"To knit one for your sister?"

She recalled that much about him, that he enjoyed knitting for Amy. "Right."

"Actually, we wondered if you'd be interested in coming to our house for dinner. We could show you the pattern then."

"Really?" Jeff put off contemplation of the ideal-colored sock yarn he should knit up next. "I go back home next Friday. I guess it'd have to be before then."

"My last final's on Wednesday. We were thinking that evening. Kind of a pre-Christmas celebration."

"I'd like that."

"Five o'clock?"

"Sounds great. Text me the address."

Her smile made his heart race. "OK. I'm glad you can make it. We'll have lots of traditional Norwegian treats."

"I'd offer to bring something, but the kitchen in my dorm kinda sucks."

"Just bring yourself." She flashed an adorable smirk.

"That I can do."

As Sigrun wended her way back to the seating area, Jeff found himself drawn to a skein of sky-blue yarn intermingled with speckles of gold. That would make a handsome pair of socks to wear with the leather heritage boots his parents had ordered for him for Christmas. Such a pretty, brilliant blue. Yes, indeed.

Jeff arrived at the Karlsens' home on Quaking Aspen Road at five o'clock sharp. The days were getting so short it was already almost dark. Strings of white Christmas lights adorned the sprawling ranch house and its charmingly landscaped lawn, still splotched by the remains of the recent snowstorm. The sight boosted his holiday spirit.

Astrid greeted him at the door with her husband, Anders, who sported a wine-red chamois shirt over jeans, and their big Airedale terrier, whom they introduced as Freyja. Fortunately, she contained her enthusiasm over his visit enough to refrain from jumping all over him.

Astrid's gaze fell immediately on Jeff's woolen sweater. He'd hoped it would impress her. It was by far his most ambitious colorwork project: a Christmas-themed pullover dominated by fir trees in spruce green and cherry red, along with antlered deer, all arranged on a back-drop of white dotted with silver snowflakes.

"Welcome to our home, Jeff! Please, please let me have a look at this work of art you're wearing. You're incredibly talented—isn't he, Anders? Take a look at this craftsman-ship! Just gorgeous!"

As Astrid, who was wearing an eye-catching Nordic sweater of her own, gushed over Jeff's masterpiece, Sigrun approached from the kitchen in a pink but-ton-down and slim-fitting khakis, flashing a self-con-scious smile. The way she reached out to shake his hand felt stilted, as though a more demonstrative gesture would have been her preference, and diffidence had got-ten in the way.

Anders' invitation for Jeff to make himself comfort-able erased the awkward moment. Astrid indicated the sofa and offered him something to drink. "Beer? Wine? My husband is sort of a collector. He's got a room full of specialty beers downstairs, including some excellent pilsners. Would you like to try one?"

"Sure." Although Jeff's beer-drinking experience had not yet acquainted him with what a pilsner was, they were celebrating, so why not try something new?

"The Czech pilsners are the best," Anders told him. "Only the best for our guest. I'll be right back."

"Thank you." Jeff took a seat. This sofa put the one in his dorm room to shame. How would he ever be able to sit on that shabby couch again after enjoying this luxu-riously firm piece of furniture? He petted Freyja's frizzy head and took in the spacious room with its tall ceiling. The skylight above revealed the last remnants of light as the evening sky dimmed. Scandinavian Christmas décor dressed up the shelves, putting his Pagan soul into the holiday spirit. As Jeff's German roots outcompeted his Italian side for attention, he felt at home here.

Anders arrived with his beer, and the four of them sat, accompanied by Freyja, around a large, live-edge coffee table hewn from an enormous tree. They told him they'd acquired the impressive red wood table from an artist Astrid had known in Colorado during graduate school. While Jeff was accustomed to more modest surroundings, he traveled just enough to appreciate the finer things in life. The chance to enjoy the home of an artist with carefully cultivated taste was welcome.

Sigrun's parents asked about his home life. He shared about his dad's German heritage, the sheep farm once run by his grandparents, now rented out since his grandfather's passing, the outdoor gear store his family ran, and their love of the national parks that had prompted his sister to become a ranger.

In turn, Jeff learned about Sigrun's younger brother, Lars, who was working at a fast food place to save some money. Anders mentioned the local home improvement store he helped manage, called Luck's, and revealed how they escaped Prairie Plains' increasingly hot summers by spending them back home in Norway.

Astrid got up to attend to their meal. "If you brought something to knit, Jeff, don't hesitate. Dinner will be ready as soon as Lars gets home."

Jeff had started working his new sky-blue yarn into the first of a pair of socks. As he unearthed the work-in-progress from its bag, Sigrun followed suit.

Jeff admired the bold blue and white colorwork she was knitting up. "What pattern are you using?"

"It's a snowflake pattern from Norway. Do you like it?" She held it up with a charming smile.

"I do."

"I had my last exam today."

"Awesome. How'd it go?"

"It wasn't as hard as I thought." Sigrun rambled on about her preparations, what had and hadn't shown up on the test, how she'd problem-solved her way through the toughest question, as her father listened, one leg crossed over the other, with a nod or two.

Jeff thought distractedly about how the blue of the yarn he'd picked matched the blue of Sigrun's eyes. "So that was a chemistry test?" He should have gotten at least that much out of her account—his active listening efforts perpetually fell short.

Bored with Jeff's knitting, Freyja put her paw on his thigh, coaxing him to stroke her neck and shoulders.

"Of course. Have you taken any chemistry?"

Jeff smirked. "No. That's one of the subjects I generally try to avoid. No offense."

"Oh. So what classes *do* you like?"

The remark might have cut him down a peg in her eyes, but that didn't bother him. "I'm more of a philosopher, I guess. Because of my major, I have to take business courses left and right. But my favorite courses are the ones that make me think: philosophy, ethics, stuff like that."

Anders joined their exchange. "So you are a business major, Jeff?" His Norwegian accent was more noticeable than Astrid's.

"That's right—entrepreneurship, actually. I'd like to run my own business some day."

"Aha. I see you're very American in your thinking. I think this is a good plan for you."

Jeff smiled, then Sigrun took his bait and asked about his philosophy interest. "Which class do you recommend? I think I'd enjoy a philosophy course."

Jeff gave her a run-down of the intro to ethics course he'd taken, and suggested she might want to consider a bioethics course, given her major. Sigrun had plenty of brains to go along with her beauty. But to the extent that his down-to-earth sister served Jeff as a barometer of the kind of girl he should go for, the Norwegian fell short, even if he couldn't pinpoint why.

Fortunately, Lars didn't keep them waiting for long. He came in through the kitchen, having shed his coat in the mudroom. The gangly teen with his loose blond locks had worked up a big appetite and pressed his mother to get dinner served.

"If you'll feed Freyja, we can start right away."

Lars made short work of heeding his mother's command.

Jeff hadn't been sure what to expect from a Norwegian kitchen. When Astrid placed a beautiful piece of grilled lamb on the table, with red currant sauce and, to his ancestral German delight, sauerkraut, he smiled like he'd won the lottery. He'd grown up eating lamb thanks to his grandparents' farm, and sauerkraut was a regular treat back home. Aside from his mom's freshly made pasta, he couldn't imagine yummier cuisine.

Until, that is, Astrid served dessert, treating them to a fragrant almond cake accompanied by fresh berries, and a mulled wine called *gløgg*. Between the beer and the wine, the conversation flowed freely, and Jeff felt at ease among the members of this interesting family who knew how to make the most of the holiday spirit.

The family dynamic eased the pressure of making conversation with Sigrun alone. And Lars's juvenile antics, clumsily calculated to impress their "college man" guest, made Jeff giggle. His parents tolerated his pranks with good humor, as he teased Freyja with bits of lamb, exasperated Sigrun by making faces, and claimed Astrid had spiked the wine with arsenic. Jeff asked himself to what degree Sigrun shared her brother's fun-loving side. Her analytical nature was fine in a chemistry class, but less appealing on a date.

The meal finally drew to a close. Jeff had no interest in rushing back to his drab dorm room, however. "I'd love to give you a hand. Can I help with the dishes?"

Astrid beamed. "Absolutely. That'll give us more time to spend in my studio. I have some things to show you I'm sure you'll appreciate."

Jeff's eyes grew wide. He understood that Astrid made a show of respecting the level playing field observed by the members of the Flatlands Fiber Guild—she never put anyone down, regardless of how clueless they were in the crafting arena. Their members did everything from crochet acrylic baby blankets to stitching intricate lace from yak and qiviut. As far as Jeff could tell, Karlsen was far and away the most accomplished creator in the group, even more accomplished than elderly spinner and shepherd Bonnie Dittendorf, to say nothing of Tabitha Howell, whose skills as a designer and maker of shawls were respected beyond the confines of Prairie Plains.

Astrid's work occupied a different plane. Jeff had checked out the art professor's bio on the university website. She held an MFA from a competitive program, and exhibited her work not just nationally, but internationally—some was even on permanent exhibit in Minneapolis. It hadn't occurred to him that this modern ranch house harbored her studio. Suddenly, Jeff was *itching* to experience all the treasures it must contain.

He outworked everyone in the effort to wash, dry, and store away the Christmas-themed plates and glassware they'd used. Then Anders and Lars harnessed Freyja to take her for a stroll, while Jeff and Sigrun followed Astrid to the far end of the house.

Astrid opened the unassuming wooden door to reveal her atelier.

Jeff's heart pounded. "Wow! This must be almost a thousand square feet!"

"Eight hundred. Almost big enough." She laughed. "My husband is very handy. He built this entire addition for me. He's what we call 'a keeper.'"

"I'll say. This is amazing!"

As they walked into the space, Jeff felt like he'd entered a different world. Maybe the fact that Sigrun had grown up with her mother's artwork and seen her studio a million times accounted for her blasé reaction. Jeff's gushing inspired her to smirk. But it didn't matter. Astrid encouraged his desire to learn more, proving her skill as an educator and mentor.

"So on these walls we have my supplies of fiber—yarn, handspun, felting fiber, prepared wool, silk, thread, you name it."

Jeff gawked at bin after organized bin of fiber in every thickness, texture, and hue.

"And these are my weaving looms. Have you ever considered weaving?"

He shook his head, his mouth agape. "I haven't. This is all so amazing!"

"And these are my spinning wheels. I have a couple for singles, and I reserve this one for plying." She laid her hand on a wooden apparatus with a large drive wheel connected to its frame by a synthetic band. "That's my traveling wheel in the case over there, and I also have this Saxony-style wheel I refurbished for fun."

Jeff chuckled helplessly. "Fun. I mean, wow—this is like an amusement park on steroids for fiber lovers!"

Astrid laughed out loud. "I knew you'd appreciate it."

Appreciate it? Jeff was over the moon!

Sigrun, by contrast, released a pained sigh. Her mother had stolen her thunder, she seemed to be hinting. How could she possibly compete as Astrid wowed the object of her—affection?—with her "amazing" art studio?

Well, she quite possibly couldn't. Jeff stood open-mouthed as he took in the abundant stash of fiber in every color of the rainbow. This was a space he could only imagine in his wildest fiber-inspired dreams. Compared to Professor Karlsen's studio, his grandmother's warehouse spilling over with fleeces in various stages of processing was a faded suggestion of the possibilities offered by the wealth of dyed, carded, combed, and spun wool and fiber billowing from container after container in this lofty space, which Anders had outfitted with copious windows and skylights that let in light even at this late hour, thanks to its reflection off the stubborn snow blanketing their backyard.

"And here are some of the pieces I'm working on." Astrid directed Jeff to where a few finished works competed for attention with works in progress, all displaying the artist's skills in blending the crafts of knitting, felting, rug hooking, and weaving to produce objects that honestly blew Jeff's mind. Yes, he'd made up some of his own patterns—that was creative in its own way. But he stuck closely to traditional techniques in construction and colorwork, tapping his mastery of a few basic skills with each new piece. This approach seemed painfully conservative when compared to the extraordinary creativity confronting him in Astrid's studio.

"Here, have a look at this one."

Jeff followed the professor, while Sigrun leaned over a table covered in scraps of fiber, the boredom evident in her mien.

"Lately, I've been focused on integrating birds into my work. Did you know that humans have managed to reduce the population of wild birds on this continent by nearly *three billion*?"

Jeff gazed at the complex weaving. "Actually, I did hear that. It's horrifying."

"I want to celebrate the birds that are currently at risk of extinction, and draw people's attention to them with a series of mixed-media pieces. This one features waterfowl—loons and plovers." As Astrid pointed out a few salient details, Jeff admired the three-foot by six-foot weaving, whose vibrant colors and rich textures united to make an inventive retelling of a natural scene on the edge of a lake.

"This literally takes my breath away, Astrid. I'm just so amazed."

Sigrun made her own contribution to their exchange. "This one's really nice, too." She pointed out a smaller piece depicting colorful orioles in a woodland setting.

"Wow." Jeff studied how the elements of spun, felted, knitted, and hooked wool and silk painted a unified image, rich in color and texture. "I never imagined you could use wool with that kind of freedom. It's like a whole new world. How did you get the yarn outlining the trees to have all those bumps and spirals?"

Astrid followed his finger. "By spinning it that way. If you haven't tried spinning, you should. It teaches you how yarn is formed and gives you the agency to make your own thread, with any color, thickness, or character, and use it to create whatever you want."

"I really should try it."

Astrid smiled. "Don't worry. I can't get Sigrun to try it either."

"Oh, Mother…"

"It's true, Sigrun. You know it is. Don't get so annoyed. But if you decide you're interested, Jeff, I'll give you free lessons. Valerie Dittendorf will charge you forty bucks an hour, so you should really take me up on that."

Jeff chuckled. "That would be amazing. I'll see how things go in the spring. I signed up for Tabitha's Black Women's History course, and I hear she's kind of demanding."

"In a good way. She just wants her students to learn. You'll do fine."

"I'd rather not disappoint her, but I'll keep the spinning lessons in mind. I agree, I should learn more about how yarn is made, since eventually I wanna start a business in yarn production."

"You see? It makes perfect sense."

They continued their tour for another quarter hour. Jeff could have stayed here all night. Everywhere he looked, there was another hank of exotic fiber, another device he'd never seen, and another work of art delighting his eyes and hands. Astrid regaled him with fascinating facts about how different fibers behaved when they were spun, felted, or woven, how colors interacted, and the history behind her craft. Sigrun stood by her drawing table, looking on in silence, her expression subdued as her mother hogged their guest.

Lars and Anders returned from walking Freyja, their noise reminding them that the evening had to come to an end at some point. They gathered back in the living room and sat a bit longer, finishing off the mulled wine and chatting, while Jeff, Astrid, and Lars indulged in some knitting. It surprised Jeff to see that Lars was a knitter, until he recalled how Astrid had mentioned that during a guild meeting. Lars seemed so boyish and playful, but it dawned on Jeff that he was no different. He asked the teen what he was making.

Lars was determined to have a scarf in his school colors that wasn't made of acrylic like the store-bought ones. "Acrylic is stupid. Why do people wear that crap against their skin?"

Jeff laughed. "I don't know. It doesn't keep you warm, it smells bad when you sweat, and it pollutes the earth. We should start a movement."

"Yeah, we should."

"We'll call it, 'real men knit.'"

"Actually, I think that's already a thing."

"I think you're right." They traded smiles.

6

The Girl

Roc Day. Jeff had heard of this annual fiber crafting event, named after a Robert Herrick poem called "St. Distaff's Day," and celebrated to honor spinners and fiber artisans as they returned to work following the traditional twelve days of Christmas. But in spite of his grandmother's prodding, he'd never attended—he'd been just a little too cool for gatherings like that back in high school. Now, things were different.

Since the Flatlands Fiber Guild of which he was a bona fide member was serving as host group for the area Roc Day potluck this year, his attendance was important, and he was excited to go. He hadn't seen "the guild ladies" since before Christmas, and looked forward to catching up on all their fiber crafting projects when they met at the local community center that first Saturday in January.

Things wouldn't get underway until eleven, giving him plenty of time to fit in a chat with the volunteer coordinator at the Prairie Plains Humane Society, where he was eager to get more involved. He'd booked it for 8 a.m. The likelihood that he'd spend three hours figuring out how to donate a bit of his time to the homeless pets that tugged on his heartstrings was small—wasn't it? He assumed so. Erroneously, of course.

As he drove to the shelter, reflecting on how his involvement would bring him personal reward, while also beefing up his résumé, he nibbled on some jerky he and his family had prepared from the prairie chickens and partridges he'd bagged with his dad during a brief but therapeutic stay at their winter cabin before Christmas. Jeff dabbled in upland hunting with his father and enjoyed their man-to-man outings with their Gordon setter, Fritz, who, though perhaps not the best-trained gun dog in the world, still managed to combine competent pointing and retrieving with top-flight canine companionship.

It had been a nice holiday, all in all. Jeff had enjoyed sharing his adventures surrounding the fiber guild, the Karlsen family, and his YouTube channel, with his parents and sister. He'd also earned a tidy sum working at his family's store during the break, enough to get him through the spring semester if he was frugal enough.

The clock read 8:01 when he pulled into the shelter parking lot—pretty much on time, which was good. Punctuality was something the German in him valued, even if his Italian half could take it or leave it.

He entered the well-heated front office, where the smells of ammonia and traces of animal waste met his nose. The woman on duty recognized him right away from his Humane Society marketing project, and greeted him warmly. The volunteer rep was wrapping something up, she said. He was welcome to go and wait inside her office.

She showed him into the casually organized space and left him to his own devices. He stuffed his mittens into his pockets and allowed his eyes to roam over the binders stashed on the shelving and the companion-animal-themed bric-à-brac. The worker he was waiting on was one of the few he had yet to meet here. He hoped to encounter the same friendly demeanor he'd become accustomed to from the rest of the staff during his meetings with them.

Suddenly, the back door to the office opened, and in strode a practically-dressed female, accompanied by the competing odors of dogs, cleaning solutions, pet food, and disinfectant, her sturdy frame filling an orange Carhartt sweatshirt and olive-gray work pants.

She reached out to shake his hand. "You're our new recruit?"

Jeff nodded and returned the gesture. But his knees went weak, and he couldn't figure out why.

"I'm Laurel. Come with me!"

Well OK, Laurel! Let's do this! Jeff had only to put one foot in front of the other to follow her beckoning hand. But he couldn't do it. His eyes followed her, but his body refused. His mouth hung open, and he couldn't close it.

Laurel turned back and met his frozen gaze. Her dark eyes drew him in like a magnet. A smidgen of ancient Arabian blood seemed to run through her African veins. The short afro she wore framed her perfectly structured face with equally perfect symmetry. Her skin was so dark—Jeff had an urge to reach out and touch her, but fought it off, causing a pang to stir his heart. Certain that he already looked stupid enough, he was determined not to make things worse.

"You coming?" A patient smile lit up her face. He held her gaze, and her smile took on an air of desire. *Whoa.*

Sweat beaded on Jeff's forehead and butterflies fluttered in his gut. "Yeah, sorry. I wasn't expecting you to be..."

Laurel studied him. Her smile warmed even as something seemed to hold it back—condescension, disbelief, or maybe just plain amusement. An overwhelming desire to plant his lips on hers came over Jeff. He could have done it so easily. They were almost the same height, right around five foot ten. For no good reason, he grew aware of the hair growing on his face since he'd decided not to shave off his baby beard for winter. It would be fuzzy and soft against her earth-toned skin.

She raised her brow. "I wasn't expecting you to be either!"

Her words prompted him to laugh—or was that more of a cry? He felt himself nodding. "I'm coming."

Laurel stared into his eyes for a couple more seconds. Then she reached for his hand, grabbed it, and pulled him with her out of the office. "Let's do this. First, the dogs."

Jeff hung on to her like a wonderstruck kid clinging to his teen idol. They exited the building and entered the outdoor kennel facility. Apart from the dogs, the two of them were by themselves this early in the morning. A thousand barks assailed their ears.

"Hush!" Laurel uttered the word with gentle authority.

To Jeff's amazement, her command met with immediate results. Naturally a couple of rogues kept barking their heads off, but quiet descended on the rest of the pack. Laurel began introducing him to the canine inmates.

While cradling Jeff's hand in her left, she extended her right hand, pointing out a young Labrador retriever. "This is Rocky. He's only been here a couple weeks. He sits for me and also lies down. He's very energetic." Laurel looked on as Jeff extended his free hand to Rocky and rubbed his neck through the chain link fencing. "He likes you."

"Sure he does. Don't you boy?" Jeff smiled to see how Rocky wagged his tail.

They went down the line, checking in on Holly the spaniel mix, Buddy the pit bull, a trio of mixed-breed puppies with marled coloring fresh off the reservation up north, the ageing boxer Nellie, and overly sweet Petie, a golden doodle left behind when his owner had passed away.

Even after letting go of her hand, Jeff exchanged countless glances, smiles, and laughs with his guide. He'd been catapulted into a brand-new world. His body tingled, his senses were on high alert. Every smell, every touch raised beads of sweat across his body, and he grew hot in the gray cabled sweater he'd donned on this less-than-frigid January morning. He longed to have Laurel's eyes rest on him and her body close in on his, and was not disappointed.

What was happening? He knew this much: he *liked* what was happening.

Laurel grabbed his hand again. "Time for the cats. Do you like cats?"

"I do like cats. I only have one at home, but she's a sweetheart."

Laurel smiled. "I really like your hat. Is that handmade?"

Jeff nodded helplessly. His cheeks were on fire.

"Impressive." She assailed him with another sultry gaze. It seemed to last an eternity. "Let's go."

She led him back inside the building, and they entered the cat room. "We've got a couple dozen in here. Too many. I know you're working on some marketing for us, which is great. We have *got* to find homes for these babies. They don't deserve to rot away in here, even though we try to take good care of them. They're sensitive, and it's hard on them being here."

Jeff let Laurel's velvet voice with its hint of Southern charm wash over him. He didn't care what had landed her in the Midwest. He only cared that she was here. Her obvious compassion aroused his desire. "I'm eager to help any way I can."

Some of the cats roamed the space freely, others huddled in this or that corner, and the rest lingered in steel cages. As the noise of constant meowing washed over them, Laurel introduced Jeff to feline after feline.

Jasmine was a lynx-point Siamese who'd been in the cat room since Thanksgiving. Littermates Henley and Farley were due to be picked up by their adoptive family on Monday. Lucky wasn't so lucky, as he was missing an ear, part of his tail, and a few toes, thanks to frostbite—admittedly, he *was* lucky that some caring human had seen fit to bring him here, after finding him in a field while out hunting pheasants. Then there was Jude, a black cat rescued from abusers on Halloween, and Misty with her litter of tiger-striped kittens, who still insisted on suckling, even though they'd been on solid food for a week.

As they moved from cat to cat, Laurel coaxed Jeff into petting them, holding them, playing with them, listening to their purrs, and calming the cats who cowered in fear. The feeling of being on a shared mission intensified when Jeff followed her into the room for the sick and weak felines, the ones recovering from parasites, pregnancy, injury, or illness. She told Jeff each cat's story, and his heart swelled with compassion. He was in awe of the special relationship mankind had established with the creatures that accompanied people on their journey through life. He wanted to make these cats' lives better. And he wanted to do it with Laurel.

"Have a look at this little guy." Laurel knelt down beside a cage housing a small white cat with orange patches. His injuries were severe. "I named him Teddy. He was inside a car engine trying to lick the antifreeze when the guy came out to start it up. When he came in, I thought, we should just let this kitten die. But the vet said no—we can save him. He's only four months old. He wants a chance at life. She operated on this tiny boy for like a couple of hours, and put him back together as best she could. See how his jaw's got that wire on it? She had to amputate a part of his leg, but she was able to save the other one. Here, pet him. Gently—be careful."

Jeff did as she said. It scared him to touch the injured kitten, but when he petted him down his back, he purred audibly. He smiled. "He likes it!"

"Sure he does! I wanna adopt this cat, but he requires a lot of care. He shouldn't be in this place trying to get better, you know what I mean?"

Jeff nodded.

Laurel looked him in the eye. "Maybe you could help me."

Her perfectly symmetrical face with her dark, magnetic eyes, thrilled his soul. He had to nod. He would kiss her—not now, not here. But sometime, somewhere. Soon. "Count me in."

Laurel held his gaze with knitted brow. "I just know you're the man for the job. Somehow, I know."

He knew it, too. With absolute certainty! "I am, Laurel."

She rose lithely to her feet. "Well, I've got some forms for you to sign. We'll get you scheduled as well."

Jeff's eyes caught a glimpse of her footwear as he closed Teddy's cage. "Don't worry, little guy, we'll look after you." As the door latched, he realized what he was seeing. Laurel was wearing almost the exact same boots as him. "No way."

"What?"

"Your boots."

"Oh yeah—what the hell? You wear Red Wings?"

Jeff nodded with a flustered laugh.

"Fucking awesome!" Her smile was huge. "Is that the Black Prairie leather?"

Jeff nodded, his smile huge. "You really know your stuff. Looks like you've got the Slate Muleskinner rough-out I've been seeing lately."

"Got myself these babies for Christmas."

"Nice. I'm jealous." He laughed.

"Well...maybe I'll have to get you out to Red Wing one of these days."

Jeff smiled from ear to ear. "Count me in." He basked in her gaze, smiling and longing—it seemed she was doing the same.

Then they returned to the office where their eyes had first met. Laurel handed him a clipboard with forms to fill out. Jeff took the pen from her and started writing, and she leaned over his shoulder, reading every word.

"Nietmann?" She checked her pronunciation.

"Like 'neat-man'—that's right. But I like to go by 'Knit mann.'" He chuckled.

Laurel looked at him impishly. "Huh-uh. It's 'Knight-man.' K-N-I-G-H-T-man.'"

Jeff flashed a smile. "You're correcting my own last name?"

She nodded. "You're the knight in shining armor for these animals. So, it's 'Knightman.'"

He stared at her as his skin tingled and his heart fluttered. "I think that could be right."

"I know it's right." Her twang sent him soaring.

He finished filling out the paperwork.

But Laurel wasn't done with him. "Can you spare a little more time this morning? I could use some help getting the dogs their exercise."

"Absolutely." All thought of Roc Day and the Flatlands Fiber Guild had fled Jeff's mind. There was one place for him in this moment: right here with this tantalizing woman he could barely take his eyes off. "What do you need me to do?"

Laurel led him back out to the dog runs. One by one, they leashed up the canines who needed exercising and walked them around the yard, where the frozen snow had been tamped down by daily human-animal traffic. They walked Sadie and Rocky, Maple and Nellie, and eyed each other, smiled at each other, took in each other's scents, and talked to each other.

Laurel's aptitude for getting these sundry hounds to do what she needed amazed Jeff. She calmed them, trained them, entertained them, loved them. Jeff was good with dogs—they'd never not had a canine companion while he was growing up—but Laurel's know-how was seriously next-level. She seemed so young: she couldn't be more than twenty, yet with these creatures, many of them once abandoned and abused, she was an old, compassionate soul, happy to accept their foibles, their instincts, their shenanigans, their dirt, their jumping, barking, nuzzling, licking—in short their just plain being dogs, because she cared. Laurel didn't put on airs. She was as down-to-earth as they came. That was all Jeff needed in a girl.

As they leashed up the last dog, the nervous Shetland sheepdog, Russ, Laurel made a suggestion. Since she had to get lunch anyway, he might as well join her. As long as he didn't insist on satisfying some old-fashioned sexist need to spend his money on her.

Jeff smiled nervously. "Well...I can't let you spend money on me, either."

"Well, Knightman, I'll tell you what. You can buy *my* lunch, as long as I get to buy *your* lunch. Will that work?"

Jeff thought his smile would break his face. "I can tell how serious you are. It's a deal."

"Shake on it."

They shook on it.

Jeff waited while Laurel clocked out.

They decided to ride in his truck to a mutually agreeable eatery since, as she explained: "Mine's full of pet food and supplies I need to unload."

"No problem. My truck is your truck."

They talked over options—fast food was out, Chinese was out, Italian was too heavy, pub food was meh. There was a small diner open only for lunch, but it featured the closest thing to homemade goodness, the "Cowpoke Café" on Main Street. They chose that.

Jeff led her to his Chevy.

She climbed into the front seat. "Gotta be efficient. I have to be back at work by noon."

"I'm supposed to be somewhere, too." In reality, Jeff could care less about Roc Day now. He was where he wanted and needed to be.

They sat down at a corner table, peered over the menu together, immersed in each other's being, and placed their order. They talked about dogs, cats, and food, and the babbling brooks of their words washed over Jeff's senses. Nothing had ever felt more right to him than sitting in this place at this time with this girl, shooting the breeze, staring into her dark eyes, amazed that she stared into his, and three quarters of an hour passed by like an eternal minute. How could the time be over so soon?

Laurel checked her phone. "Unfortunately, I have to get back. But I'd love to do this again tomorrow. What about you, Knightman?"

Jeff's thoughts exactly. "I'm free. It's not like I've got homework, since classes don't start till Monday." Not that it would have mattered.

"It's cheaper if we cook. You could come to my place for a meal."

Her place. Sounded perfect. "Lunch or dinner?" he asked.

"Dinner. We'll have more time."

"Six o'clock?"

"Make it five. Can you cook?"

He released a chuckle. "Sort of. I make a mean knoephla soup."

"OK, well I don't know what the heck that is. So why don't you come over tomorrow and show me?"

"Deal."

They left the diner and climbed back into Jeff's truck. He revved up the engine and pulled out onto Main Street. As they headed out of town toward the shelter, he realized their time together was about to end, and his heart ached. The traffic thinned, and trees and fields replaced the buildings and parking lots. The railroad track was visible up ahead. Jeff noticed a shiny ribbon wending its way toward Prairie Plains. Then the crossing gate began to descend. The giant diesel engine rumbled, and the train sounded its 120-decibel horn.

Jeff followed the urgings of his heart, put the truck into park, and released his seatbelt. Laurel glanced at him, then released her own belt. They thrust themselves at each other furiously, indulging in impassioned kisses, all but sucking at each other's souls as the train rattled noisily over the tracks in front of them. Time was short—they made the most of it. The train passed, the gate began to rise, and they let each other go, exchanging gazes of amazement, then resumed their drive.

Jeff got Laurel to the shelter right at noon. His soul hurt with the knowledge that she would climb out of his truck and disappear back into the shelter. He envied the dogs and cats Laurel would look after for the next several hours. If he were Teddy, the injured kitten, she would enter the sick cats' room and find him there in his cage, pick him up, hold him tenderly, and make him purr. He released a laugh.

"What's funny?"

"Just wishing I could go in there with you. That's all."

"But you've got some place you've gotta be?"

"I do." *Damn it.*

"Well, see you tomorrow, Knightman. Do I need to buy any ingredients for your soup?"

"I'll take care of it. Text me your address?"

Laurel retrieved her phone, collected his contact info, and texted him. "Got it?"

"Got it."

"See you tomorrow."

"Right. Five o'clock."

She melted him with her stunning smile.

7

The Gathering

It felt as though the air had gone out of him. *Back to reality.* Jeff took one more look at the door the volunteer coordinator had closed behind her, and his fluttering heart turned to lead. He tried to resurrect his excitement about Roc Day, and the expected space full of fiber enthusiasts who were like automatic friends, because they shared his obsession. His grandmother would be thrilled to know he'd finally taken part.

But then he thought back to Rocky, and Maple, and Russ, and Sadie, and wanted nothing more than to be walking them around the yard behind the shelter with Laurel, exchanging glances, words, and an occasional kiss.

Jeff backed out of his parking spot and turned to go down the highway. By now, he'd arrive at the gathering an hour and a half late. But the guild members were counting on him. He'd armed himself with some kettle corn—his modest contribution to the potluck. The idea of the Laurel-less world he'd known just a few hours ago flooded his mind as he drove. What an absurd world, as empty of meaning as a dried-out husk. There was one thing, and one thing only, that mattered now, and that was Laurel. He didn't even know her last name—it didn't matter. She was the astonishing center of his revolutionary new universe.

Jeff was almost surprised when he landed at the community center parking lot. He heaved a sigh, grabbed his container of kettle corn and his project bag, and got out of the truck. He stood on the asphalt, taking in the cold air, and recognized with pleasure that his heart had resumed fluttering. The challenge he faced was more simple than maybe he'd imagined: he had only to integrate his wondrous new reality into his familiar old life.

He called to mind the things that had mattered to him before this morning: his passion for knitting, his entrepreneurship studies, his growing rep as a rurex video personality, and his standing as a guild member who'd come to enjoy mutual respect with the collective. All those things were still there, anchoring his happiness. It was just that now, there was a fresh anchor, one that bound him even faster to the projects and ambitions he pursued in the name of a good life. One that had him completely under its romantic spell.

He took another breath, then trudged across the ice-strewn parking lot and into the warm building, where the smells of assorted hot dishes intermingled as they wafted into his nostrils.

Wouldn't you just know it: Sigrun Karlsen was the first person to accost Jeff the moment the glass door shut behind him. "There you are! We've been wondering where you got to!"

"Sorry, Sigrun. I got waylaid."

"Is that what you call it?" Such a buzzkill. A wave of nervousness passed over Jeff as he realized how not interested he was in this tedious person.

Astrid came up behind her, and he shook off his discontent. "We're just glad you're OK, Jeff." She took his container of kettle corn in one hand, and hooked her other hand around his arm, ushering him into the gathering area as Sigrun tagged along. "No doubt you're getting in a little extra sleep before the semester cranks back up. You're a student, it's absolutely what you should do. Come on in. There are a lot of people who want to meet you, but first you need to eat. There's so much delicious food to try! I even slow-cooked some lamb just for you, since I know how much you like it." She smiled warmly at him as Sigrun pouted and sulked.

"Sounds nice, Astrid." As the professor found a home for his potluck contribution, Jeff asked himself how hungry he was—after all, he'd just eaten. In reality, though, he'd more or less nibbled at his food while taking in Laurel's being as they'd sat at their corner table in the Cowpoke Café. He would do what it took to accommodate his fiber-crafting colleagues' expectations, whose importance in his life it would be a mistake to deny, even as he loathed how his memory of that kiss shared with Laurel by the train tracks was shedding its sharpest contours.

Astrid shepherded Jeff as he entered the spacious meeting room with its composite tile floor and fluorescent lighting, taking in the aromas of everything from slow-cooked lamb to rum-soaked cake to peppermint tea, and the sight of a few dozen people engaged in eating, drinking, chatting, spinning, knitting, crocheting, weaving, and milling around. As he came down from his intoxicating high, he adapted to this strangely familiar environment of not just a handful, but a roomful of people taking part in the crafts that were his lifeblood.

Valerie was perched behind her ornate castle-style wheel, drafting some magenta roving into the orifice, when she looked up over her half glasses and smiled. "Hi, Jeff! I'm so glad you could make it!"

"Better late than never," he quipped. Then his eyes found Tabitha, knitting away on a cream-colored triangle.

Her expression warmed the second she met his gaze. "I must admit, you had us a little worried, Jeff. But here you are, and all is well."

"Sorry. I didn't mean to be so late."

Brenda was sitting beside Tabitha, pre-drafting a lap full of black wool. "You're here. That's all that matters. Our group just isn't complete without you!"

Jeff felt a bit like a minor celebrity. Not only had his delayed arrival induced multiple guild members to succumb to abject worry on his behalf, his videos were really making the rounds. Crafters were taking notice of him on YouTube. The Extreme Knitting video he'd made at Uncle Henry's Christmas tree farm had gotten over twelve thousand views. Based on their comments, the scenic film had boosted viewers' holiday spirit and inspired them to go out themselves and try knitting in the falling snow. Jeff had been clever to stitch on a Christmas stocking for the video, which had gained him over two thousand new subscribers. Long before he even had a chance to start selling his own yarn, he could be earning enough from YouTube to add a tidy supplement to whatever he picked up from his primary gig.

Astrid escorted Jeff through the gauntlet of fellow crafters to the tempting potluck spread like a mother duck leading her duckling, while Sigrun looked on with a frown. Ah, Sigrun. She and Jeff had blown many an hour texting back and forth over break, beginning with her complaints about her mother's interference in their "relationship," and Jeff's defense that he saw a mentor in Astrid. She was a professor after all, that was what she did—mentor people.

Sigrun had finally relented: *I suppose.*

Then she'd launched into a campaign of sharing funny Airedale videos, some of them straying into the area of animal abuse, which Jeff had pointed out, thus ticking her off. And by the way, she'd come back, she was finding the endless parade of possible knitting projects he'd kept sending "a little tiresome." In the end, they'd limited themselves to occasional texts about their holiday activities, ending with Sigrun: *I can't wait to see you at Roc Day,* to which Jeff had replied: *See you there.*

And now he was seeing her here, and he saw likewise that he'd have to get real with her, especially after the morning's events. Their future lay in either friend-ship or no-ship—he'd have to make that clear.

Well, that could wait for the moment.

As Astrid took Jeff under her wing, guiding his hand while he filled his plate, he took comfort in her supervision. After his world-rocking tour of the dog runs and cat rooms, he had zero willpower to guide his own destiny. He joined the Karlsen women at the table where a few other latecomers were indulging their appetites, his plate piled high with meats, casseroles, pastas, breads, salads, and whatever else he could fit there. He'd filled a second plate with cookies and cake, topping it all off with a big glass of water. As he ate, a raft of friends and strangers alike regaled him with greetings, insisting they should discuss their mutual love of fiber the minute he was done eating.

After he'd stuffed his gullet to bursting, Jeff heeded Astrid's encouragement and approached the circle of crafters. Sigrun's interest in shadowing him seemed to have waned—she took a seat, whipped out her phone, and started scrolling.

A woman in a Christmas-themed cardigan looked up as Jeff passed. "I adore your sweater! It's so Irish! Did you knit that?"

Jeff ran his hand over the weathered wool of his gray pullover and nodded.

"You did a *beautiful* job with the cables."

"Thanks. I appreciate it." He thought back to the challenge of getting the complicated cabling right throughout the project, while keeping the gauge consistent. "Do you enjoy knitting cables?"

"I'm a huge fan. That's a lovely wool. Is it British?"

"Actually, it's from Australia. It knits up really well." And it did, too—it was the kind of yarn Jeff hoped to produce himself one day. Yarn that held up to the elements, but also softened and puffed with repeated handwashings, making for rugged yet comfortable garments a person could wear over and over again, well into the future.

Then Astrid introduced him to a couple, one of whom, a slender man in a cashmere sweater and pleated trousers who peered at his hands through oval-framed glasses, was knitting a tiny, rose-colored sweater.

His idle companion, a portulent, middle-aged man with neatly trimmed beard, seemed to recognize Jeff. "We so love your videos! You guys are a hoot to watch. Where did you learn to knit like that?"

Jeff felt himself blushing. "From my grandma on my dad's side. She raised wool for forty years."

"That's amazing. My name's David, and this is Dan."

Dan interrupted his stitching to give Jeff's hand a shake.

"Nice to meet you. Is that a doll sweater?"

Dan's smile was warm to a fault. "A Barbie sweater, that's right." He reached into his bag and withdrew a similar project already completed.

Jeff took it and admired how the doll sweater was knit from fingering-weight wool. It was a perfect replica of an adult-sized cardigan. "Incredible. Do you use size zero needles for that?"

"Exactly."

Astrid touched Jeff's elbow. "Dan has knit and sewn an entire wardrobe of fashion for his Barbies. I met him at a doll show in Minneapolis. He does astonishing work."

"You're too kind, Professor Karlsen."

"Not at all, Dan."

Jeff returned the miniature sweater to its maker. "It was a pleasure to meet you."

"The pleasure's mutual!"

Astrid then introduced Jeff as their latest new guild member to a crafter named Ralph Cadotte, who was finger weaving. "Have you ever seen this kind of craft?"

Jeff shook his head as his eyes roamed across the green, white, and yellow chevrons Ralph was forming down the length of his work. "It's a first."

"Ralph is an Ojibwe artist from northern Minnesota. His work is devoted to preserving traditional weaving techniques and the culture surrounding the craft."

Seeing these crafters at work made Jeff glad he'd managed to come here today. "Inspiring." Because it really was inspiring to take in so many versions of fiber crafting, especially since seeing Astrid's studio back in December. It made Jeff wonder about all the directions his enjoyment of yarn could possibly take him in down the road. The possibilities seemed endless.

The weaver sat up in his chair. "By the way, Jeff, I have a suggestion for your YouTube channel. Have you ever heard of Dead Man's Trail?"

Jeff shook his head. It floored him to think everyone and his uncle knew about his extreme knitting video adventures.

"It's up near Thief River Falls, in Minnesota."

"Oh, yeah—I've heard of that." Thief River Falls was actually known for its snowmobile trails.

"People say the trail's haunted. It would make a great video if you followed that trail up a ways as you're knitting."

Haunted—sounded interesting. Might make for some fascinating viewing. "Thanks for the tip. Sounds like an awesome idea." He studied Ralph's work as the next row of his sash took shape. "You do all that with your fingers?"

"Yes, I do." Ralph rose from his chair. "Here, let me show you how." He invited Jeff to take his seat behind the simple weaving frame and instructed him on executing the next row.

Taking direction this way was just what Jeff needed. He was too pleasantly exhausted to direct his own actions.

Ralph's art enchanted him. He asked himself what he might gain by diving deeper into exploration of Native American fiber crafts. It amazed him how rich life was, simply because humans had stumbled upon a way to spin fiber into yarn and thread, and weave, knit, and sew that thread into garments and artifacts and works of art.

It made Jeff a little jealous of Astrid's profession. Her whole career was devoted to this kind of exploration. Her obvious interest in mentoring him warmed his heart. He was determined not to let Sigrun's dysfunctional attempts at turning their relationship into something it wasn't get in the way of that.

Tabitha approached Jeff before he settled down with his own crafting, stealing him from his mentor so she could introduce him to a member of the area fiber festival board. Maria Aguilar, a thirty-something with a Central American accent, was spinning a cloud of yellow wool into thin, even yarn. She wrapped the twisting thread around her orifice hook and rose as Tabitha told her Jeff's name. "This is the young man I wanted you to talk to. If we're looking for fresh blood on the board, I think Jeff could be it."

He eyed the women expectantly, then Maria explained. "Professor Howell tells me you're a business major, as well as a skilled knitter. We thought maybe you would be interested in joining us on the fiber fair board. You're young, you're smart, and I hear you're ambitious, too. It could be a great experience for you."

Tabitha looked him in the eye. "No pressure, Jeff. But we'd love for you to think it over. Your skill set matches the board's needs. You'd also be a fine candidate for offering a class or two at this year's festival. It would mean a little extra money in your pocket."

Jeff basked in the realization of how many supporters he was accumulating. He'd led the life of a loner his first two years of college, and now it seemed all he'd had to do to change that was embrace his identity as a knitting genius to find not just friends, but admirers. And not just any admirers, but boosters who had real pull in the world. "Wow. It sounds like a great thing to be involved in." When he thought about it, the business angle made enormous sense. And it would look great on his résumé to have this experience. "Can I get more information? I don't want to commit until I know I can do the job right. But I'd really like to give it serious consideration."

Maria promised to send him the link to the website. "Dr. Howell said you're in her class this semester, and she's on the board too, so we'll get you all the info you need. Thank you, Jeff."

"My pleasure. I really appreciate your thinking of me. Sounds like an awesome opportunity."

"Great. Well, enjoy today. It only happens once a year that we get to gather together with so many knitters and spinners and weavers in one place."

Maria was right. As Jeff finally sat down to knit, with Astrid on one side and Brenda on the other, it dawned on him what a special day this was turning out to be, between meeting Laurel and spending the entire morning with her, and now being surrounded by fellow fiber crafters all afternoon. He began guiding his fingers through another row of colorwork on his sweater project, and swelled with appreciation for how good life was.

Tomorrow, he assumed, it would get even better, when he had his first date with the girl of his dreams.

8

The Date

CLASSES WERE A DAY away from starting, and Jeff had yet to purchase his books. He was good at getting caught up in his side projects and reserving the adulting stuff for the last minute. He might be sorrier if it weren't for the fact that trivial concerns like having his books ready to go the first day of class now paled in comparison with his urge to nail his preparations for his first date with Laurel.

Fortunately, he wasn't hurting for time—he might as well get the text-buying behind him. He took a break from his morning knitting and headed across the wintry campus to the bookstore. With any luck, the required texts wouldn't break his budget. Those tomes for business classes in particular could cost a king's ransom. But when he got to the store, Jeff saw that his accounting and business law professors were looking after the students' needs, having assigned inexpensive course packs. He felt a little richer upon discovering that.

As he looked for the history section to find the texts for Black Women's History, he realized this class might end up being more useful than he'd imagined. Who'd have thought he'd stumble on a goddess like Laurel, who just happened to be Black, the weekend before he began studying the history of Black women? He took it as a sign and made sure to snag pristine copies of the required books, so he could mark them up freely.

Then it was time to attend to his dinner date. He devoted an hour and a half to buying the ingredients for knoephla soup, a traditional favorite on his dad's side of the family. The dish was so peculiar to their Germans-from-Russia heritage that it wasn't even widely known in Germany. He chased down red potatoes, fresh carrots, celery and onion, heavy cream, chicken stock, butter, flour, and a raft of herbs and spices.

The sum Jeff laid out for these goodies made the cost of his textbooks seem like a drop in the bucket. But given his determination to make a good impression on Laurel, he bit the bullet. With his wallet now a ghost of its former self, he drove to her apartment, nervously contemplating the evening ahead as the cheerful January sun illuminated his thoughts.

The complex where she lived looked modern and well-maintained. It struck Jeff as recently built, likely with rents to match. A fenced-off dog park was clearly getting some use, even with its now weeks-old coating of snow. *Of course* this place would have to allow pets for Laurel to live here. He wondered what animals shared their home with her—a dog? A cat? Maybe both? He was already jealous of each and every pet she had.

He parked his pickup and texted her that he'd arrived, his blood rushing madly through his arteries. Was he dressed all right? Should he keep his trademark beanie on or take it off? Were his teeth clean enough? He quickly checked them in his rearview mirror—yup, they were good. But he wasn't wearing any scent—was that a mistake? As he read her response: *Great, just ring my bell,* he figured with any luck, the fact that he'd made his burgundy sweater by hand would make enough of an impression to render any faults in his appearance immaterial. If some hair was out of place, or there was a salt stain on his boot, or he smelled of those onions he'd bought, he could point to his pullover and say, yeah, but I knit *every stitch* of this baby, so shoot me.

He got out of his truck, gathered his groceries, and looked for the entrance to Laurel's building. She'd given him clear instructions, making his job easy. As he searched among the neatly labeled doorbells for her apartment number, he tingled all over. 203, 203, 203—where was it? Then he found it. Ah—he extended his finger to press the button, and jumped back with a start. *What the heck?* He read the name beside the number once, twice, then a third time. There was no mistaking it. The block letters said one thing, and one thing only: L. HOWELL.

No fucking way! Jeff thought back to all the times he'd shot the breeze with Tabitha. He'd never heard the professor say word one about having a daughter, or a niece, or even a much, much younger cousin. What was going on? Admittedly, it wasn't like "Howell" was a rare last name—lots of people had that name. Pure coincidence! On the other hand, Prairie Plains wasn't exactly a magnet for Black people. There were more Native Americans in this town than Black folks, suggesting it was more than a coincidence that Laurel was both Black *and* a Howell. But if Tabitha was her mother, her aunt, or even a distant cousin, why had she never mentioned her? Jeff stared at the button with wrinkled brow. "This is crazy!"

Then suddenly Laurel was *right there*, dressed in jeans and a forest-green crewneck, opening the door and letting him into the hallway.

Jeff greeted her abruptly: "Hi!"

Laurel flashed an adorable smile. "What's crazy?"

Jeff thought his heart would pound its way through his chest. "The price of food these days. Look what I brought!" He released a breath—pretty nice save.

Laurel peered into his bag of grocery finds. "Yum! But wait till you see what I brought, Knightman!"

The sight of her smile and the sound of his nickname set him at ease. "What?"

"You'll see!" She drew him gently along by the elbow, down the hall with its faint new carpet smell, to her apartment, then opened the paneled door and invited him inside. "You can set your things there." She pointed at the granite counter top, and Jeff set his bag down. The kitchen was spick and span—everything sparkled in the bright overhead light.

"Nice place!" He looked around, trying to tame his jitters. He was now in *her apartment*. All thought of Laurel's surprising last name was overtaken by the astonishment of being surrounded by her domain.

Laurel gave him a peck on the cheek, making his heart skip a beat. He eagerly returned it. Then a small black dog sauntered up and started sniffing his Red Wings. "Who's this little guy?"

"That's Pearl. I rescued her."

Jeff reached down to pet the pup, whose tail waved furiously—how happy she was to be Laurel's rescue dog! He couldn't make out any obvious breed. It seemed Pearl was just a cute, short-haired canine with perky ears and a very, very active tail. "You're as sweet as you can be, aren't you?" Then he noticed a fluffy-haired cat sitting circumspectly on Laurel's plaid sofa. "Does your cat like visitors, too?"

"She's pretty friendly. Her name's Olive."

"Olive. Can I pet you, Olive?" As Jeff approached the feline, she sniffed his outstretched hand and let him rub her soft, striped neck. In the back of his mind, he wished Laurel's companions could speak for her somehow, could augur her willingness to let Jeff run his hands over her own shapely form.

Laurel clapped her hands softly. "OK, pets. I've gotta show my date our new arrival. Come this way."

Jeff followed her like a lamb, his pulse racing all over again, towards a closed door beyond the bathroom.

She opened it quietly. "Come inside."

Jeff basked in the spell she cast. They entered her spacious bedroom, and his eyes immediately fell on the injured white and orange kitten she'd introduced him to at the shelter. "It's Teddy!" He worked to suppress his excitement and keep his voice down.

"I adopted him." Laurel clicked the door shut on poor Pearl—keeping her other pets away from the fragile feline made sense. "Look, Teddy! Daddy's here, too!"

Jeff let the affectionate label wash over him as he went up to the purring kitten, who looked at him with wide green eyes from his spot on Laurel's bed. "Hey, little guy!" He leaned down and gently stroked Teddy's back. The patient had improved dramatically in just twenty-four hours. "I think you're a miracle-worker, Laurel. Look how good he's doing!"

She smiled. "All it takes is some extra loving care. I feed him with a medicine dropper—he absolutely craves his kitten formula. And he gets around when he needs to. He just loves life, in spite of everything. Kind of inspiring, really."

"I'll say." It amazed Jeff how such a small creature could survive getting knocked around by an engine's fan belt.

He lowered himself carefully onto the paisley comforter, keen on petting Teddy as much as the kitten seemed to appreciate it. Laurel sat and petted him from the other side, occasionally touching Jeff's fingers as loud purrs emanated from the animal's healing body. Jeff's eyes met Laurel's a few times, and they exchanged smiles.

He began looking around. Before he could draw many conclusions regarding Laurel's private empire, his eyes were pulled like magnets to the wall opposite, where a huge bulletin board was propped on her desk. At first glance, it resembled one of those investigation boards from a crime show. What "crime" could Laurel possibly be investigating? He started sorting things out.

On the top left, an index card showed the name "HOW-ELL" in block letters, while on the right he read "BEN-NETT." Below these, he made out a family tree displayed in organic fashion, with arrows and photos and captions and question marks, all going back what looked like a couple hundred years.

Each side of the family was headed by a contemporary photo of what Jeff assumed were Laurel's parents. His eyes grew wide the second they fell on the photo atop the Bennett side. There was no doubt about it: *that was Tabitha Howell.* Bennett must be her maiden name. He cast a sideward glance at Laurel. Should he say something? Share his fiber guild connection with the woman who was obviously her mother? Or wait for her to do the talking?

Laurel petted Teddy patiently as Jeff studied her handiwork. She seemed to have no issue with his taking in her family tree. She even asked: "Have you any idea how hard it is to trace your roots when you're descended from enslaved people, on *both* sides of your family?"

Distracted from his effort to make sense of her research, Jeff met her gaze. "Not on both."

Her eyes grew huge. "Huh?"

He'd said the wrong thing—put his foot in it—again! "Sorry, Laurel—that didn't come out right." His own ancestry was a dizzying jumble involving oppressed people risking what little they'd had to seek out desperately needed opportunity. While comparing his roots to Laurel's seemed wrong, Jeff's family history involved its own brand of trauma. But the last thing he wanted was to come off as insensitive. "It's just that, in my dad's family—we're Germans-from-Russia—the people who came here to the US in the 1880s did pretty well. But the ones who stayed behind were mostly dragged off to forced labor camps in Siberia and Kazakhstan under Stalin."

Laurel stared at him. "Are you shittin' me?"

Jeff released a helpless laugh. "No. Not at all. Most those people died there. The conditions were deplorable. My dad's family got lucky. But Laurel," he asked, gently stroking Teddy's uninjured leg as he continued studying her ancestry project, "why are the photos of your parents so tiny? Those are your parents, right? The photos on the top?"

She nodded. "Who else?"

"All right, then, so they get these little passport pics, and everyone else gets to have three-by-fives. Is there a reason for that?" As in, is there a reason why your mother never so much as talks about you? As *though you didn't exist?*

Laurel released a huff. "Well, let's just say, my folks and I aren't on the best of terms."

Apparently! Jeff subjected her to a lengthy stare.

"You see... Oh, Knightman, I don't wanna burden you with my family problems."

Hopefully she had *someone* she could burden, then, because Jeff was gaining the impression that these "problems" had gotten out of hand. He didn't want that for her. "It's OK. Actually, Teddy and I have a little confession to make." He looked back and forth between his date and the kitten, wondering if having Teddy share the "blame" would be as helpful as he hoped. He took a breath. "I know your mother."

Laurel's dark eyes pierced him like ray guns. He held her gaze, thinking this might be the end of their date.

She exhaled heavily, causing Jeff to follow suit. "Well, seein' as how there're like ten Black folks in the entirety of Prairie Plains, I guess it's not too surprising that you would've seen her around. Wait—did you take a class from her?"

A logical conclusion that was also expedient. He'd rather she not know at this early juncture just how friendly he'd gotten with Tabitha the shawl knitter. "I start one with her tomorrow."

An evil grin lit up Laurel's face. "Well, I hope you're a damn good student, 'cause she don't put up with no bullshit. You're seriously taking her class?"

He quirked a smile. "I bought the textbooks right before I came over here."

"Which class?"

"Black Women's History. I signed up last fall. I need it to fulfill my history requirement, and she sort of recruited me. Said she had too few white males taking her classes."

Her grin bloomed into a snicker. "Sounds about right. But seriously, dude—my mother's a hard professor. I think you're gonna need a tutor. So it's a damn good thing we met yesterday."

Jeff's face lit up as he contemplated Laurel as his tutor. Now he was downright *excited* he'd signed up for the course. "I'm counting on you."

"'Cause I know how she gets when she thinks her students are lettin' her down. 'Oh my God, Laurel,' she'd say, 'those students can't even cobble a paragraph together, much less an essay.' Or 'those students could no more apply a theory to a fact than they could apply a rule to their juvenile behavior.' And especially the ones who skip class: 'What's goin' through those students' minds? Don't they realize they're payin' for this class, and they don't even carve time out of their day to show up?'" Laurel studied Jeff's face, her own still registering a good-natured smirk.

"It's just one more reason for me to feel lucky we met yesterday. But Laurel, I'm sorry if you and your parents are struggling."

"Well, let's just say that, in the battle between career and family, family lost out in our case."

"That hurts."

"Damn straight! I mean, I spent my entire life growing up in Atlanta. And then, overnight, before my last year of high school, my mom's like, 'I got this great job offer, big promotion, awesome salary, I just can't turn it down.' And boom! We move to this freakin' *tundra* where I don't know a soul, and my mom's this rock star professor the university can't live without. And my dad and I are like, what about us? So my dad takes her cue, can't find what he wants over here, says 'Laurel, you're a high school grad now, I'm gonna teach economics in Dubai. Go find yourself.' And off he goes."

That was not quite the story Jeff had been expecting. "Dubai?"

"Dubai! Fuckin' *Dubai*! 'Cause, you know, the money's just too good, gotta follow my dreams, life is short, blah blah blah."

Laurel's pithy account of her family break-up made Jeff shudder. "So did your parents divorce, then?"

She shook her head. "For now, they just lead their separate lives. Who knows? Maybe they'll get back to-gether. I don't fuckin' know. It's like this drug: success, accolades, money, prestige...I mean, I get it. You work hard, spend a decade earning a doctoral degree, you got ambitions. Great—go after them. But in the meantime, you got a daughter here that you brought into the world, and she's not doin' so well. But you got papers to grade, and research to conduct, money to earn, a reputation to build, and she finished high school—she can find herself."

Jeff took in her defeated stare. "I'm sorry, Laurel."

"I don't know, maybe I complain too much. After all, my dad pays my rent, and there're plenty of people worse off than me."

"No, but I get it. I feel really lucky. I spent my whole life in the same town, the same *house*. My parents have owned this outdoor sporting goods store since the dawn of man. It's all I ever knew until I came here for college."

"You *are* lucky. You really are. Maybe some of your luck'll rub off on me."

"Do you ever think about returning to Atlanta?"

"Do you know how freakin' expensive Atlanta is?"

No, he didn't. But he could imagine. "I guess."

"At least here I can work a modest job and get by—finding myself."

"You're gonna find gold, I predict it." That elicited a smile from Laurel's perfectly symmetrical face.

Jeff's eyes fell back on her ancestry project. "Who's that woman there, three rows down on the right? Roberta?"

"Roberta was a school teacher in Virginia. My great aunt. The Bennetts mostly hail from Virginia, and the Howells were in North Carolina."

"Mind if I take a closer look?"

"Go for it. I've been spending the last two years working on this family tree, and you're the first person to see it besides me. Might as well show it off."

Teddy was fast asleep. Jeff rose and stood in front of the bulletin board. As the first person ever to be a party to Laurel's research, he felt responsible for getting everything out of it he possibly could. He surveyed the various images, names, and arrows, and his eyes seized on a vintage picture of a young man with a mustache—it must have dated back to the Civil War. He looked at Laurel as he pointed it out. "What about Percy here?"

Her nod suggested he'd chosen a cherished ancestor. "Percy's a distant uncle who worked on the railroad. You know, a lotta Black men helped build all those tracks. A really important part of history."

"I can't imagine that backbreaking labor. I think I'll stick to knitting." He chuckled nervously.

Laurel treated Teddy to a few prolonged pets. "That's right, you do knitting." Her eyes rested on the beanie he wore—he almost never went without that headgear in winter, indoors or out. "Check it out, you made that?" She took in the spruce green wool he'd knit into intricate cables.

"Yup!"

"My mother would be impressed. She loves knitting."

Jeff released a breath. He might as well show all his cards. Doing otherwise would hardly conduce to a healthy relationship, if that was where this was headed. "Well, I actually know that about her. I joined the fiber guild she goes to."

Laurel's jaw dropped. "Shut the front door! That is honestly insane. You do know my mother, then!"

He nodded and took a step or two toward her. "I had no idea you were connected when I saw you yesterday. Seeing these pictures, you clearly take after your father more. But you have your mother's eyes. I'm sure I don't have to tell you that."

"Her eyes maybe, but not her let's-just-jump-on-the-ambition-train-and-forget-about-that-kid-I-brought-into-the-world mindset."

"No, that's true." He thought of how Laurel was with the abandoned dogs and cats she worked with day in and day out. It dawned on him how she could readily identify with the animals she cared for.

Laurel got up. She drew him in with her dark-eyed gaze and furrowed brow. "And if you let on to her that we're seeing each other, you won't just know my mom. Your behind will know the toe of my boot!" She kicked with her foot to strengthen her point.

Of course she was playing. But her anger was palpable. "Mum's the word!" Jeff said that, yet it bothered him to conspire in keeping Laurel estranged from her mother. They were both important to him. And in spite of her obvious anger, he felt it worth the risk to push Laurel on the issue of their broken mother-daughter relationship. "You're not gonna keep this up forever, though—?"

Her shoulders sagged as she let out a breath. She reached for his hand. "I know, I know. She's my mother. Heck, she's got to be lonely." She looked him in the eye. "It just takes time, you know?"

Jeff nodded his reassurance as her eyes teared up. She leaned in toward him, and he wrapped her in his arms. "I'm sorry you're going through this."

"It's just so hard." Laurel sobbed as she returned his embrace. "I'm so glad I met you. I've been so fuckin' lonely!" Her chest heaved against his and her tears wet his sweater. It was several minutes before her calm returned. "I'm sorry, Knightman. This probably wasn't what you had in mind when you met me yesterday." She wiped her tears and spiked her words with a half-hearted chuckle.

Jeff's sole mission in life now was to be there for her. "I feel like maybe I'm the guy you need. That actually makes me happy, Laurel." As he realized the power of his embrace to calm her, it sent an unexpected shiver of pride up his spine.

Gradually the clouds parted, and they resumed their contemplation, hand in hand. Jeff studied more images from Laurel's ancestry project, eager to learn as much as she was willing to share. He pointed out a photo of enslaved women at what must be a plantation. "Tell me about them."

She wiped away a few remaining tears. "I'm pretty sure they're relations. I work with a couple of genealogists, and we're confident that's the plantation where some of my father's ancestors worked. That photo was taken right around 1860 in North Carolina."

"Incredible. You've really been doing awesome research."

"*Someone* has to do it. I wanna know my roots, you know? My mother won't touch this history with a ten-foot pole. Sure, she'll teach you the basics—slavery, emancipation, Jim Crow, Civil Rights—but get down and dirty with her own ancestors? Not her. Theories, distance, perspective, analysis, all that, fine and dandy. But backbreaking labor like you said, dysentery, rape, beatings, bullet wounds, sweat, drudgery, fleeing and getting hounded by slave catchers, the really visceral, hurtful truths of what a lot of our ancestors endured—she struggles with that. That's why her research is all about the Civil Rights era. That she can take. And she's really good at it, too. She's like a world expert on Shirley Chisholm, and she's interviewed Mary Berry several times. But if you ask me, what you don't know *can* hurt you, and I wanna know it, no matter how troubling it is."

Jeff wrapped his arm around her again. "It's really important work." He zeroed in on a more modern photo of a man from the Bennett side. "What about him?"

"That's my great uncle, Charles Bennett. He studied at Howard University and was a member of the Non-Violent Action Group. Here he's getting ready to go on a Freedom Ride to Mississippi to try to help register people to vote."

"Amazing. I feel like I should take *your* history course, Laurel. It seems like it's just as good as the one your mother's gonna teach me."

Laurel chuckled. "Maybe." Her smile conveyed her pride in her accomplishment. "But there are still so many questions. I feel like this is gonna be a life-long project. Thankfully, there are a lot more resources nowadays than there used to be. I even got my dad to do a DNA test so we could find more of our ancestry. And between his DNA and mine, I'm finding a growing number of current relatives scattered across the country. I even have white relations whose ancestors sired children with mine—it's just crazy. Isn't that crazy?"

"It just goes to prove that, in the end, it really is a small world. We're all connected, often by a lot of trauma."

"Small," Laurel agreed, "and beastly. Why do people have to treat each other so shittily? I mean, apparently it's not just my people, but Stalin was out there destroying your people, and you've got modern-day slavery...there's just so much greed and brutality in the world. It's sickening."

"Now you know why I knit all the time." Jeff was almost surprised his quip elicited a laugh.

"I get it. It's why I spend my days petting cats and walking dogs."

"If you ever want to add knitting to that list, you know who to contact." He grinned at her.

"I'll keep that in mind. Say, are you gettin' hungry? I think we should get started on that soup of yours."

He actually was. "Good idea. You can really work up an appetite contemplating the ravages of history."

"Let's do this." Laurel gently returned Teddy to his quilt-lined crate, and he immediately settled to sleep. Pearl greeted them, her tail wagging like a hummingbird's wing, when they returned to the kitchen. They unpacked Jeff's groceries and started preparing knoephla soup.

"What the heck is a 'neffla,' anyhow?" Laurel flashed a crooked smile.

Jeff laughed. "I only had one year of German, and we didn't cover that word. But my grandma told me it means 'buttons' or something like that, because this soup has small little dumplings. It's basically a dumpling soup."

"To be honest, these may be the first dumplings I've ever eaten."

"There's a first time for everything, right?"

"Right."

They set about washing, slicing, dicing, sautéing, mixing, rolling, and cooking, with Pearl officiating, making sure no scrap that made its way to the floor went to waste.

Their conversation meandered to Jeff's college studies. He touched on his entrepreneurial ambitions, but also put in a plug for his theoretical interests in philosophy and ethics.

Laurel listened attentively, warming Jeff's heart every time she met his gaze. "I think you made a good choice taking my mother's course. If you can write and you can think, you've probably got it made."

Jeff liked hearing that. "Let's hope so. Nevertheless, you've got me a little nervous. My roommate had her last year, and he didn't do so well."

"He probably skipped class or showed up late or just neglected to turn things in. A familiar story."

"What do you mean?"

"Because I've been there."

That was news. "Really?"

Laurel nodded with a hint of disgust. "My freshman year was a shit-show. That's why I never went back."

"Was that when your dad went to Dubai?"

"Yes, it was. I was so fuckin' depressed, I could barely function. I was thinking about goin' to vet school. But unless you've got a 3.999 GPA or higher, there's no way to get in."

"You want to be a veterinarian?" It made so much sense!

"Want*ed* is more like it. With the kinda grades I got, you can forget about it."

"But wait." Jeff set his dumpling mixture aside. "You said you were depressed."

"And how! But who cares? It is what it is."

"Not necessarily. I had this friend from high school whose parents went through divorce after she graduated. She went directly to college and it was a complete disaster. But she told me later that she went to a psychologist, who diagnosed her and sent a letter to her university. Somehow or other, they found a way to erase all her Fs from her records. So she started over again, and the last thing I heard, her studies were going much better. Maybe you could try something like that." He tried to infuse encouragement with his gaze.

Laurel looked at Jeff as though he were hawking a miracle cure. "They took all her F's away?"

"That's what she told me. Let's see, I think she's a soc major. Our moms know each other, and that's what Mom told me. Wants to go into counseling, maybe. In any case,

Laurel, you would make an awesome vet—are you kidding me? Those animals need you. I mean, you can't go on forever earning peanuts at the Humane Society and letting your father pay the rent. You should try to fix this and move ahead with your plans."

Laurel pondered that with furrowed brow. "A psychologist. I never thought of that. Do you think the university would really change my records if they got a letter from a psychologist?"

"It's certainly worth a try. I mean, you were just crying in my arms a little bit ago. I can tell you're depressed. And based on what I've seen, the university wants students to succeed. They don't wanna penalize people for things they can't control."

"They're not gonna just put me on some drugs—I wouldn't want that. Drugs scare me. I saw what those can do to a person back in high school."

"Then just do therapy. But the important thing is, get a diagnosis and get the letter, so you can go back to school. I mean, look at that research you've been doing! You're clearly smart enough to earn a 3.999 GPA." He winked at her.

Laurel smirked. "A letter. Just like that." She heaved a sigh. "I don't know, Knightman. Seems a little unrealistic."

"But you'll try it, right? It can't do any harm..."

She looked at him as the wheels turned in her brain. "You've got a point. But Jeff, who can I go to? Got any Black psychologists in this two-horse town?"

He shrugged his shoulders. "Does it really matter? There have to be some women, at least. But really, anyone who's licensed and sympathetic should be able to help. Could you ask around at work?"

"No. I'd rather they not know about all this. Kinda makes me look bad."

"I'm not sure you're right on that, but I understand. I could ask around on campus—"

"—I don't want my mother to find out."

"Got it. I'll be super careful. If you trust me, I'll try to get an answer for you." It was the least he could do for her. "The business school is a little isolated from the rest of campus in my experience. I think I know someone there who can recommend a good psychologist. What do you say?"

Another breath escaped her taut chest. "It's a little scary, you know? Spilling my guts to a stranger who might or might not know the *famous* Dr. Howell, on the off chance that it might do me some good. On the other hand..."

On the other hand... "You've gotta do something, Laurel. I've only known you a short time. But if my opinion's worth anything, you can't go on like this. The animals need you!" He reached for her arm, and thought about how she was too smart, too compassionate, and probably too driven to stay where she was, working her ass off at an animal shelter in a town she didn't like with little emotional support.

Laurel studied his face and swallowed. "All right, Knightman. You're right, actually. But just please be careful. I'm not ready to bare my soul to my mother. I'd rather word didn't get out. You understand?"

"Completely. You're in charge. But I feel like this could really work if we're bold enough about it. And it makes me happy that you're willing to let me pitch in." He was determined to earn her nickname for him, to be her knight in woolly armor.

She smiled, and his heart fluttered again. "Thanks, Knightman. Let me know what you find out." The hug they shared was steeped in compassion.

They resumed their cooking and tried to relax. Their collaboration resulted in a delicious knoephla soup that was every bit as good as that made so often by Jeff's father and grandmother.

After their meal, they returned to look in on Teddy and give him a meal of his own. His energy reserves were growing. He tumbled around clumsily on Laurel's bed with his tiny splint and missing paw. While the kitten aroused their pity, he also earned their admiration with his determination to thrive in spite of his grievous injuries. After some cautious play and lots of petting and purring, Teddy was returned to his bed. They fed Olive and Pearl, and bundled up to walk Pearl around the parking lot in the frigid January air.

When they reached his truck, Jeff sighed. He'd have to say so long at some point—now was likely that point. The good news was that, since he'd signed up to volunteer at the shelter three mornings a week, he was sure to see Laurel in a couple of days.

But just as he said: "Well..." with a resigned shoulder shrug, Laurel accused him of trying to leave. She didn't want that. That was fine with Jeff. It wasn't like he had homework, since classes had yet to start.

They returned to her apartment and occupied the sofa with a can each of pop. Laurel asked Jeff about all this knitting madness he was engaged in. He showed her his YouTube channel, and she immediately subscribed.

"I never thought a man could knit like that. It just goes to show how wrong I was. If you knit me a sweater, I'd wear it day in and day out, especially in this godforsaken weather."

"Is that a hint?"

"Take it how you will," she said with a grin. "And by the way, my favorite color is purple. My mother hates purple, but I love purple. Lavender, plum, violet, orchid, amethyst, I'll take all of that. Just sayin'!"

"Hmmm...but I have a lot of gray yarn in my stash. Would that be bad? What about blue? Or brown?"

Laurel shook her head. Her smile would convince a car salesman to slash ninety percent off the MSRP.

"Or maybe orange?"

"Huh-uh."

"Neon green, then."

She shook her head again, smiling away. "Where's that stash at, Knightman? I'll add some purple to it. Then you won't have any excuses."

"You will now, huh?"

"Uh-huh. I can shop online with the best of 'em."

"OK, deal. I'll give you some pointers. I know a good yarn shop or two."

Laurel raised her hands and clapped. She was adorable.

They turned to the topic of music. Jeff wasn't a huge listener. Knitting to ambient noise was just stimulating enough. But Laurel—Laurel adored music. She was obsessed with jazz. They took a deep dive into her favorite artists, from Duke Ellington to Miles Davis, Ella Fitzgerald to Billie Holiday. She even threw in some Snarky Puppy and the Ezra Collective for good measure.

She was an avid collector of vinyl. Jeff marveled at her "stash" of LPs, which included a wide variety of artists, both classic and contemporary. She got up and down off the sofa, playing cut after cut on her turntable as she shared this rich musical culture with him. Then she told Jeff it was time to get their groove on.

"You mean dance?"

"Yes, Knightman, dance. You dance, don't you?"

He flashed a crooked smile. "If you mean with knitting needles, then sure. I'm an awesome dancer."

"You don't use no knitting needles in this kind of dancing, fool. You got to swing! Come on now, let me show you."

Laurel took off her Red Wings so she could step and sway without damaging the laminate flooring. She began with a few solo moves, but that didn't satisfy her. "Come on, join in, Knightman. I know you can do it."

Dancing had never been Jeff's thing. For Laurel, he was willing to change that.

He tried his best to imitate her moves without looking any more ridiculous than he had to. She giggled and teased him mercilessly, and he blushed to beat the band as he struggled to meet her most basic standards of jazz dance. After more giggling, laughing, starting, and stopping, than he imagined possible, Jeff caught on to some straightforward moves and managed to dance in sync with his accomplished partner. Inevitably, the lively cuts ceded to slower, more romantic numbers. They started dancing arm in arm in their stocking feet, with Pearl looking on jealously, while Olive ignored them and flounced away to eat more kibble.

It took two hours of dancing to wear Jeff out. Their date had turned into a five-hour stint of emotional revelations and shared enjoyment. The thought of leaving Laurel and returning to his dorm to sleep across from the roommate he barely knew weighed on Jeff's mind. Nor had his lust fully cooled—on the contrary. As tired as he was, the thought of lying in bed with Laurel in his arms aroused him. "Are you tired?"

Laurel looked at the clock. "Not really. But I try to get to work by six."

"That's early."

"Makes my day more productive. It helps me to get lost in my work."

"Got it."

"You can stay here if you like."

Jeff suppressed the cry of joy that sought exit from his throat. "I'd like that."

He spent the night with Laurel Howell, holding her contentedly under the watchful eye of her many ancestors.

9

The Mission

"How busy are you this evening?" Laurel handed Jeff a banana and a granola bar to complement their hazelnut coffee.

Jeff looked at the clock—5:20 a.m. Even at this ungodly hour, he felt surprisingly at home in Laurel's cheerful kitchen. They'd just given Teddy his formula and cleaned his crate. "I can get a lot done during the day. So I'm actually free." And even if he weren't, he would fix it so he were.

"Wanna come back here, then?"

"Absolutely. What time?"

"Five? Six?"

"Let's split the difference. I'll come at five-thirty."

"Perfect." Laurel left Jeff to eat while she bundled up and took Pearl outside. Then she joined him back at the table, where they sat a little sleepily, absorbing each other's presence.

Jeff studied his surroundings. In addition to her pets, Laurel had several lush houseplants spilling over the kitchen windowsill. A rural landscape extended beyond the window, looking precisely like the "tundra" she'd complained of the day before. They took in a few news reels on her phone—a purple portable speaker perched beside a stack of mail delivered the sound. A bowl of fresh fruit sat beside that, filled with mangoes, bananas, apples, and oranges. Jeff smiled to realize Laurel took good care of herself.

"Don't hold back, Knightman. Take an orange for the road."

Jeff complied. The thought of keeping Laurel's mandarin orange with him as he faced the day was a comfort. "Guess I better go."

Laurel's shoulders sagged. "Yeah. But it was a great night. Did you know, I've never been late to work? Not even once?"

Jeff called to mind Laurel's devoted rapport with the shelter pets. "Duty calls. Well, see you tonight."

That prompted a smile. "Tonight. Exactly." They stood and hugged, working to tame their passions. They both faced the challenge of making it through the day on inadequate sleep and energy. Jeff donned his parka and mittens and headed to campus, while Laurel went off to work.

Jeff's next undertaking was an invigorating shower. He didn't have Black Women's History until nine—it crossed his mind to take a nap. But he was too keyed up, so he used the hour before class to take a brisk walk and let the ten-degree air clear the cobwebs from his mind. The knowledge that Tabitha Howell was Laurel's mother had him tied up in knots.

But when nine arrived and Jeff found himself in the space where Laurel's mother would instruct him for the next fifteen weeks, other thoughts plagued him. The professor entered the room, dressed in a boldly-colored top over brown slacks. She was all business. Doubtless Howell expected to find her fellow fiber guild member sitting in the back row, knitting out of eyeshot of the other students. But indulging in that soothing routine was the farthest thing from Jeff's mind. The stifling classroom was smaller than those he was used to in the business school, and packed with students whose collective lack of diversity stood in jarring contrast with the diversity-minded course content.

Of the eighteen people Jeff counted as he sat in the front right desk, his leg shaking to beat the band, there were all of two Black students, one the only other male: Randall Cobb from the basketball team, who did a mean impression of Kevin Durant every time he scored a dunk. The team had a solid academic reputation, so Jeff figured Randall would succeed in a course taught by a reputed hard-ass. That left over a dozen students who were both female and white, or possibly Latina. The last time Jeff remembered being surrounded by ninety percent women in a class was back in high school, when he'd taken child development. The eyes of all those females felt like lasers zeroing in on him, demanding to know how he dared invade their feminine realm with Randall Cobb.

Dr. Howell attempted to warm the group up by asking them one by one what had brought them here. Jeff was petrified. He pushed himself to picture Tabitha at a meeting of the Flatlands Fiber Guild, knitting meditatively on a shawl as they casually talked alpaca, handspun, superwash, and colorwork. He tried to replace the learned expression stiffening her features with the contented smile that accompanied her stitching away over a cup of hot tea. It was useless.

Relieved that the professor had begun her poll at the opposite end of the room, Jeff dreaded the moment when she finally came around to him. He had every reason to fear some heedless impulse would make him blurt out: *Your daughter's obsessing over her enslaved ancestors, and I wanna help her untangle her roots.*

"I wanna be a community advocate," a couple of girls responded.

"I want to be an elementary school teacher," said another, "and this class will be useful for that." The red-haired student looked enviably comfortable in this academic space.

"I'm a soc major," another said.

Then Randall announced: "Hey, I'm here for the girls."

Dr. Howell responded with a frown. "We'll see about that, Mr. Cobb."

She went on to the next girl, and the next, and Jeff cursed his brain, which refused to toss any thoughts his way besides: *I want to learn more about Percy Howell's railroad-building work. I'm intrigued by Roberta Bennett's teaching career. I'd love to explore Isaiah Bennett's WWI military service. The enslaved Howells on that plantation in North Carolina. Laurel Howell's nagging depression...*"

"How about you, Mr. Nietmann?" As the professor looked at him, Jeff was assailed by the sight of Laurel's eyes staring into his. His blood pressure shot through the roof.

"Me?" His brain flailed for a response that would not make him look like the *imbecile* he happened to be in that moment. Finally, it delivered: "I like history." He breathed the biggest sigh of relief he'd breathed since his mother had found his fake ID, showed it to him, then said, "Use it wisely," and mercifully dropped the subject.

"Excellent, Jeff." Howell's remark brought him instant relief.

But it refused to stick.

As the professor went over the syllabus and fielded questions, every glance of hers that came Jeff's way had him convinced she knew what he least wanted her to know: that he'd spent the night *screwing her daughter.*

Desperate to suppress his nervous leg and the bile rising in his throat, Jeff scribbled notes that were so detailed, Howell might as well have dictated the entire syllabus. Every period of Black history she named had one of Laurel's ancestors attached to it. All this history had become painfully personal to him overnight, and here Tabitha was, listing off period after troubling period with the coolness of a scientist anatomizing a lynching victim. He couldn't fathom how this erudite Black woman could survey what he now regarded as Laurel's personally traumatizing history with such calculating distance. The sight of Laurel's eyes in his professor's face compelled Jeff to imagine Laurel standing there, reviewing the eras they would cover. It would make infinitely more sense, it would be so intimate and real. Tears welled in his eyes.

Keen to prevent his thoughts from streaking in all their nakedness past the analytical professor and her shallow students, Jeff shut his eyes and conjured the most benign image he could think up. He seized on the lush houseplants spilling over Laurel's windowsill. That enabled him to hold back his tears.

Dr. Howell's—Laurel's!—eyes lingered over him, more than they did over the other students. She was concerned—that's what he was forced to conclude. *She's onto me...I barely got the condom on in time...* But he had, he was certain of it. If he could just get the hell out of that classroom, he could devote the rest of the day to burying himself in the assigned books, then return on Wednesday, just as cool and calculating in his mastery of the content as Dr. Howell was herself.

He finally exhaled when Tabitha let them go. Only not him, *oh no*. She *had* to approach him at the end of the hour, 'cause she was clearly worried, and force him to engage in a chat, which he could only hope to do without spilling his blameworthy guts. *Fuck!*

Tabitha bathed him in her warm gaze. "I'm so glad to have you in this class, Jeff. I didn't have a chance to ask you about your holiday. Was it nice?"

"It was great." Jeff pushed himself to accept the sight of his girlfriend's dark eyes beneath his professor's elaborately braided hair. "How about you?"

"Oh, it was fine I guess. I took a little trip to Dubai."

The word was like a punch to Jeff's gut. Every muscle tensed up as he asked: "Really? Did you enjoy it?"

She scoffed a little. "Truth be told, it's not my favorite country. My husband took a job there and wanted to see me. But I was honestly relieved to get back here to Prairie Plains. Isn't that crazy?"

Ahhh, now she had Laurel's voice! *Laurel's accent!* "Yes, ma'am." He turned beet red—now he had Laurel's accent, too! He had no fight left. He yearned to give in to flight... "See you on Wednesday, then?"

"Sounds good. Take care, Jeff. And remember, you're welcome to knit in my class."

It was the *farthest thing from his mind*. "Yes, ma'am. I'll remember."

"All right then." With detectable hesitation, she let him go.

Jeff walked numbly down the hall, wondering if Laurel's eyes were following him. He started jogging. Then running. He found the men's restroom, practically knocked a guy down as he stumbled into a stall, and threw up everything he'd eaten that morning. After that he felt a little better. But it would be days before he considered eating again.

Crazy! Tabitha's word rattled around in his brain. *This whole fucking situation is crazy!* Jeff was suddenly the fulcrum of the Laurel-Tabitha seesaw. Fate had elected him as the unwitting—and possibly completely witless—instrument of their reconciliation. He'd slid onto the tile floor by the toilet and sat there, like a lavatory philosopher, contemplating his situation. He had every reason to expect it would grind him down to an emotional pulp. It was unbearable, yet he would have to bear it. Because if he walked away from this job, the stunning star that was Laurel Howell might literally implode.

He leaned against the unforgiving wall, trying to ignore the urine smell rising up his nostrils. *Well, after all, fixing people's relationships is a dirty job,* he acknowledged, chuckling helplessly. But he was a complete greenhorn in this area. Laurel was right when she'd said how lucky he was. He'd only had one real relationship. That had been back in high school with Caitlin, the Ojibwe girl he'd gotten to know in art class. After all the hustle and bustle surrounding going to prom together, their romance had petered out over the summer. By senior year they'd both moved on, barely saying a word about what had gone wrong.

And while Jeff had encountered the usual bullying along the way, because he wasn't a jock but was an admitted knitting nerd instead, he'd had a pretty quiet emotional life, tested only by the passing of his paternal grandfather, whose death to heart failure had been hard, but not unanticipated. And now he was being shredded to pieces by a mother and her estranged daughter, both of whom deserved to be happy. It was clear to him now that Dr. Howell was as sad as Laurel was. She just hid her emotional life behind a wall of academic accomplishment, with a little knitting on the side.

This was hardly the personal path Jeff would have chosen for himself. But when he thought about it, he wasn't at a total loss when it came to a way forward. Laurel herself had conceded that seeking a strategy to undo the damage her depression had done to her college career made sense, and Jeff was optimistic enough to believe they had only to tap into the right resources to make that happen. And seeing as how no one besides him was privy to Laurel's dogged quest for her place in the world through her ancestry research, and the surprising connection of that to Tabitha's own celebrated scholarship, which had ended up landing Laurel in an emotional desert, the task had fallen on Jeff to mend these women's bridges. And there could be a wonderful prize in it for him if he succeeded, namely Laurel herself, with whom Jeff had fallen head over heels in love.

He pulled himself up off the floor, washed at the sink, then left the humanities building for the business school. Resources, resources—that's what he needed now. He'd worked with the same academic advisor since the start of college. Surely that man could recommend a psychologist for Laurel to visit with. Jeff knew exactly where to find him, and went straight to Mr. Halperin's office.

The advisor greeted his visit with a smile. Halperin asked if he was all right, saying he looked a little pale. Jeff reassured him, then shared a few details about a student he knew who might benefit from the help of a therapist.

"I know someone who's done good work with students over the years," Halperin told him. "She's a bit frumpy, but she's been at it a long time. She should be able to help your friend." He shared the contact information for a Dr. McCoy. Jeff shook Halperin's hand, thanking him profusely.

This little victory lifted his spirits. He even felt confident enough to devote an hour or two to studying at the library. He was on a tear to be the best student who'd ever darkened Professor Howell's classroom door. Proving himself would keep Tabitha from deciding she should be disappointed in him. If she respected him as a student, she might respect him as an agent for getting her and Laurel talking again. In fact, he outdid himself. He read three times the number of pages assigned for Black Women's History this week, getting almost all the way through bell hooks' Black feminist treatise *Ain't I a Woman* over two concerted hours.

A message from Laurel briefly interrupted his work. As promised, she was checking in during her lunch break. Jeff hadn't so much as looked at his phone since texting Laurel that he'd arrived at her apartment yesterday afternoon. As he responded to the alert, he saw to his dismay that Sigrun Karlsen had messaged him over and over again. *Oh, geez.*

He exchanged a few reassuring messages with Laurel. He couldn't wait to see her tonight, and would she please give his regards to Teddy. She promised she would, appending a laugh emoji to a string of dog and cat images.

Jeff rubbed his forehead as he pondered the messages from Sigrun. He'd come to regard Astrid as an important mentor—he couldn't very well ignore her daughter's frantic efforts to communicate with him. He tapped on the thread of text after text, moving all the way back to the top. *What r u up to?* he read. That had come in around 9 p.m., when he and Laurel had been dancing in their stocking feet to Count Basie. Further down, he read: *Jeff, you really need to get back to me.* Then, at 10:41: *If something's up you should let me know.* And just before midnight: *I don't understand how you can ignore me like this.* She must have gone to bed at that point, because the subsequent message: *I hope you know how much it hurts that you can't even respond to a simple text from me,* had been sent at 7:20 a.m.

Jeff sighed heavily. "I just *have* to do something about her." He got up his nerve and decided he should invite her for coffee. Ignoring all her demands for an explanation, he simply typed: *We really need to meet.*

Yes, we do, she texted back. *Where have you been all weekend?*

He'd dated Sigrun all of a couple times—what was she expecting from him? *Out. Let's meet at 3 at the coffee shop.* He didn't even give her a say in the matter. Either she would come, or that would be the end of it. Jeff had more important concerns than Sigrun's bruised ego.

Shortly after management class, he went to the coffee shop and found Sigrun waiting for him.

"Oh my God. I thought something'd happened to you. Don't scare me like that, Jeff!" What a welcome. She didn't even reach out toward him—how upset could she be?

"My bad." Not that Jeff really felt that way. But he did feel the need to get this over with. "What can I get you to drink?" He moved toward the counter.

Sigrun followed. "You don't have to buy mine. I know you probably don't have much money."

Jeff groaned inwardly. "There is such a thing as chivalry."

"Well, OK. As long as you can afford it."

"That's beside the point." He furrowed his brow as he glanced into her sky-blue eyes.

Sigrun shrugged her shoulders.

Jeff bought her an Americano. He ordered a mocha with four espresso shots for himself. Then he realized he hadn't had a bite to eat since losing his breakfast after Professor Howell's class, so he ordered a jumbo-sized poppy seed muffin. All this time, Laurel's mandarin orange had been hibernating in his coat pocket. He smiled and got that out to eat as well.

They found a table and sat across from each other.

Sigrun was scowling. "What in the heck have you been up to, Jeff?"

He was in no mood for her huffiness. "It's been a long weekend."

"I mean, couldn't you at least pick up your phone and respond to me? It's really kind of rude to just leave—"

"—Look, Sigrun." He drilled her with his eyes, simultaneously peeling Laurel's orange.

She stared at him. "How come you're so pale?"

The sudden question briefly derailed Jeff's thoughts. He must really need an infusion of calories if she was inspired to compassion by the sight of him. "It's nothing. I'm just hungry. Look, I wanted to meet with you because I'm not the kind of person who breaks off a—well...let's just call this a friendship—with a text message—"

"What do you mean, 'break off'? And what do you mean, *'friendship'*?"

Jeff bit off a third of his poppy seed muffin. He made her wait for him to swallow half of that while he wiped the crumbs from his mustache. Then he met her gaze. "Sigrun, *I'm seeing someone.*"

"Yes, me!"

He shook his head and finished swallowing. "Not you. Someone *else.*"

She stared at him with huge eyes. "I don't understand."

Her pout would have looked adorable on a six-year-old. But since she was nineteen, it put Jeff off. "I've met someone." There was every chance Sigrun Karlsen and Laurel Howell had crossed paths, given the friendship between Astrid and Tabitha. If he shared who this "someone" was, it could have devastating consequences, given Laurel's urgent need to keep her distance from her mother.

Sigrun supplied him with the perfect opportunity to keep his girlfriend's identity a secret when she guessed: "Is it a guy?"

He interrupted his effort to chew a few orange segments.

"It *is* a guy! Isn't it?"

Jeff abruptly downed the orange and followed that up with another third of his mocha. Letting her believe this was just too expedient. "Don't be so judgmental."

"Why in the heck wouldn't you say anything, Jeff? You just let me go on thinking all this time that..." Then she slapped her hand down on the table. "Well, I should have known! I mean, all the guys I've ever seen who like knitting are gay. *I'm such an idiot!*"

Her acute drift from the trail that would have led her to "the other woman's" identity caused Jeff to sigh in relief. He guzzled more espresso-laced coffee as he took in, wincing a little, her rather bigoted train of thought.

But that train took a surprising turn as Sigrun decided she was the first person he'd chosen to come out to. "You should have told me. Oh my gosh, Jeff. Why didn't you say something? Did you think I wouldn't understand? That's actually kind of sweet, that you would choose me to be the first person to know."

Jeff wiped his mouth. He was disappointed to have finished his mocha, and sorry he hadn't brought any knitting along to calm his nerves, which were quickly responding to the espresso shots. "Look, Sigrun. I'm really sorry. I mean, you're just so self-contained, so independent. You make me feel like I'm not needed."

"Huh?" She arched and furrowed her brow simultaneously.

"I just hope we can be friends. I have enormous respect for your mother as an artist. I really do wanna take those spinning lessons from her. If we could just move on from this, it would be a huge relief."

She let out a breath. "I guess I understand. Who are you seeing, anyhow? Do I know him?"

He conjured a safe reply. "I doubt it."

"Is he a student here?"

He could honestly say: "No."

"Is he a knitter, too?"

"Sigrun, I have to go." In truth, he *wanted* to go. He was determined to get to the yarn store before the place closed, so he could buy something to knit Laurel a sweater with. He rose to his feet.

Sigrun followed suit. She looked a little crestfallen, but her mien conveyed sympathy. "I hope I get to meet him sometime."

Jeff tossed his cup and wrapper into the recycling. "No doubt. See you on the fiber trail?"

She nodded slowly. "Sure."

Jeff consented to a hug and a peck on the cheek. As he watched her exit, a shiver ran up his spine. The impression he'd left her with, that he was dating a guy, could have interesting repercussions. On the other hand, she was the one who'd reached that conclusion, a product of her own unresearched assumptions. And at the end of the day, it didn't matter. Gay or straight, people were people, all just trying to make the most of their daily journey around the sun on this crazy, miraculous planet called Earth.

Jeff's next stop was Dee's Yarn & Fiber Emporium. He'd barely given a thought to his knitting since meeting Laurel. But now he was downright excited to spend time planning his approach to stitching a purple sweater for her. The yarn shop was only half a mile from campus. Jeff contemplated his knitworthy girlfriend as he drove toward College Ave.

She was right around his height, but more slender and—of course—shapely. He was confident a little positive ease would go over well. Laurel was active, she worked hard, and was very physical, even if she didn't exercise for the sake of it. Exercise was a luxury for people who sat behind desks all day long. For people like Laurel, it was a luxury she couldn't afford. Her purple sweater needed to be as comfortable as it was beautiful. If he chose a DK-weight yarn, he could easily include a colorwork yoke. It would be amazing if he could incorporate kittens and puppies to celebrate her love of animals. He was certain he could devise straightforward repeated patterns to accomplish this end.

He entered the yarn store, his frayed nerves immediately responding to the cozy atmosphere of this fiber-filled space. He was relieved to find he was the only customer and Ms. Dee was manning the brightly-lit shop herself. What he didn't want was for fiber guild members to discover he was embarking on a new project and interrogate him regarding the intended recipient.

Bonnie was spinning contentedly when Jeff arrived. "Well, who have we here?"

Jeff waved with a smile. "Hi, Ms. Dee!"

"Welcome! Just let me know if you need any assistance, Jeff."

"If you could point my way to the DK yarn in shades of purple, I should be able to take it from there."

"I think we have what you need. Is this for a sweater?"

Jeff nodded. "How did you know?"

Bonnie chuckled. "I'm a good guesser. I've been sitting here for the past hour, apparently waiting for your arrival.

You're giving me a good excuse to get up off my duff." Her cheerful tone warmed Jeff's heart.

He reached out to give her his arm. It amazed him to see her still running this shop at ninety years old.

Bonnie reached for her cane. "Come over here, young man." She led him down a haphazardly stocked aisle to some lighter-weight yarns. "We just replenished our supply of these Norwegian wools." The remark drew Jeff back to his unnerving exchange with that daughter of Norway, Sigrun. He knew this brand well, however, and asked Bonnie if she had any additional colors.

"How many colors do you need?"

"As many shades of purple and lavender as you've got."

"Purple and lavender, purple and lavender, yes—the colors of royalty."

Jeff flashed a smile. "For my princess!" He figured he was safe sharing that much with Bonnie, who surely had better things to do than speculate over who he meant.

"Well, I see about five shades of purple here with this yarn. We also have some yarn from Montana—did you want rustic or superwash?"

That was a good question. Laurel's sweater should be soft on the one hand, but hard-wearing on the other. Perhaps most importantly, it had to keep her *warm*. She clearly wasn't fond of Prairie Plains' winter weather. If he knit a sweater to be worn over, say, a turtleneck, he could afford to use a woolly wool that would excel in the warmth department. "Rustic."

Ms. Dee had to go and complicate things. "You know, I do have a yak-wool blend that would offer equal degrees of softness and wooliness, as well as superior insulation.

But...well, you're a student. It might be too expensive." Her owl-like eyes rested on his.

In the end, maximizing Laurel's happiness was more important than heeding the limitations of his budget. "At least let me take a look."

Bonnie smiled. "Come this way." She hobbled toward the front of the store where she kept the luxury yarns. "There are four hues of purple and lavender with this brand. But you could also accentuate those by adding in a white or a yellow, couldn't you?"

"Actually, that's a good idea, Ms. Dee. Yellow would bring out the purple, wouldn't it?"

"It would. But I would go with something light." She handed Jeff a skein in royal purple.

The gorgeous yarn would suit his purpose perfectly. "How much is it?" He tensed in anticipation of her response.

"It's right at fifty dollars a skein."

Jeff swallowed. He asked himself how much yarn he would need, and whether he could buy some now and some later, since it would take a few weeks to finish the project. During that time, of course, it could sell out—after all, it was some of the nicest yarn he'd ever come across.

Bonnie smiled. "Since you're in the fiber guild, Jeff, you get a ten percent discount. That might help you out a little."

Jeff knew for a fact there was no ten percent discount for fiber guild members. He'd bought yarn from Ms. Dee before, and that had never come up. She was simply being kind. Did she suspect how much the project he had in mind meant to him? Could be. Her gesture deserved honoring. He also realized that, if he put the yarn on his pitiful student's credit card with its thousand dollar limit, he could pay it off from his YouTube earnings, which were growing by the month. Suddenly, splurging on Laurel and buying all the skeins he needed at once made perfect sense. "Sold!"

"You're sure?"

He nodded deliberately. "I'm sure."

Bonnie helped him pick out the purple, lavender, amethyst, and orchid he needed, with a skein of "lemon chiffon" to round out the palette.

"Oh, and Ms. Dee, I don't usually knit sweaters at school—all my long circulars are back home. Could you sell me a few needles in a size four?"

"Of course. Bamboo, wood, or metal?"

"Bamboo or wood would work great. The metal ones make my fingers kinda sore."

"I have just what you need." She handed him a few samples in various lengths to consider.

Jeff made his choice, took a deep breath, and brandished his credit card. Three hundred and fifty dollars later, he was on his way back to campus with the goods needed to knit Laurel Howell a colorwork sweater worthy of an animal-rescuing princess.

He realized he might no more return to his dorm room tonight than he had last night. He took the precaution of packing a few items to take along to Laurel's apartment. Armed with these and his bag of luxurious yarn, Jeff hopped into his pickup, and embarked on the mission of earning his princess's love.

10

The Reprieve

It was five-thirty on the dot when Jeff arrived at Laurel's place. She buzzed him into the building. When he reached her door, she let him in with a spoon in her hand and the injured kitten on her shoulder. She was just getting the pets fed. "We're so glad to see you!" She worked around Teddy and gave Jeff a careful hug.

Jeff stroked Teddy on the neck. "Just look at you. You're making Daddy so proud!"

Laurel's smile was like a sunrise parting the fog on a January day.

"Oh, I've got something for you." Jeff found the card with Dr. McCoy's information.

Laurel reached for it. "Where'd you find out about her?"

"From my academic advisor. No problems with confidentiality. He knows all about students and privacy, so I thought he'd be a great person to ask. He said Dr. McCoy is 'a bit frumpy,' but she's been helping students out for years and knows what she's doing. Said you should be able to get in to see her soon."

Laurel stared at the card, finally nodding after a brief silence. "Thank you. I'll give her a call."

"You'll make an awesome veterinarian, Laurel. It's all about the future."

She met his gaze. "You're right." She invited him to take off his coat and sit down, then gently handed Teddy to him. She grabbed a couple sparkling waters while Pearl looked on, wagging her tail with her usual happy energy. Then she took a seat on the sofa beside Jeff, inviting Olive to take over her lap.

Jeff let Olive sniff his hand. "Wanna know something funny?"

"Sure!" Laurel took a swig of her water.

"You know Sigrun Karlsen, I assume, right?"

She practically choked. "Uh, yes. You could say that."

"You have a history?"

She smirked. "Tell me what's funny."

Jeff took in her confirmation of his assumption that she and Sigrun were hardly strangers. It made what he had to share all the more interesting. "I may have given her the impression I was gay."

"Really?" Laurel stared at him, a smile doing its best to override what Jeff took to be her contempt. "That's insane."

"She's been trying to involve me in this really dysfunctional relationship via text, and I just had to get real with her. So when she said she thought I was seeing a guy, I sort of didn't deny it."

Laurel's stare persisted. "Is she still a little...well, shall we say: *bougie*? A little stuck on herself?"

Jeff laughed. "Yeah, you could say that. I mean, she's nice and all. I just don't think she's ready for a relationship. So, do you know her through your mom, then?"

"Oh my God—my mom and Sigrun's mom are like best friends. Plus, Sigrun was a junior when I was a senior in high school here."

"Aha. Then it's a good thing she thinks I'm dating a guy."

"I can't imagine you with a man. No way. Just goes to show you how self-absorbed she is."

Jeff responded to that by kissing Laurel on the head. "Tell me more."

"What's to tell? Other than that girl has a way of just sucking all the oxygen out of a room." Laurel pushed Olive onto Jeff's lap beside Teddy and jumped onto her booted feet. "She just kind of saunters, you know what I mean?" She fanned her arms out to indicate Sigrun's long flowing locks, then strutted about like a peacock. "And she's just like, oh, I'm here now, let's get this party started." She gestured with her hands, suggesting an imaginary heir to the throne prompting her subjects to bow down to her. "I'll never forget science fair in the spring of my senior year. I got first prize. But she was so impressed with herself that she got second place, as a mere junior, and she practically shoved everyone else aside as she stood there, like she'd earned an Olympic gold medal or some shit. Let me show you."

"Wait—you won first prize at the science fair?"

"Oh, baby—back in Atlanta, I was the science fair diva!" Laurel sat back down, whipped out her phone, and scrolled through some photos. She found one that showed her, Sigrun, and two other students at Prairie Plains High School accepting their science fair awards. Just as she'd said, Sigrun had found a way to stand so it looked like she'd won first prize instead of Laurel, whose blank expression failed to mask her irritation. "Let's just call this one of those winning-the-science-fair-while-Black moments."

Jeff released a grunt. It angered him that Laurel had had to put up with Sigrun's arrogance. "I definitely picked the right girl."

Laurel seemed quite pleased with herself. "I got the *real* prize." She said it with a throaty, self-satisfied tone, looking right into his eyes. "You have no idea how happy it makes me that I got something she didn't. She can think you're as gay as Lil Nas X. You'll always be *my* Knightman." She kissed him on the lips as Teddy and Olive purred to beat the band beneath their chins.

Apparently, Laurel had quite the illustrious past. Jeff was proud of her. "Tell me about all those science fair projects."

"You wanna know about my science fair projects?"

"I do. And so does Teddy." He lifted Teddy's good paw and waved it in front of her, then manifested his inner kitten and spoke for their rescue pet: "Tell us about your scientist work, Laurel!"

Laurel laughed. She got up and beckoned to him. "Come into my boudoir." Her tone bore a hint of raunch-iness.

Jeff placed Olive on the sofa arm and flashed a smile at Pearl. "See you kids later." He carried Teddy on his shoulder and followed Laurel into her bedroom. When he closed the door in front of her, poor Pearl protested with a series of whimpers.

Jeff set the kitten down. He was able to hobble about on his own now, a freedom he seemed to enjoy.

Laurel opened a drawer in her desk. "These are the certificates." She handed him a stack of awards. "The trophies are still over at my mom's house."

Jeff sat on the bed and leafed through these souvenirs of Laurel's youthful accomplishments. They were all in the area of animal biology. The topics she'd investigated ranged from how dogs communicate with their barks and the best strategies for keeping squirrels out of bird-feeders, to more specialized issues of dermatophytes in canine claws, the impact of neighborhood cats on the local bird population, all the way to advanced topics like "The Influence of Age on GI Microbiota in Cats" and "The Impact of Dog Ownership on Home Dust Microbiota."

Jeff admired Laurel for her smarts. "Microbiology. Looks like college-level stuff."

Laurel sat down beside him. "I suppose. I kind of miss taking science classes."

"All the more reason to see that psychologist sooner rather than later, and make your case to the university about letting you start back with a clean slate." Their eyes met just long enough for Jeff to gaze some encouragement into her. "Laurel, this stuff is really impressive. If I wasn't the knitting genius I am, I'd be downright intimidated. If it hadn't been for my fascination with fiber, I wouldn't have won a single thing for any of my science fair projects."

Laurel arched a brow. "But you did win *something*."

Jeff assumed the competitive spirit within her was rooting for the man who'd dumped Sigrun Karlsen. "I did. I got second place for my research on toxins in synthetic fiber. My work on that taught me why I want to stick with fiber from animals and plants."

Laurel nodded. "OK. Sounds like you pass the test." She rewarded him with a kiss.

Jeff's stomach embarrassed him by emitting a loud growl.

Laurel giggled. "Sounds like you're hungry, Knight-man."

"Starving! I spent my whole lunch hour reading a book for your mom's class."

"I told you she was hard!"

"That's why I just have to be harder. She assigned fifty pages this week, but I've already read *Ain't I a Woman* from cover to cover." He noticed Teddy clawing at some papers and reached out to distract him.

"That's good. Stay ahead of the class. And it's good you've had philosophy. She's really big on theory."

"Yeah, I saw that. I think I've got practically the entire syllabus memorized."

Laurel smiled. "Then you've earned a nice steak dinner. Want me to get us some sirloins? They've got some yummy grassfed beef at the market."

"Or we could eat out. Might be quicker."

Laurel met his gaze. "Did you know that lunch the other day was the first time I've eaten out in over a year?"

"What? Why?"

She shrugged her shoulders. "I just don't get out much."

"We need to change that. People should see you. I mean, you're...you're so beautiful, Laurel."

She scoffed. "Beautiful in my unmade-up face, my ranch-hand hoodie, and my leather boots."

"So...put on your dress boots, then."

"These *are* my dress boots." She laughed.

Jeff took a gander at Laurel's Iron Rangers. They were in severe need of conditioning, thanks to all the dirt, shit, pee, and cleaning solutions they encountered day after day at the shelter. "They do need a little mink oil, don't they?" He leaned down and ran his hand across the vamp and heel of her right boot. "I'll bring some over next time I'm here. We'll have a little conditioning party."

"Sounds fun."

"In fact, we could even go directly to Red Wing and get you some new dress boots." The thought of taking a road trip with his new love caused Jeff's imagination to dance.

"As I told you before, I would be open to that." Her words were music to his ears.

"So should we go out?"

She nodded. "I'm sure I won't be the only one dining out in a ranch-hand hoodie around these parts."

"If I have my way, it won't be long before you're dining out in a handknit sweater, 'cause I picked up the yarn for that today."

That elicited a big smile. "You really did?"

He nodded. "It's out in my truck. You can check it out while we're on our way to that steakhouse. I'll drive."

Laurel clapped her hands together. "Come on Teddy. Let's get you back in your cat house, so Daddy and I can go out to eat."

They took Pearl to do her business, locked up the apartment, and headed to town.

When they got inside the Cattleman Steakhouse, one of Jeff's classmates was working as host. She welcomed them, and Jeff enjoyed being seen in public with his new girlfriend—something he hadn't experienced since high school. He wrapped his arm around his casually dressed partner as he greeted Ashley from management class. "Two, please."

"Sure, Jeff. Table, or booth?"

He looked at Laurel. "Booth, please."

"Come this way."

The restaurant was fairly full. The warmth, the smell of sizzling steak, the hubbub of relaxed conversation, combined with the western-style décor, aroused Jeff's contentment as well as his hunger. As they sat across from each other in the privacy of the green leather booth, they exchanged gazes and basked in togetherness.

They talked about Red Wing. Jeff proposed that Laurel should accompany him on his next "Extreme Knitting" video trip. It would bring him and his friends all the way to northern Minnesota. Maybe they could follow that up with a swing down through Red Wing.

"You really do all that traveling in the dead of winter up here?" Laurel shivered as she raised the thought of driving for hours in bitter cold.

"Sure! We already checked, and the weather is looking really good for the end of the month. A big dome of Canadian air is parked over the region. All the main roads'll be clear, and we could go snowboarding!"

"Say what?"

"You haven't tried snowboarding?"

Laurel frowned. "Honey, I can barely ride a skateboard."

"You skateboard?"

"Not much since I broke my wrist as a high school freshman."

"Ouch!" The thought of Laurel breaking a bone had Jeff shivering now.

The waiter came to take their drink order. He, too, was familiar to Jeff—Micah Okstad was a leader among the campus LGBTQ students and made sure everyone knew it. "What can I get you two tonight?" He looked quite dapper in his pink hair and turquoise bowtie.

"Not sure." Jeff looked at Laurel.

Laurel looked at Micah. "What have you got?"

"Well, let me tell you: we actually do have a few really nice red wines. If you'd like, I can let you try a couple."

Laurel drilled Jeff with her eyes. Neither of them was twenty-one.

Jeff kept his cool. The thought of adding wine to their meal out appealed to him. "Have you got a good cabernet?"

"Absolutely."

"We'll take a bottle of that."

"Excellent. I'll bring it right out." He left them.

Laurel leaned across the table and whispered: "What are you doing?"

"Don't worry." Jeff had zero concerns. The fake ID his mother had let him keep was right there in his wallet. "Besides, I'll be twenty-one next month. So it's close enough for jazz, if you ask me."

"Next month?"

Jeff nodded.

Laurel smiled. "Me too."

"No kidding!"

"When's your birthday?"

"February 15th. My parents are coming out. You can meet them."

"Well, if they're anything like you, and I'm sure they are, I'd love to meet them."

Jeff searched through the photos on his phone to give Laurel a peek at his family. He shared a few Christmas pics with her.

"Geez, how tall is your dad?" Laurel squinted at the tall, lean, light-haired man with gold-rimmed glasses draping his arm across his dark-haired son's shoulders by their Christmas tree.

"He's six-three. And my Mom's five-five. That puts me right in the middle. Crazy, huh?"

Laurel smiled broadly. "I can't believe it. Your mom looks so sweet. And that's your sister?" She peered at Jeff's park ranger sibling with her outdoorsy allure.

"Yup! That's Amy."

"And she's really taller than you?"

"No, not at all."

"But she's definitely taller than you. She's wearing moccasins, for Christ's sake." Laurel flashed a saucy smile.

"OK, you dragged it out of me. She's five foot twelve."

"That's six feet, dumbass."

"Granted, but it sounds shorter when you say five foot twelve."

"You're silly." Laurel laughed. "But seriously. You have a beautiful family."

"Thanks. I can't wait for them to meet you."

"So they're coming here on the 15th?"

"Yup! Sans my sister—she has to work. What about your birthday? It's also next month?"

Laurel scowled. "Don't even go there." She busied herself with unrolling her silverware from the cloth napkin.

"Why not?"

"Just don't." The defiance in her voice contrasted provocatively with the smile that insisted on forming across her lips.

Jeff waited. She could only look away for so long. Then he thought of something that might motivate her. "How will I know if I get your sweater made in time?"

She huffed. "OK, fine. February 14th."

Jeff flashed a big smile. "Really? Valentine's Day?"

She nodded. "Don't shoot me."

"I think it's adorable!"

"You do?"

"Absolutely!"

"But I'm the most unromantic person who ever roamed God's green earth."

"No. Not true."

"Well, we'll see. So now you know." She managed to smile again. Jeff enjoyed her discomfort. He had no need for a girl who was cock sure of herself.

The waiter arrived with their wine. He opened the bottle and poured a taste into Jeff's glass. "*Monsieur?*" Micah's debonair flair contrasted jarringly with the haute rustic Western décor.

Jeff took the glass as his companion looked on, furrowing her brow. "Need to see my ID or anything?"

Micah shook his head. "I know you. You're fine." It was true—they'd taken the same macroeconomics class a year ago. Then the waiter looked at Laurel. "I believe I know you as well, right? English class? Freshman year?"

The scales seemed to fall from Laurel's eyes. "Oh, yeah. Camus."

"*L'étranger*—'The Stranger.' Awesome discussion."

Her face lit up. "I remember." Her warm tone caused Jeff to conclude she must have thrived in that particular class.

Micah turned back to Jeff. "So? Do you approve?"

Jeff took a big swig of the cabernet. "Delicious."

"Excellent." He poured them each a glass, then asked regarding their dinner selections.

They wasted little time, as they were both set on indulging in the classic broiled sirloin. Jeff ordered a baked potato and Caesar salad to go along with his.

Laurel said: "Same for me," and Micah left them.

She took a swallow of her wine, then renewed their conversation. "You never told me how the Black Women's History class went today."

"Oh, yeah. To be honest, I was kinda nervous."

"I hope I didn't scare you too much."

"No, I just...I don't wanna disappoint your mother. Plus, I couldn't stop thinking about last night. And your mom has your eyes—I couldn't stop seeing you up there. It was incredibly distracting."

Laurel burst out laughing. "Poor baby! Well, if you need a leg up, I have a couple dozen of her books in my apartment."

"You do? So you borrow her books at least?" Jeff wondered if that amounted to actual communication between the two of them.

"Not that she knows about it. I just need certain books for my research on the family, and she happens to have them. So I go over there with my key and get them."

Jeff studied her self-satisfied expression. It disappointed him to think Laurel and Tabitha exchanged no words over these illicit transactions. "But doesn't she notice they're missing?"

"Hard to tell. She's reduced that house to a veritable *pigsty.* I have no idea how she keeps track of anything in that place. But I guess I'm not too worried about it. I changed my phone number, so it's not like she can call me and confront me."

A pigsty? Jeff found that hard to imagine. "And she's never there when you take them?"

"I make sure of that." She eyed him circumspectly, then took a breath. "Look, Knightman. In case you couldn't tell, I have a lot of anger surrounding my parents."

Jeff frowned. "I know."

"You want to know, and I appreciate that. It means a lot, believe me. But you have like this perfect little family, all lined up in perfect harmony in front of the Christmas tree. I can only dream of a family like that."

Jeff pushed himself to listen to Laurel's words. He was itching to refute the perfect part. His traditional Italian mother had struggled mightily with his sister's Lesbianism, his father had almost lost his store back in 2008, and his grandfather's passing had left his grandmother in a deep depression. But he knew in his heart of hearts he truly was fortunate, and Laurel was in many ways not so fortunate. She deserved to be heard. So Jeff listened.

"Plus, you can't imagine how much easier everything is for you as a white male. I don't mean anything personal by that—it's just a fact. And I'm sorry, Knightman, because I know what I'm saying upsets you. But I have to experience everything from *this* angle." She gestured toward herself. "As a Black woman. The same with my mother. And it's not always easy, you know what I mean?"

Jeff tried to suppress his tears. He needed to hear this. They were embarking on a relationship harboring many unforeseen challenges that would never arise if, for example, things had gone differently between him and Sigrun.

Laurel barreled ahead with her editorial. "Any man that I might end up having a child with—whether he's white or Black or Latino or whatever—that man will be the father of a *Black child*. There's no getting around that. I'm only saying this to prepare you, Knightman. We're all humans, race is a construct, everyone's made of star dust, blah, blah, blah—I've heard all of it." She waved her hand in a gesture of dismissal. "But whether we like it or not, it just isn't that simple." She looked at him, raising her brow, like a professor checking her student's understanding.

Jeff let her words ring in his ears. He contemplated her exquisite beauty and recognized with relief that it outweighed by far the gravity of her speech. "No one wants to understand you more than I do. If you're willing to teach me, I'm willing to learn. No matter what it takes."

Laurel seemed on the point of tears. "It won't always be easy."

He held her gaze. "It'll be worth it. If nothing else, when things get really hard, we'll have each other's shoulders to cry on." He extended his hand across the table, inviting her to grasp it, which in the end she did. "Love will find a way, Laurel."

She managed to agree with that. A waitress bustled past them, giving them a second to retreat from the intense exchange. Laurel clasped his hand. "That was the luckiest day of my life when you showed up at the shelter on Saturday." She swallowed, and her lower lip trembled. "Thank you, Jeff."

He smiled. This was the first time she'd called him by his actual name. "That goes double for me. I can't tell you how thrilled I am that I met you."

They indulged in their wine, seeking refuge from all the emotion.

Micah arrived with their salads. "Here you are, *mademoiselle*." He set an inviting bowl of mixed greens in front of Laurel, doing likewise for Jeff. "Your steaks will be out shortly. *Bon appétit!*"

They dug in with relish—all that seriousness had sharpened their hunger. They turned to more benign topics of conversation as their meal unfolded, deliberating in particular over the projected Minnesota trip that would combine Jeff's plan to do a video in Thief River Falls with travel to Red Wing, where they could visit the flagship boot store, as well as introduce Laurel to the outdoor sports that allowed Jeff not just to survive the harsh northern winters, but to thrive in them. Her willingness to give winter sports a try boosted Jeff's spirits. Laurel seemed genuinely ready to move forward in her life with him at her side. They were embarking on something truly special.

This realization received corroboration from their waiter once they'd finished eating, as he returned Laurel's credit card and requested her signature. "You two," Micah said with a wave of his hand, "you make an absolutely *adorable* couple. I'm so jealous."

Jeff smiled. "Thanks." He looked at his girlfriend, pleased to see that her smile was even bigger than his.

When they arrived back at the apartment, Jeff was exhausted. The day had been long, but it was too early to go to bed. Laurel helped him find a place for the items he'd brought from his dorm. Then he made a suggestion. If he got started on her sweater, they could turn the work into a knitting lesson.

Laurel's relationship with knitting was obviously tarnished by her anger toward her mother. Nonetheless, she obliged him. They sat together on her plaid sofa, working to prevent Olive from eating the lavender yarn dangling in front of her. Jeff explained the long-tail cast-on technique and gave Laurel a demonstration. Once she had it down, he insisted she take a turn at adding some stitches.

He looked on as her fingers worked. "Your mother would be so proud."

"Oh, shut up." Laurel's scowl quickly turned into a laugh.

"I feel like we should document this momentous event with a selfie. What do you think?"

"As long as you promise not to post it on social media."

He wouldn't hurt her for the world. "Promise. It's just for us."

"All right, then."

"Say cheese!" Jeff snapped multiple pictures of the two of them, storing them in a new album on his phone, which he labeled: "Knightman Princess Pics."

11

The Ancestor

JEFF AWOKE THE NEXT morning to hear Laurel crying. He rose up on his elbow and leaned over her as she faced the wall. "Laurel, what's wrong?"

She was sobbing so hard she couldn't speak. A few fruitless attempts to get at the bottom of her tears later, Jeff rested his head next to hers and just let her cry.

Finally, Laurel passed her phone to him. "Here. Read."

He found it opened to an email with the subject: "Hattie Bennett." A family history center in South Carolina had sent it. Jeff assumed this must be one of the genealogists Laurel was working with. He scanned the message together with the accompanying attachments. One of these was a fugitive slave advertisement from a plantation in Virginia. It described a "negro girl named HATTIE," who was "about five feet eight inches high, slender and sprightly, with very black eyes and bushy hair...about seventeen years old..." Jeff knit his brow as he discovered her attributes included being "a fine spinner and knitter."

According to the email, this same Hattie Bennett had turned up a decade or so later on the Underground Railroad, where she'd taken shelter in St. Paul, Minnesota, on her way to Canada, with a young daughter in tow. The genealogist had a theory that this Hattie Bennett was identical with a fugitive with the same first name who was mentioned as an employee in a woolen mill along the Mississippi River in Ontario. Apparently, Canada had its own Mississippi River—this was the first Jeff had heard of that. If he was right, then Hattie Bennett had spent the rest of her life there, raising her daughter alongside other fugitives who'd likewise found refuge in Ontario.

Jeff scratched his head. Why did this hugely revelatory information have Laurel sobbing into the wall? He was afraid to jump to any conclusions, especially after her cautionary speech last night. Yet saying nothing ran its own risk of being misinterpreted. He settled on: "I'm sorry, Laurel." Not that he knew what there was to be sorry about, but there must be something. Otherwise, she wouldn't be lying there, bawling into her pillow, instead of giving Teddy his kitten formula.

Finally, Laurel managed to string a few words together. "She brought her up here to *save* her!" Then she continued her heartbreaking wailing.

Jeff's thoughts darted back and forth. Hattie Bennett had fled from the South and brought her daughter up North to the "tundra" to give her a better life. "You mean like your mom? Bringing you up here?"

"She wasn't trying to hurt me." Laurel shook as she sobbed.

"No, I'm sure she wasn't." Jeff sat up and placed his hand on Laurel's back, rubbing it with a slow and steady rhythm.

"Always knitting, knitting, knitting, knitting..."

Jeff racked his brains. Hattie Bennett was a spinner and knitter. An image of his own grandmother flashed across his mind. Knitting and spinning, knitting and spinning, out of love for her family. How many garments had Jeff worn growing up that had been knit by his grandmother, at least half of them from wool she herself had spun? A lot. "Out of love."

Laurel nodded weakly. "I'm such a fucking ingrate."

Jeff was weirdly struck by the vastness of Laurel's vocabulary—not many people ran around calling themselves "ingrate" instead of more common, everyday slights, like "asshole" or...even worse. He rubbed her shoulder. "No. You're just a little angry, like you said."

"I just wanna go away and die!" She sobbed so hard, she was choking.

Jeff was seized with anxiety. "You're gonna call that psychologist, right?"

Laurel let out a deep, shuddery breath. "I thought she didn't really care." She turned toward him, her perfectly symmetrical face streaked with tears.

"Of course she cares."

"All she ever knits are those damn shawls. Nothing else! No sweaters, no hats, no dresses—just shawls. That woman has knit like a thousand shawls over the years!" She drilled him with her tearful gaze.

"Gorgeous shawls," Jeff agreed. He thought about the projects he'd seen Tabitha stitch at the fiber guild meetings. She really knew her way around intricate lace and stunning color combinations.

"Those people were wearing shawls left and right! Like Sojourner Truth—you ever seen that photo of her?"

"Of course. It was warmth against the cold." Jeff prayed inwardly that his words were helpful.

Laurel nodded as she held his gaze. "How could I not see that? She's like, *manifesting* those people with her hands!"

This was clear as a bell to Jeff. His grandmother said repeatedly how working with fiber bound her tightly to the German-Russian pioneers who'd risked everything to leave their homeland for a better place to look after their families. "It's true. Honestly, I feel the same way when I knit. It connects me to my ancestors."

Laurel stared at him. "You really do get it."

He nodded encouragingly.

Her mien suddenly darkened. "I don't think I can ever look that woman in the face again."

"What do you mean?"

"I'd rather put a bullet through my head!"

A jolt shot through Jeff's chest. "No, Laurel. Stop. You're scaring me."

She started sobbing again. "I'm sorry, Jeff. I just feel so horrible."

"It's OK. We'll figure this out. You're feeling guilty—it's normal. We'll work through it, OK?"

Laurel managed to nod. She reached around and held him.

"Hattie Bennett." The name slipped out of Jeff as he reciprocated her embrace. He tried to process the significance of this ancestor, one of Laurel's four-times great-grandmothers, according to the email. She'd fled enslavement in the South and journeyed to the North, doubtless facing extraordinary risks, with a child she must have brought into the world around 1850, the year when, as he'd learned from the genealogist's email, the Fugitive Slave Act had come into effect. Hattie had been known for her fiber-crafting skills, which had served as her main livelihood, thus as a means of surviving, perhaps even thriving.

Jeff got an idea. "We could go to St. Paul. It's less than an hour north of Red Wing."

Laurel studied his face. "What would we find?"

"We can research the answer to that question. It says here they hid in a barbershop."

Laurel shuddered. "Thank God they didn't get caught. That would have been disastrous!"

"True! It seems like she really did save her daughter."

This had her sobbing all over again. Jeff waited for the storm to pass, rubbing her gently. They would work it out, do more research. It would be OK.

"Are you really sure you wanna be with me?" Tears fell from Laurel's eyes.

"One hundred percent. And stop being so hard on yourself. I'm *honored* to be on this journey with you, Laurel."

She shed more tears onto his chest as she hugged him. "My Knightman. I'm just glad you're going to work with me this morning."

"Yeah. Me too." Jeff was determined to stay by her side for as long as it took to feel sure she wouldn't do anything drastic.

With a fragile state of calm restored, Jeff took the quickest of showers while Laurel washed up and fed Teddy. Out in the kitchen, he kept a watchful eye over Laurel as they fed Olive and Pearl and explored their breakfast options.

It bothered him to eat up all her food. "I'll bring some groceries over here later. I don't wanna keep raiding your fridge."

"Don't worry about it."

Her apathy was disturbing. Jeff must keep encouraging her until they found the answers she needed. "Dr. Mc-Coy's office opens up at eight. Promise you'll call then."

She nodded as she put some grounds into the coffee maker. "I promise."

"And Laurel, forward that email to me. OK?" Jeff thought of his dual capacity as Laurel's boyfriend and Tabitha's student. Somehow, he knew the information about Dr. Howell's three-times great-grandmother would be useful in attempting to restore their relationship. He just had to figure out how to take advantage of it.

"Should I use your student email?"

"Better use my Gmail instead." Jeff told her the address. A reassuring ping signaled the arrival of her message.

After a quick breakfast, Laurel took Pearl outside while Jeff got dressed. He used her absence as an opportunity to brainstorm. How in heaven's name could he leverage his role as Howell's student to build a bridge between her and Laurel that would not jeopardize Laurel's fragile mental state? Marching up to Tabitha and telling her Laurel needed help was out of the question. There were issues between them Jeff dared not pretend he understood. Any steps he took *must* be authorized by Laurel. But doing nothing was also not an option. He had to come up with a strategy that would meet her emotional needs, which were hardly transparent.

What he did know was, there must be a reason why he'd happened to meet the professor's daughter the weekend before starting her course. "Laurel's research," he mumbled to himself as he laced up his boots. "That's the key. I have to get that up in front of her mother."

He tried to call the Black Women's History course syllabus to mind that he'd practically memorized the day before. Maybe he could use one of the assignments to showcase the ancestors Laurel had managed to trace, thanks to her past two years of research. Would that constitute "cheating"? To integrate Laurel's work into his own? *Fuck that. This is about her, not me. So who cares?* Besides, he had a lot to learn, and learning it would require much diligence on his part, so there. It would be fine.

Laurel returned with Pearl, whose tail wagged excitedly no matter how sad her owner was. That was a comfort.

Jeff reached for his backpack. "It just dawned on me, we both have to drive. You have to get back here to check on the pets, and I have to go to campus." He didn't like the idea of Laurel's driving to work unaccompanied in her state of mind. But they had little choice. "I'll follow you. OK?"

Laurel nodded. "Sounds good. Thanks."

At least she'd regained her composure. That was a relief. Doubtless the cold air outside had done its part to energize her.

It was ten till six and still dark. They got into their separate vehicles and drove to the Humane Society. As they worked their way through the morning, with Jeff assisting Laurel in his volunteer capacity as they looked after the dogs, fed them, watered them, walked them, and cleaned out their kennels, he checked in on her regularly. To his relief, the canines under Laurel's care appeared to lift her spirits. Her love for the animals brought meaning to her life—that was clear from her firm and playful interactions with them.

Meanwhile, he racked his brains, trying to solve the puzzle of how to leverage his role as Tabitha's student to repair their mother-daughter relationship. By the time he had to head to campus for his nine o'clock class, Jeff had come up with a scheme. He figured he could use Laurel's fifteen-minute break to share it with her.

She was just letting Rocky back into his run when Jeff tapped on her shoulder. "I think I have a plan. Can you spare a couple minutes?"

She latched the kennel shut. "You do?"

"I think it might work. Maybe we could talk it over outside." Because there, they would have some privacy, which could come in handy if Laurel decided she needed to shed more tears. Anything he proposed might set her off. Regardless of how sincerely Jeff tried to figure out what was best for her, his understanding of her perspective was doomed to be imperfect. After all, he'd only known Laurel for three days, even though down deep he felt like he'd known her forever.

Laurel followed him beyond the dog runs to the edge of the shelter property. An empty cornfield extended beyond the chain link fence, blanketed in white.

Jeff reached for her gloved hand. "Did you call the psychologist?"

She nodded. "I'm meeting with her on Friday afternoon."

"Good." He would have preferred that she'd gotten an appointment for today, but they had to take what they could get. "I think I may have a good way to ease you and your mother back into a conversation, by taking advantage of the fact that I'm in her class."

Laurel eyed him skeptically. "I like the 'ease' part."

Jeff chuckled nervously. If she hated his idea, he wasn't sure where he could turn next. "I really think your mother would be interested in your ancestry research. I have this knitting channel on YouTube, and—"

"Right." She actually smiled. "I watched all your videos. I really liked them, Jeff."

"No kidding. You did?"

She nodded. Her admission was a huge boost to his pride. But they weren't here so she could stroke his ego. They had a serious job in front of them. His words were unraveling like a tangled skein of yarn, but he kept going, trying to weave the strands of his plan into a coherent web. "Your mother has a multimedia project on the syllabus we can do in place of one of the research papers."

"For real? Boy, she really is losing her edge." Laurel flashed an unexpected scowl.

"What do you mean?"

"Multimedia? What happened to those book-length essays she used to assign?"

He resisted the urge to scoff. "I think maybe it just means she's keeping up with the times."

"Well, there's that."

Jeff shook off her resistance. "In any case, here's my idea. Instead of Freeman doing the narration with me, you're going to do it. And we're gonna talk about Hattie Bennett and any other ancestors that fit in with her. We can take the video series to the plantation where she was raised in Virginia, and then to St. Paul, and even to Canada." Laurel's brow was creased with furrows, but Jeff pressed ahead. "According to the email from the genealogist, that plantation is still accessible today. I wanna get permission to film there, and hopefully involve local experts in the project."

She snugged her hood around her head as a shiver ran through her. "That's crazy! How're we gonna do all that?"

"It'll take a lot of planning. Have you got a passport?"

"Yeaaah." She drew the word out, giving voice to her hesitation. "My dad keeps thinking I'm gonna show up at the Burj Khalifa one day and meet him for coffee or some shit."

Jeff was glad to see her sense of humor remained intact. "OK, that's good. I went with my family to British Columbia a couple years ago. So at least we don't have to worry about crossing the border into Ontario."

"Let me get this straight. You wanna make a video for your channel about my ancestors?"

Jeff nodded with all the encouragement he could muster.

"And turn it in to my mom for your class?"

"That's what I had in mind." He hoped against hope she would agree to it. After all, neither of them had any better idea for reuniting her with her mother.

"That's gonna be a hell of a lotta driving."

"It'll be a grand adventure," Jeff replied, sweeping with his hand from left to right. "But here comes the sticky part. My channel's all about 'extreme knitting.' Hattie Bennett did knitting and spinning, according to that fugitive slave ad. And you were saying earlier about how your mom 'manifests' her ancestors with her knitting. I want for *you* to manifest them in the video." He gazed into her eyes, trying not to get distracted by their beauty as he attempted to instill her with confidence.

"But I'm not a knitter."

"That's where Astrid comes in."

"What do you mean?"

"I'm gonna take spinning lessons from Astrid Karlsen. I want you to take them with me. Learn how to spin." He arched his brow and reached for her hand.

Laurel shook her head. "There's no way that woman doesn't hate my guts by now."

"Hate your guts? Why?" A chill ran across Jeff's back as a cold breeze nipped at his cheeks.

"She's my mother's best friend. You think they haven't had *words* about me?" She used emphatic air quotes. "About how I've failed her as a daughter?"

"Laurel, Astrid can't possibly hate you. If your mother and her are the close friends you say they are, then Astrid is by far the *best* person to involve in this project."

"She meets my mother week after week for lunch. I'm sure my mom has told Astrid in every way possible how I've hurt her. And besides, that daughter of hers will find out and spread gossip about us far and wide."

Being a good listener meant Jeff couldn't discount Laurel's suspicions. There were reasons behind them he had to take seriously, even if he didn't understand them. And yet, he was convinced Astrid must appreciate how depressed the move from Atlanta to Prairie Plains had made her friend's daughter. She was also the one person most inclined to welcome a strategy for returning Laurel to her mother's arms.

The more Jeff thought about Tabitha Howell, the more certain he was she was lonely. Her work as professor and her involvement in the fiber guild were probably the only two outlets that kept her going, after effectively losing not only her daughter, but her husband, too. "That's not impossible, I admit. But I'm equally sure Astrid would support any effort to get you and your mother back together one hundred percent."

Laurel sighed as she rubbed her face. "This is so risky."

"You're right. It is risky. And there's no doubt I'll have to think carefully about how to explain everything to Astrid so she can keep our secret from your mom—and from everyone in her family."

"Especially Sigrun."

"Especially Sigrun. Worst case scenario, we may have to hope Sigrun has grown out of her high school gossip phase and would have no reason to hurt you or your mother today."

Laurel let out a sigh as she glanced across the snow-covered field. "I don't know. You're probably right, Jeff. Sometimes I feel like everybody hates me. But then I stand back and realize how fun it is to play the victim and assume all my problems are somebody else's fault. Stupid, huh?"

Jeff smiled and put his hand on her shoulder. "I think maybe you're ready for those conversations with the frumpy psychologist."

Laurel managed a chuckle. "So you want me to learn how to spin wool? Like Hattie Bennett?"

He patted her shoulder and nodded. "This could be the most amazing video, Laurel. The two of us could go to these stations on Hattie's journey through life and compete with each other to see who can spin the most thread."

"Compete?" She flashed a crooked smile. "You'll win that contest in a heartbeat, *Knitmann*."

"But I've never spun an inch of yarn in my life! My grandmother has tried over and over again to get me into it, and I just haven't had the energy."

Her face lit up with an evil grin. "OK then, you're on! But when're we gonna do all this, Jeff? I'd have to take off work."

"Do you think you can do that?"

She weighed her response. "Seein' as how I've accumulated a lot of vacation time I've never used, I probably can."

"Spring break is the second week of March. That gives us seven weeks."

"You know this is absolutely crazy, don't you?"

Jeff nodded. "That's how I know it'll work." He winked at her.

She responded with a helpless smile. "I love you, you crazy loon."

"I love you, too." They indulged in a kiss, using up the final seconds of her fifteen-minute break. "Text me every half hour, Laurel. Otherwise I'll worry myself to death."

She agreed. "So you're gonna talk to Astrid, then?"

"The sooner the better. I owe her an apology for misleading Sigrun yesterday, anyhow. It'll give me the perfect excuse to look her up on campus. Hopefully, she's got some office hours today."

Laurel's enduring skepticism wasn't lost on him. But they both knew her efforts to get beyond the mother-daughter impasse had yet to yield any better plan than this very hair-brained one. She assured Jeff she was on board, and would contact him every half hour to let him know she was all right. "Are you coming back over tonight, then?"

"Of course. I'm thinking I should bring over a few more clothes. Is that all right?"

Laurel nodded. "I'll talk to the landlord, tell him I have a boyfriend. I'll try to get you a key."

Jeff exhaled in relief. Laurel's willingness to embrace his caring concern boosted his optimism. "See you this afternoon."

"Good luck with Astrid."

"Thanks. I can definitely use it." He kissed her once more, and they parted ways.

12

The Meeting

Jeff disliked having to leave Laurel at work. But her mood had improved among all the abandoned dogs and cats, those welcome role models who embraced life unquestioningly and surrounded her with their barks, their meows, their wagging tails, their eagerness to eat, drink, and be merry in their own canine and feline ways. *Those animals are the ones who've kept her going,* he mused. It relieved him to realize there was a solid place in the world where Laurel knew for a fact she belonged. She was a modern-day St. Francis.

The shelter animals needed her as much as she needed them. And it lay within Jeff's power to ensure Laurel could continue her work of compassion. On his way to his nine o'clock accounting class, he swung by the fine arts building, a rare event since he'd finished those graphic design courses a year ago. He looked up Professor Karlsen's office, hoping she would be available to consult with him before the day was out. To his relief, she had an office hour at 2 p.m. He would arrive early to maximize his chances of getting in to meet with her, before other students decided to hog her time.

Until then, he had plenty to occupy him. After accounting, he had a free hour. He used this to pay his dorm room a visit. His roommate was out—perfect. Jeff grabbed several days' worth of clothes, toiletries, and supplies, and loaded them into his truck. Having spent a fair bit of time in Laurel's apartment by now, he knew her sparse wardrobe took up minimum closet space. Her austere lifestyle did little to allay Jeff's concerns regarding her mental state. But on the plus side, it left plenty of room for his own belongings in her orderly accommodations.

Their relationship was moving forward with lightning speed, which would have made him nervous, were it not for the profound connection he felt to Laurel. Plus, she *needed* a friend just now. And what Laurel had to offer that friend was worth a king's ransom. Nothing was more obvious to him than that the two of them belonged together.

He went to entrepreneurship at eleven, then put in some study time for business law. When he visited the cafeteria to take advantage of that expensive meal plan his parents had bought him, he found his cameraman, Colin Milliman, in the dining hall, jamming calories into his young man's body the same way Jeff planned on doing.

Colin hailed him as he entered the space with a tray full of food. "Knitmann!"

"Hi, Colin!" Jeff smiled to see his friend wearing the yellow and blue beanie he'd knit for him for the blizzard video last fall. He sat down, placing his tray loaded with roast beef, egg noodles, green beans, corn, carrots, rolls with butter and, for good measure, a slice of institutionally-prepared apple pie on the table. "How's it goin'?"

"Great! What's the latest on Thief River Falls? Is your Native informant still gonna meet us?"

"Ralph? I think so. Say, Colin, I'm thinking about bringing my girlfriend along. We wanna go down to Red Wing after the Dead Man's Trail project."

"No kidding. You got a girlfriend?"

Jeff nodded. It felt good to have that news to share. He took out his phone with a big smile and showed Colin one of the selfies he'd taken with Laurel the night before.

"Whoa, dude! She's a dead ringer for Tiana."

"Tiana?"

"Yeah. From that Disney movie? *The Princess and the Frog*? Sorry—dating myself. We have the DVD. My sisters love watching that, even if all the frog stuff goes on and on forever and a day."

Jeff chuckled. "I'll have to watch it."

"Fuck that, Knitwit! Looks like you've got the *real* princess there. Don't waste your time."

That was actually a good point. "Thanks, dude. We were wondering if you wanted to tag along and go to Red Wing, or drive separate vehicles or whatever. 'Cause that's gonna be a long drive—all the way up to Dead Man's Trail, then down to Red Wing, with maybe a stop in St. Paul, and then back here."

"I'd be down for the longer trip," Colin replied, his mouth full of macaroni and cheese. "What are you planning in Red Wing?"

"I wanna show her some winter sports stuff. She's more of a Southern girl. Hasn't made friends with the winter yet. Snowboarding is a must, and maybe some snowshoeing, depending on how much it costs to rent the equipment. Plus, she likes the same kind of boots as me, so we'll make a point of going to the boot store."

"Yeah, she definitely looks like a rugged version of Tiana. Perfect fit for you, Jeff! Freeman is an awesome snowboarder. I'm guessing he'd love to spend the extra day, as long as he doesn't have to pay for the gas."

Jeff laughed. "No problem. I saved up a decent amount of money over break. And I'm sure Laurel'll be glad to chip in."

"That's her name? Laurel?"

"Yup."

"Nice."

"And don't worry, she makes her own money. We're still dividing the YouTube take three ways."

"No worries. All I do is run the camera and edit. To be honest, I never thought we'd make any money off of this. I think it's crazy we're actually earning, like, *real dollars*, for having fun!"

"Lucky us!"

Once Jeff had taken in that welcome infusion of calories, he worked in some study time before Astrid Karlsen's office hour. Nervous fears kept invading his thoughts—Astrid would be out sick; eight students would be waiting in line to see her; she'd pick up her phone and dial Tabitha's number the moment the name "Laurel" tumbled from his mouth. The urgency of recruiting her help in the effort to restore the connection between Laurel and her mother bore down on Jeff. If for some reason she refused to help, or took issue with his strategy, he wasn't sure where he could turn next.

He headed to her office a full ten minutes early. If there happened to be a raft of students wanting to confer with her, he would be first in line. When he arrived, he was alone. But not for long. Wouldn't you know it, two minutes later, Astrid approached her office accompanied by none other than—*Tabitha Howell*. Jeff's blood pressure shot through the roof as he spotted the professors approaching him. As tempted as he was to run off with his tail between his legs, he held his ground, praying that all the upheaval he and Tabitha's daughter had been through over the past seventy-two hours weren't written all over him for the two friends to read. "Hello, professors!"

"Why, it's Jeff Nietmann!" Dr. Howell proclaimed warmly. "How are you doing today? You seemed so—so distracted yesterday. I hope you're feeling better."

Jeff released a nervous chuckle. "Thank you. I'm sorry about that. I actually got sick right after class. But I'm feeling much better now."

"Well, good."

Eager to avoid a conversation that could generate unwanted revelations, Jeff clammed up. A chill coursed through him as he noticed that Tabitha's warmth was complemented by a correspondingly cool reception on the part of her best friend, who was drilling him with her eyes. "Did you come to see me, Jeff?" Astrid's question felt like the prelude to a disciplinary hearing.

"Actually, yes." Jeff half wondered whether the whole dating-a-guy rumor might have found its way to Laurel's mother. Well, would that be the worst thing? Throwing Tabitha off the real trail seemed advantageous, if also rife with potential pitfalls.

Astrid gave Tabitha a quick hug. "I'll see you on Thursday."

"I look forward to it." Dr. Howell aimed her gaze at Jeff. "Take care of yourself, young man. I'll see you in the morning. And bring your knitting this time, all right?"

He suppressed a shiver and nodded. "Absolutely."

She waved and headed down the hall, leaving Jeff alone with Astrid.

The art professor seemed downright eager to coax some explanations from him. He swallowed. He was doing this for Laurel. Whatever it took to keep her safe and moving forward was what he would do, no matter how much it complicated his own life.

"Come on in." Astrid ushered him into her office.

To Jeff's relief, they were very much alone. "Mind if we close the door?"

"Good idea." She directed him to take a seat. In contrast to her home studio, Astrid's office was small and cramped, filled mainly with books on various aspects of the fiber arts, crafting through history, treatises on materials, and illustrated books about birds. Jeff recalled the art pieces Astrid had shown him in December, so that lined up. But his contemplations were brutally interrupted when his mentor all but shouted at him: "There's no way you're dating a *guy*, Jeff Nietmann!"

His heart beat wildly. If this meeting went badly, it could spell disaster for his emotionally fragile partner. "You're right." He wondered how Astrid could just know that about him, that he was as straight as the day was long. "I'm really sorry. But for the record, it was Sigrun who jumped to that conclusion." It occurred to him that there must be some—the only word his mind dredged up was *unfortunate*—prejudice on Sigrun's part that could have led her to conclude that, based solely on the evidence that he was a knitter. "I never told her I was seeing a guy."

"But you didn't deny it?" Astrid stared him down with her striking blue eyes.

How Jeff wished he was instead looking into the warm, dark eyes of his girlfriend now! "Look, Astrid. Something's going on that Sigrun simply can't know about."

"I see." She left it at that, and waited.

Jeff was starting to feel sick again. But he refused to abandon his faith in Tabitha's closest friend. Accepting the enormous risk he might be taking, he retrieved his phone from his pocket, his hands shaking, opened the gallery app, cued up the best of the selfies he'd taken with him, Laurel, and Teddy, and showed it to the art professor.

Astrid looked on with furrowed brow as Jeff fumbled with his phone. Then she took in the image of him smiling his most radiant smile, and her best friend's daughter doing the same. Her peeved expression suddenly dissolved into one of amazement. "Laurel Howell? *Really?*"

Jeff nodded. Having finally laid his cards on the table, he let out a huge breath.

Astrid looked at the photo and at Jeff in turn. "I can't believe it. How in the world did you two meet?"

"At the Humane Society." What a relief it was to see her kind demeanor restored.

"I see... Yes, of course, that makes sense." She shook her head, knitting and unknitting her brow. "I understand now why you were playing games with Sigrun."

"Astrid, I'm really sorry. Laurel's just struggling so much with her relationship with her parents. I can't tell you how hard it is to be caught in the middle. I just *have* to put her needs before mine. And right now she needs a lot of space."

She acknowledged that with a nod. "It's been almost two years since I last saw her." She studied the photo. "Laurel is still as beautiful as ever. Who's the little cat?"

"That's Teddy. We adopted him."

Astrid took in the photo another second or two, then handed his phone back. "Would you like some water to drink? Or tea? Coffee?"

"Water's fine." His temples finally stopped pounding.

Astrid rose to grab a couple bottles from her mini fridge. "Have you been seeing each other for long?"

Jeff closed his eyes and took a breath. The whirlwind nature of their relationship stayed blissfully hidden from view when he was with the girl his passions had seized on. But when he looked on it as a student baring his heart to his mentor, it came palpably to the fore. "We met on Saturday."

"Just this past Saturday?"

Jeff nodded.

"Wow! You're really smitten, then!"

He smiled. "You could say that. I had no idea she and Professor Howell were even related until the next day."

"Actually, this makes me very happy for her. I can't tell you how worried Tabitha's been. It just breaks her heart. Laurel was deeply depressed when they moved up here. It cost her all her friends, and then on top of that their dog died, and students gave her a ridiculously hard time in school. She absolutely refuses to speak to her mother. She even changed her phone number to avoid talking to her. It's been incredibly hard on Tabitha."

Jeff took in this information with a heavy heart. It corroborated everything Laurel had shared. "She wishes they could have waited a year before leaving Atlanta."

"I know. And I agree with that. The fact is, the university was desperate to hire her mother. I wasn't on the hiring committee—I just served as Tabitha's faculty mentor when she arrived. But I heard they were willing to go to almost any lengths to bring her here. You have no idea how hard it is to hire people of color away from the big private schools that have more resources. It's so unfair to think that rich kids who can afford to pay their way to attend schools like Washington University or the University of Chicago have access to a diverse faculty. But the kids who can only afford to go to state schools, especially up here, don't get that advantage. There are still just too few Black PhDs on the market. They made Tabitha a full professor with automatic tenure and nearly doubled the salary she was making. Jerome told her over and over again it would be a huge mistake to turn that down, so Laurel was overruled."

Jeff wondered what influence Laurel's father could have had in dragging her out to Prairie Plains as a high school senior. "I have to imagine Professor Howell was really torn about what to do."

Astrid confirmed that. "She hoped against hope the move would end up being something positive for Laurel. She did everything she could to support her when they arrived. They bought a beautiful home, tried to get her involved in engaging activities, catered to her every whim. But at the same time, Tabitha's profession is very important to her, you have to understand that. She had two competing interests ripping her apart, both equally legitimate. In the end, it was her daughter who lost out."

"Why do you suppose things were so hard for Laurel at the high school here?"

"I mean, there were a million reasons, right? She was new, she had no allies she could count on, she was beautiful, she was talented, she was smart, she was female, and she was Black. It's one thing to be marginalized. But when you're marginalized *and* you don't have allies, you're sort of screwed in a place like this."

Unaccustomed to hearing the adults around him speak so bluntly, Jeff chalked Astrid's frankness up to her European sensibilities. He'd already witnessed how she pulled no punches in decrying the sometimes wretched state of the world. He welcomed this opportunity to gain as full a picture as possible regarding what Laurel was up against, and encouraged Astrid to share all she was willing to. "She told me she won the science fair. She seems to really excel in that area."

"Oh, yes! She was taking every AP course she could get into, dual credit, college credit, honors courses, because ultimately she wanted to go to veterinary school. But her success inspired so much jealousy on the part of other students—to my shame, even Sigrun didn't spare her." She shook her head and frowned. "It bothered her to no end that Laurel outcompeted her on task after task. Her AP test scores were higher, her research was more sophisticated—and how could that be, since she was, quote-unquote, a *Black girl*? Jeff, I can't tell you how mortified I was when word of this remark reached Tabitha! How does this even happen?" She leaned in toward him, nearly spilling her water. "I didn't raise my kids to think that way! How could she draw a conclusion like that, that race, or our 'idea' of race, has anything to do with how intelligent a person is?"

Jeff met her tearful gaze. He had his ideas about how this could be—he'd seen this kind of thing before. And his encounters with injustice poked uncomfortable holes in his American pride. "If you ask me, I think that's called 'being raised in the United States.'"

"Yes, but *why*? After everything this country went through—enslaving human beings decades after the Enlightenment had come and gone, the absolute devastation of the Civil War—and people still can't prevent their kids from sharing attitudes like that at a *high school*, for God's sake?"

Tears welled in Jeff's eyes as he listened to Sigrun's mother share this troubling episode from her not-so-distant past. "To be fair, it does seem like racism is more or less of a worldwide problem. And it's up to all of us to fight it. My parents worked hard to provide diverse role models for me and my sister. My dad practically forced me to become a tennis player in high school, because the tennis teacher was the only Black coach at the school. I wasn't very good, but I sure did learn a lot from Mr. Wilson. When I shared with him how kids teased me for knitting all the time, he said: 'Nietmann, if you let the haters decide who you're gonna be, then you'll never be who you're supposed to be.' And that advice has stuck with me ever since."

"I wish Sigrun had had a coach like that. Her track coach kept telling her she had that 'Nordic physique,' and consequently was cut out to excel as a distance runner. Why would you tell a kid something like that? I mean, isn't that kind of racist?"

"Sounds like it."

"All I could think to do was lecture her, and ask her what she was thinking, and try to get her to spend more time with the Howells. But by then the damage was done, and Laurel started withdrawing into her shell. Her freshman year in college was a complete catastrophe. And when she flunked out of school, that was basically the end. She just gave up. And then it was like, oh my God, Dr. Howell's daughter flunked out of college, and somehow Laurel's failure was Tabitha's failure, and there was just this cascading series of disappointments and confrontations. Jerome finally gave in to Laurel's demand to live on her own, and he got her that apartment over in Prairie Acres. Of course, by then he'd decided to abandon the family, and he took a job as an economics professor in Dubai."

"Laurel told me about that. So he and Tabitha—I mean, do you think they'll get back together at some point?"

Astrid took a swig of water and shook her head. "No idea. He's one of those men who, when you meet him, you feel like, oh, he's such a fun person, he's so—in Norwegian we would say '*omgjengelig*,' like charming, or I think you could say 'affable' in English. You feel like you could sit around with him all day, gabbing and drinking and just hanging out. But once the party's over, he retreats within himself and gives you the cold shoulder and doesn't want to have anything to do with you. He's the type of person who wants to be seen and appreciated, but he's not very good at seeing others, if you know what I mean. He just had zero room for Laurel's issues—they didn't interest him. I suppose it wasn't fun to listen to her crying at night or asking questions about why she had to forfeit all her friends, or be the target of her peers' suspicions and envy.

So he just tosses money at her and tells her to go figure it out herself."

It made Jeff's heart bleed to hear all this. But he was grateful for the information. "That helps me understand Laurel's anger at him."

"Of course. And Tabitha is absolutely devastated. She throws herself into her work. And when she's not preparing her lessons or working on research, she just knits her shawls. Her house is an absolute wreck. She never lets anyone over there. She just goes to the guild meetings and sits on the board for the annual fiber festival. That and the committee work she does here on campus, those are basically her only social outlets. So there you have it, Jeff." Astrid heaved a sigh. "I feel strange sharing all this with you. It would probably be best if you didn't tell anyone about our conversation. But you have no idea how exhausting it is to watch a family I care about so deeply simply self-destruct—and no one has any idea how to pick up the pieces. My husband is tired of hearing about it, I can't share it with my kids, I have no one to bare my soul to. Every time I see Tabitha, that's her primary topic of conversation: how she let her daughter down, and how there's no way she can fix it. The only evidence she has of Laurel's existence is that she sneaks over to her house from time to time and takes away a few of her books. That's it. Nothing else."

Jeff took in Astrid's words with a sober mien. But he saw an opening in her last sentence to introduce his strategy. "Laurel told me about that, too. Actually, I think Tabitha would be proud of her. She's been researching her family history."

This got Astrid's attention. "Really? But isn't that enormously difficult? Tabitha has told me multiple times it's almost impossible to gather any real information about her ancestors. There are simply no records to speak of. And that's why she contents herself with looking at the broader picture, to at least have a *sense* of what their lives must have been like."

"Sounds a little like *my* ancestors. My great-great grandfather Albrecht left two brothers behind in the Russian Empire when he decided to come over here with his cousin. Almost all the people who descended from that branch of the family were deported to Siberia and more or less murdered. Any records of their fate are buried in the heart of Russia and pretty much impossible to get at."

Astrid shook her head. "I didn't know that about you, Jeff. That's horrifying."

"It is. But Laurel has succeeded in turning up lots of details about both sides of her family, going back more than two hundred years."

"Wow! Sounds like she's actually managing to outdo her mother, then—which would be quite a feat. But on the other hand, it doesn't really surprise me, given how smart she is."

"The apple doesn't fall far from the tree—that's what my dad always says. Laurel has this huge bulletin board up in her bedroom where she posts the gist of her findings about the two sides of her family. It's full of amazing history."

Astrid furrowed her brow. "What a tragedy that she isn't sharing that with her mother. Tabitha would do anything to know what Laurel is up to. We have a really big problem here, Jeff. But what are we going to do about it? We have to get these two people talking to each other again!"

This was the moment Jeff had been waiting for. He took a swallow of water and wiped his mouth. "That's actually why I'm here, Astrid. Laurel kept telling me you must hate her, and Sigrun would gossip about us and I shouldn't come to you. But I tried to convince her you're on her side, and you'd actually be the best person to help her move forward until she's ready to talk to her mother again."

"In that case, she is wrong, and you are right. So we are team Laurel, now. Tell me, coach, what do we do?"

"OK, so now I'm really glad I came." Jeff opened his email app. "Laurel managed to identify a plantation in Virginia where some of her maternal ancestors were enslaved before the Civil War. One of the genealogists who's helping her found records about her four-times great-grandmother, a woman named Hattie Bennett, who escaped and possibly made it all the way up to Ontario. He has a theory linking her with an employee at a woolen mill in Canada who escaped enslavement. I'm gonna forward the email to you that they sent her this morning."

"I'd love to see that." Astrid woke up her computer. Jeff watched as the documentation sketching the outlines of Hattie Bennett's journey showed up on her screen. "Sounds like a very brave woman. Actually, there was a fairly well-established woolen industry in that part of Canada in the mid-nineteenth century. That's fascinating that Hattie might have made it there on the Underground Railroad, so she could monetize her skills."

"Laurel and I want to do a video to showcase Hattie's skills. My plan is to turn that into an assignment for Tabitha's course I'm taking. We want to share it with her as a way to open the door to rebuilding their relationship."

Astrid looked over at him as she contemplated his scheme. "Sounds clever. Does that mean Laurel's thinking about learning to spin and knit like her great-great grandmother?"

"More or less. I told her I was gonna take spinning lessons from you. If she learns along with me, we can turn it into a competition, like on my videos. We can explore the sites of Hattie Bennett's trek from the South to the North, and bring her handwork to life by spinning wool on film as we talk about her history."

Astrid smiled. "Jeff, this is brilliant. So Laurel is really ready to take this step? Because it would be a huge weight off her mother's heart."

"Don't get me wrong. She's terrified. But after she saw this information about her ancestor this morning, and how Hattie saved her daughter by fleeing to the North, I think it made her realize Tabitha didn't mean to hurt her by pursuing her own ambitions. So now she's dealing with guilt on top of the anger."

"That girl has been through so much. But Jeff, I have to tell you—this project has potential beyond just that of repairing their relationship. You're wanting to do this as an assignment for your course, is that right?"

Jeff nodded. "Multimedia project."

"Because this research holds importance well beyond Laurel's immediate family history. And you're planning to travel to Virginia? To Canada? That could get expensive!"

That was undeniable, and a definite source of concern. "Well, we both have a little credit, and we're willing to do things as cheaply as possible."

"OK, that's really generous of you and all—but you should seek *grant funding* for this."

Nothing like that had remotely crossed Jeff's mind. "Grant funding?"

"The university has undergraduate research funds. You should apply. When are you thinking of traveling?"

"Spring break."

"That gives us only six or seven weeks. Cutting it close. But if you get started right away, it can be done."

Jeff considered the idea. "But how could I apply without Dr. Howell finding out?"

"Oh yeah. Shit." Astrid mulled the situation over as Jeff sipped on his water. Suddenly her face lit up. "You're going to learn to spin wool from me. Right?"

"Right."

"Perfect. Then I'll sign you up for an independent study. That way, you'll be my student, and I can help you apply for the grant funding."

Now Jeff's face lit up. "You could do that?"

"Of course. Part of my job here is teaching students these ancient arts. People across the world have been spinning fiber for thousands of years. It's a vital part of human history. Would Laurel like to earn some credit as well? Is she thinking about resuming her studies?"

"Actually, yes. We're gonna try to get a psychologist to diagnose her and document that she had depression when she started college, and GPU should remove those F's from her record."

Astrid did a facepalm. "I'm so dense! Why didn't I think of that? Of course, that's absolutely what she should do! One of my students went through that same exact process last fall. What in the heck is wrong with me?"

Nothing that Jeff could see. She stood firmly on their side, ready to meet their most urgent need. "Maybe it's like not seeing the forest for the trees."

"Jeff, you are like a knight on a white horse, riding in and saving everyone. How do you do it?"

Jeff enjoyed it when Laurel called him "Knightman," but he was more or less an emissary, an ambassador. "I'm gonna disagree with that. Laurel has been working on her ancestry for almost two years. This is honestly just her doing this work. All I'm doing is helping her connect a few of the dots. If anyone is saving anyone, it's Hattie Bennett. Laurel got this email about her this morning, and it seems like it was just the information she needed to change course. It's like Hattie saved her daughter, and now she's saving her four-times great-granddaughter, too. I can't wait to learn more about her."

Astrid studied Jeff with a tearful smile. "Point taken. Let's get you signed up for that independent study."

These words were music to his ears. "Sounds like a plan."

They wrapped up their meeting, then Jeff left the fine arts building and gave his girlfriend a call. "All systems are go, Laurel. Astrid is completely on board with everything, and our first spinning lesson is scheduled for this coming Friday during your lunch break."

"Seriously? And she promised not to tell my mother? Or her daughter?"

"She understands what you've been through, and she approves our plan. She even told me there may be a way to get grant money from the university. I'll tell you all about it when I get over there."

"That's insane! Grant money?"

"Yup! We're gonna make sure Hattie Bennett's true place in history receives the acknowledgment it deserves."

Laurel's reaction was part chuckle, part sob. "I love you so much."

"I love you more. See you in about an hour."

Jeff signed off and went to pick up some groceries. Tonight, he and his girlfriend would celebrate their plans with another home-cooked meal.

·❤·❤·❤·❤·❤·

13

The Spinning Lesson

HAVING SAT THROUGH HIS entire first meeting of the Black Women's History course on Monday more or less shaking in his boots, Jeff's experience during the class on Wednesday was much more relaxed.

The night before, he'd cooked a delicious chicken cacciatore for his girlfriend using his mother's recipe. They'd let Teddy out of Laurel's bedroom for the first time to hobble around on his splinted leg. After half an hour of cheering him on and giggling over his antics, Laurel had fallen asleep on Jeff's shoulder as he'd finished the ribbing on the body of her sweater and begun knitting the stockinette portion in the deep purple she adored.

Bolstered by the confidence that things were going as they should, Jeff boldly brought that sweater project with him to knit on during Professor Howell's class. He arrived early, sitting in the front row as he had on Monday. But this time he could care less whether his stitching distracted the other students. Keeping an eye on Tabitha and making sure she was all right was far more important, after everything he'd learned from Professor Karlsen about her family life.

When Dr. Howell walked into the room with her usual generous smile, Jeff nodded at her, drawing her attention to his knitting.

She reciprocated his nod as she set down her bag and laid a couple books on her desk. "It's good to see you."

It would be nearly two months before Tabitha would take in the video project he and Laurel hoped to share with her. In the meantime, things promised to limp along in her life as they had for the past two years. Until they got their film ready, Jeff would make it his mission to provide her with moral support. This included being the world's most attentive student and making sure his fellow students treated his girlfriend's mother right.

This proved to be a two-way street, however. For as the only white male in a course on Black Women's History, Jeff discovered that being taken seriously was not a given in his case.

Today's discussion, for example, centered around the slavery era they would be focusing on for the next few weeks. Jeff found it impossible to ignore the connections between this topic and Laurel's—as well as Dr. Howell's—own family history. Over dinner last night, he and Laurel had discussed the notion of race as construct. Coming to an agreement regarding how "real" race was had been next to impossible, because Laurel's experiences had borne out the concrete consequences the "idea" of race had for those who were marginalized due to their skin color. Jeff decided this was the perfect class to debate the issue in.

After an efficient yet insightful lecture, Dr. Howell opened the floor to questions. Jeff was the first to raise his hand.

Tabitha met his gaze. "Mr. Nietmann?"

Jeff recalled a quote from a book Laurel had shared with him. "The historian, Eric Williams, argued that race was the *result* of slavery and not its cause. Where do you stand on that?"

That drew a comment from the one Black female student in the class, Angela Curtis, who happened to be sitting behind him: "Hear the white man speak!"

Just as Jeff turned even whiter than he already was, his professor stood up for him. "We are all equals in this course. There will be no denouncing other students, however surreptitiously, Angela. Yes, Jeff. This is an ongoing debate. My stance is that race is indeed a construct, and that blackness and whiteness fall under this category to equal degrees. In order for Europeans to justify their enslavement of the people they relied on to provide free labor for their capitalist enterprises, they needed to draw artificial lines between themselves and those whom they enslaved. Doing that on the basis of skin color afforded them a seemingly simple justification for deeming certain people as eligible for enslavement, while others were not. I hope that answers your question."

"Yes, thank you." It was certainly a good answer, even if it didn't exactly line up with what Laurel would have said. It made Jeff wish he could hear Laurell and Tabitha take on this debate together.

Randall Cobb injected some levity into the exchange. "Chalk one up for the guys!" He invited Jeff to high five him. They were the only males there, after all, making their contributions to the course unique. And Jeff happened to know the basketball star was dating a white girl.

Doubtless his interest in the issue at hand was genuine, in spite of his attempt at humor.

When class ended, Jeff anticipated Tabitha's checking in on him, but today he didn't dread it like last time. In fact, he followed her out into the hallway.

"That's a gorgeous purple sweater you're knitting," she remarked. "At least, I assume it's a sweater."

She'd drawn precisely the conclusion Jeff frankly desired. "A sweater. Exactly."

"Are you knitting it for a family member?"

He immediately admitted he was, affirming his heart's conviction that Laurel was now a member of his family.

"You know, purple is my daughter's favorite color. Your project reminds me of her."

Jeff's heart skipped a beat. "Really?"

"Yes. It's been a while since I last laid eyes on her. She's sort of living her own life these days. But I'm going to enjoy watching you knit on this project during class."

He greeted that with a smile. "No problem." He was glad he'd brought Laurel's sweater to work on. Until she authorized him to disclose their relationship, he would honor her wishes and keep it a secret. But now he knew his classroom knitting was a source of comfort to Tabitha. That made him feel a little less guilty for withholding the arguably pleasant news of her daughter's love interest.

And Laurel's own mental state was definitely on the mend. Having discovered an ancestor whose life trajectory bore meaningful similarities with her mother's professional journey, Laurel now had a helpful perspective for considering Tabitha's choices. She slowly set aside her grievances and viewed her mother's actions through a more objective lens. Her readiness to move forward in life eased Jeff's mind.

And when a phone call from his parents interrupted their necking one evening, Laurel's insistence that he take the call struck him as another positive sign. Regardless of their efforts to keep what was happening between them from Laurel's mother, at least she showed no reluctance when it came to sharing it with his own parents. The timing was good as far as Jeff was concerned. It was high time his parents knew he'd found a path that promised to lead him out of the woods of bachelorhood.

He let the phone ring once more as he met his girlfriend's gaze. "You're sure?"

Laurel nodded assertively, and prodded him to pick up.

The call came from his mother's phone. "Hi, Mom!"

"Hi, Jeff! We thought we'd check in to find out how the new semester's going."

The new semester was just a few days old, and a whole month's worth of events had transpired. He'd have to prioritize the most obvious ones, to avoid getting sucked into an hours-long exchange, given the importance of the activity he and Laurel had just been engaged in. "Great, Mom! Say, do you mind if we do this on video? I've got someone I want you to meet."

She didn't hesitate. "Sure. That sounds great."

Jeff glanced at Laurel. "Are you ready for this?"

"Um-hmm." She was in remarkably high spirits. She pretended to primp her very casual hairdo as Jeff tapped the video icon.

He waited for his mother's image to appear, then dove in. "I've met someone. Mom, this is Laurel. Laurel, this is Mom."

"Hi, Mom!" Laurel waved playfully, smiling as she took in Jeff's mother, Rose.

"And this is Teddy." Jeff aimed the camera at the kitten sprawled across his lap. "We adopted him last weekend. He lives over here at Laurel's place."

"Oh, how sweet! I look forward to getting to know you, Laurel!"

Jeff filled her in a little. "She works at the Humane Society. We met when I was signing up to volunteer over there."

"I see. Then you must be an animal lover."

"She wants to become a veterinarian." Jeff said that like it was destined to happen, which he was convinced it was, and Laurel should think no different.

His mother was certainly on board. "What a wonderful ambition!"

Jeff's dad came into view. "Hi, son!"

"Hi, Dad! I want you to meet Laurel Howell."

"Nice to meet you, Laurel Howell! So your stint as a celibate monk is ending, eh?" John Nietmann quipped.

His parents' readiness to embrace the change in his relationship status warmed Jeff's heart. "You could say that."

"Glad to hear it. College is a good place to meet members of the fairer sex."

"I know it worked for you and Mom."

"Yes, it did. Twenty-six years and counting! I'm very excited for you two."

"Thanks, Dad. So you guys are coming out for my birthday?"

"That's the plan. We'll take you two out to dinner, if you'd like."

Jeff took in Laurel's smile as it showed up on the screen of his phone. "'Cause Laurel's birthday is the day before mine. We'll have lots to celebrate together."

"Sounds that way," Rose said warmly. "Congratulations, Laurel. We can't wait to meet you in person!"

"Me too." Laurel glanced at Jeff. The glow on her face told him all he needed to know regarding how happy his parents' welcoming reception made her.

As Jeff processed John and Rose's eagerness to acquaint themselves with his new love interest, contrasting that with the awkward situation holding sway between him, Laurel, and Tabitha, he was grateful to have the parents he did. It was important not to take them for granted.

His thirst for Laurel's affection, however, had yet to be slaked. So he kept his reports on his new courses, his video-making plans for Minnesota, and his goal of learning how to spin, brief and to the point. "Be sure and tell Grandma about that. I think she'll be glad I'm finally taking that particular plunge. Laurel's gonna learn how to spin, too."

John greeted that with a smile. "No kidding! We'll be sure and tell her. You know, I bet she'd be willing to part with one of her wheels for you, if you're interested. Keep that in mind."

Interested was putting it mildly! "Will do."

They signed off with multiple assurances of their familial love. As Jeff set his phone down, he studied the contented expression on Laurel's face.

She reached over to pet Teddy, who'd taken in the exchange in total repose. "Your people seem really cool,

Jeff. That helps explain how cool you are yourself." She rewarded him with a kiss on his fuzzy cheek.

"I'm excited for you to meet them in person. I think it's safe to say they've been kind of wondering if I'd ever meet someone who...well, let's just say, who meets my high standards."

Her smiling eyes rested on his. "That's so sweet. That deserves another kiss!"

It took some persuading, but Laurel ultimately agreed to coming up with the funds needed for a one-credit course as Professor Karlsen's independent study student. While she was far from ready to resume her undergraduate career, Jeff persuaded her to at least consider it. Besides, the spinning class was only a few hundred bucks, and if they succeeded in pursuing Astrid's grant funding idea, they would recoup far more in the way of expenses for their research travel than she would pay in tuition for one measly credit.

They'd arranged to meet at Astrid's home studio. Almost all her spinning equipment and supplies lived there. When Jeff pulled up in front of the Karlsens' sprawling ranch on Quaking Aspen Road, this time in the bright winter sun of a January day, he didn't have to wait long for Laurel's Equinox to pull up behind him. He met her at her car.

Laurel closed the driver's side door and reached out to hug him. "I'm so nervous! I feel like I'm doing the right thing. But I haven't seen Astrid in ages—I'm just scared to see her again. I mean, what have she and my mother been saying about me all these months, week after week, you know?"

Jeff gave her a reassuring kiss. "It'll be fine. She wants to help—that's all that matters. Come on." Jeff recalled how Laurel had been the one to lead him along on their tour of the animal shelter less than a week ago. Now it was he who took her by the hand and drew her along on the path toward progress.

When they reached the front door, Astrid flung it wide open before they had a chance to knock. She had on yet another knitted masterpiece, a colorwork sweater in gray, brown, beige, and white, with an ornate yoke. Her eyes landed on her best friend's daughter. "Oh, my God!" She surrounded Laurel in her arms. "I can't believe it! Jeff, come in, come in." She ushered her students out of the cold, then shut the door and reached out again to hug the stray sheep who'd gone through so much. "You look gorgeous! Laurel, I swear—you're the one person who can turn a heavyweight hoodie into a fashion statement!"

"Well, you know me, ever the practical tomboy!"

"Yes, and you found Jeff here—it's unbelievable..."

At that moment, Laurel spotted Astrid's Airedale, whose tail was waving to beat the band. "Oh my gosh—is that—that's Trixie, isn't it?" She knit her brow.

"We adopted her!" Astrid flashed a sunny smile.

Laurel held out her hand. "C'mere, girl!" But when the giant terrier tried to jump on her, she quickly set her straight. "Uh-uh—sit, girl! Sit!" The dog obeyed her immediately. "Shake! Come on, shake!" It took seconds for Laurel to cast her spell over Freyja and give her a hug on her disciplined terms. Jeff had to admire her gift for winning animals over.

Astrid watched as Laurel doted on the dog. "I kept hoping we'd catch a glimpse of you at the shelter when we arranged to adopt her. But we weren't that lucky."

"I was probably out back, working in the runs. I'm so glad you adopted this big girl. She was really hurting for a home. A lot of people are scared of Airedales. They think they're too big and energetic."

"I didn't realize Freyja was adopted," Jeff put in. "I thought surely you'd gotten her from a breeder—she's such a beauty."

"We were astonished to find a purebred dog like this at the shelter. When Sigrun and Lars saw him, they were insistent. We just had to adopt *that dog*, and no other dog. But of course, Sigrun couldn't stand the name 'Trixie,' so we gave her a Norwegian name."

Laurel ran her hand back and forth over the Airedale's wiry coat. "Aren't you just the lucky dog, Freyja! After losing your owner so tragically, you get to call this home now! Thank you, Astrid, for taking care of her. I can tell she's doing great!"

"She's been a wonderful addition to the family. You know how it is—dogs are fabulous company for teenagers. I remember how hard it was on your family when you lost Lady."

"It's true. I cried and cried about that."

"Who's Lady?" Jeff asked.

"She was our Doberman. I still miss her."

"You had her for a long time, didn't you?" Astrid recalled.

"Thirteen years. I mean, I knew she wouldn't live forever. But let's just say, the timing was bad."

"I know. I felt awful for you. How about now? Have you got another dog?"

"Yes, I have Pearl. She's also a shelter dog. She's small, since I'm in an apartment. But she's a sweetheart."

"What about you, Jeff?" the professor asked. "Surely there's a dog in your life?" She made it seem like owning a dog was a badge of honor.

Jeff nodded, glad he could pass this test. "Fritz. He's our Gordon setter."

"Those are beautiful dogs. Do you take him hunting?"

"Occasionally. But mostly he's just a big goof." Jeff laughed.

Astrid laughed, too. "OK, well, I could go on and on about dogs. But we have a job to do, and only so much time in which to do it. Why don't you two hang up your coats." She pointed out the hooks beyond the front door. They took her cue, then followed her through the living room, with its massive built-in bookcase—doubtless the work of her husband—filled with colorful tomes on all things art. "Come on, Freyja. Let's head to my studio."

Laurel smiled. "Ah, the *inner sanctum!*" Apparently, she was acquainted with Astrid's astonishing fiber-art haven. "I can't wait to see what you've got going on in there!"

"Well, now you can see." Astrid led them down the hall, then opened the door to her creative space. "Come on in. I made some hot cocoa for you. I hope that works."

Jeff was still shaking off the winter cold, so he was all for that. He followed the professor's cue to take a seat near one of her spinning wheels, and Laurel sat beside him.

Astrid reached for some earthenware mugs and began filling them with cocoa. "I still can't believe you two found each other. It must be fate. Do you believe in fate?"

Laurel agreed without hesitation. "In this case, yes."

"She calls me 'Knightman,'" Jeff revealed with a chuckle.

"'Knightman.' I like it! OK, Freyja, go lie down. You know the drill." As the dog found a handwoven rug to lie on, Astrid handed them each a mug full of cocoa. "Freyja thinks she should have hot cocoa too, because of the milk—she doesn't agree with it being on her list of banned beverages." She laughed.

Then she grabbed a chair and sat across from them. A crate with various fiber-crafting tools stood at her feet. Jeff couldn't help noticing that, while Astrid wasn't the boot aficionado he and Laurel were, she at least had the good sense to sport quality leather footwear. The minimalist design of her shoes suggested they may be as Scandinavian as she herself was. "All right, let's talk about spinning. I did a little research, and there's a high probability that your ancestor, Hattie Bennett, learned to use a drop spindle when she was small, perhaps around four or five years old. So I'm going to start you two off with the same skill. I have a selection of spindles, which were also called 'rocks' back then, for you to check out. We're going to spin some lovely Bluefaced Leicester wool."

Jeff wondered if that was the origin of the name "Roc" for St. Distaff's Day.

"Exactly, Jeff. That same word was used to refer to the distaff on flax spinning wheels. Interesting, isn't it?"

"Absolutely."

Jeff and Laurel set down their mugs and examined the wooden spindles Astrid showed them. They were clearly antiques, turned by hand. Astrid shared additional information—she'd done her research well. "Leicester Longwools were a breed of sheep very popular in Virginia back in Hattie's day. But I don't have any of that wool on hand—it's rather rare these days. Maybe when you travel to the plantation, you can try to lay your hands on some. In any case, this BFL wool will get you started."

She showed them how Hattie Bennett would likely have made a "leader" to attach the fiber to the spindle and start the process of spinning it into thread. She gave them each a handful of wool and had them pinch off a little and rub it back and forth against their thighs. This produced a length of thread they attached using a hitch knot to the shafts of their spindles. She prompted them to draw the leader through the notch and around the hook at the top. At this point they could try their hand at attaching and gently drafting the fiber, while applying twist by rotating the spindle clockwise.

She followed their efforts attentively, demonstrating for them as needed. The way she brought out the realness of historical experience, by having the two of them partake in the craft Laurel's four-times great-grandmother had engaged in, made its mark on Jeff. He might forget three months' worth of lecturing on the part of a long-winded expert, but he would never forget the feel of this BFL wool as he attempted to turn it into yarn the way Hattie Bennett had.

Astrid added contour to their activity. "People have been spinning this way for at least ten thousand years. Spindles have turned up in archaeological digs across the world. Without the fiber produced like this by human hands, there would have been no textiles, and none of the items made from textiles that have enabled people to survive and thrive over all those millennia. Clothing, tents, ships' sails, nets—anything made from cord, yarn, or thread first began as fiber spun by hand."

Jeff let that information sink in. A profound realization occurred to him. "We're literally making history!"

"Exactly!"

Their efforts proceeded in fits and starts. Astrid coached them with enthusiasm as the couple egged each other on.

Laurel caught on to the craft with lightning speed. "This is fun!" she exclaimed more than once. She seemed to have a genuine knack for using the spindle. Her competitive spirit came to the fore as she eyed Jeff from time to time, whose insistence on engaging the same perfectionism he demanded of himself as a knitter slowed him down in the unfamiliar skill. "How much have you got, Jeff?"

By that point, she'd spun at least half again as much yarn as he had. "Not a lot. But mine's smoother, so hah!"

Laurel laughed.

Astrid smiled encouragement. "I'm amazed at how fast you're learning, Laurel. That being said, there's an interesting form of resistance that researchers have documented on the part of enslaved people who were expected to produce a certain quantity of thread on a daily basis. They were often capable of making much more than was asked of them. But they deliberately slowed their work to avoid giving away any labor they didn't have to to their enslavers."

Laurel drafted additional wool and gave her spindle another twist. "That's actually really interesting. My mother used to talk a lot about 'agency.' I like to think my ancestors were able to exercise at least a small amount of agency, to play some role in determining the course of their lives. It makes me glad to know they could cheat the system a little. On the other hand, this is now, and you know me. I like to be on top of the competition." She shot an impish glance at Jeff. What a show-off.

"I can't take the pressure!" he quipped.

By the end of their first spinning lesson, the two of them had mastered the basics of turning a handful of wool into a useful length of yarn. And they also knew a lot more about how that work could have fit into Hattie Bennett's nineteenth-century life. It had meant survival, protection, clothing for her family, as well as the theft of her labor and agency on the part of those who'd claimed to "own" her. Laurel told them she liked to think that, in fleeing her captors, her four-times great-grandmother had succeeded in reclaiming her birthright as a maker of thread and garments to secure her rightful place in the world.

14

The Ghost

Friday evening. Jeff and Laurel were fast approaching the one-week anniversary in their relationship. Today, Laurel had managed to squeeze in a visit with Dr. McCoy. Jeff wondered if it had been helpful. "How'd your meeting go with the psychologist?"

They were standing in her kitchen, grabbing something to drink. "That woman had me turned into a freakin' faucet!" Laurel held Teddy against her shoulder as she waited for the microwave to heat up her tea water. "I mean, I haven't wailed like that in I don't know how long. But once we moved on to my genealogy work and our relationship, she told me she felt like I was on a really good path. And she didn't see any point in shipping me off to a psychiatrist, so that was a relief."

"That's good to hear." Jeff opened his bottle of kombucha and continued listening. He liked thinking his skills in this area were improving.

"She did seem a little surprised at how quickly our relationship is moving. But I told her I couldn't help it if you were the perfect man for the perfect time. It just happened, and I had no intention of throwing that away." She dunked her tea bag in the hot water, then met his gaze.

Jeff smiled. He certainly liked hearing those words. "Don't look a gift horse in the mouth." He moved in for a kiss. Teddy was right there as always, ever the intimate observer of their shared acts of tenderness. His little splint was now gone, removed by the generous veterinarian who donated her services to the animal shelter, along with the wire from his tiny jaw. Though still a bit groggy, the small yet mighty survivor seemed to know he'd landed well in Laurel's home.

Jeff's next "Extreme Knitting" video was slated for filming the last weekend in January. The weather promised to hold from Prairie Plains all the way out to Minnesota's Thief River Falls. Freeman and Colin had made sure Jeff knew how excited they were to be joined by his girlfriend for the exploit—they welcomed the infusion of female energy into their video exploration. And they welcomed Jeff's willingness to do the driving. In spite of the occasional need to top off the oil supply in his ageing Silverado, he was the best winter driver among them, and in January up here, that was a skill they knew to appreciate—literally anything could happen.

It had been years since Laurel had left Prairie Plains. While she didn't hide her nervousness about leaving the pets behind, she acknowledged her eagerness to escape this godforsaken tundra, even if was just for another corner of godforsaken tundra. She hadn't explored that piece yet—the sheer novelty of it would make leaving

Pearl, Olive, and Teddy in the care of a Humane Society coworker worth the sacrifice.

They headed out of town after Laurel got off work that Friday. The drive would be long and cold. But they had each other for entertainment, and their shared enthusiasm acted as a welcome contagion.

Jeff distracted them with lore about the site they were headed to, and where finger weaver Ralph Cadotte had agreed to meet them in the morning. Thief River Falls was located where two rivers met: Red Lake River and Thief River. The latter name was based on an Ojibwe word referencing an attempt on the part of Dakota tribes to "steal" land along the river, which they'd occupied until the Ojibwe had chased them out.

Legends of hauntings around those parts circulated far and wide. Ralph had shared with Jeff the touching story of a Native woman who'd attempted to use a trail along Red Lake River as an escape route with her child. Realizing that carrying her baby was slowing her down and threatening their escape, she'd laid him beside the river. But upon returning after the threat had passed, she'd discovered the child had been washed away. And this child, she'd come to believe, had been destined to be the next tribal chief. Her grief over his loss had shattered her, reducing her to a wailing spirit sentenced to reside at the site of her son's demise. Those who hiked along what was now called "Dead Man's Trail" occasionally reported hearing her ghost bemoan her fruitless attempts to locate her drowned child along the river bank.

After eyeing him with furrowed brow as he shared this tale, Laurel had a question. "Are you saying we're gonna get haunted while we're making this video?"

Jeff released a chuckle. "Hopefully."

"Hopefully nothin'! I'm not sure how keen I am on hearing some distraught mother who was foolish enough to leave her baby lying at the side of a river moan at me while I'm freezing my ass off following her trail."

Colin laughed. "Don't worry. If she doesn't moan, I will. Just to make sure the viewers get what they're paying for."

"Through those ads they have to watch?" Jeff quipped.

"Right."

Laurel folded her arms. It looked like she was shivering a little. "You people are crazy."

"Do you believe in ghosts, Laurel?" Freeman asked.

"Whether or not I believe in 'em isn't the point. The point is, do I want to encounter them? And the answer to that is 'no.'"

Jeff tried to reassure her. "Maybe we'll luck out."

Colin had a different opinion. "For our viewers' sake, I hope not."

They arrived at their lodgings shortly before midnight. Everyone was so tired after the long drive in the dark, they more or less fell into bed. Jeff sheltered Laurel in his arms for the better part of the night. She seemed anxious. She was away from the pets who depended on her, away from the place she'd come to call home, regardless of its shortcomings, and her mind was ever drawn to the ancestors whose often troubled existence had led to her own. Thank goodness she was finally talking to others about the people who'd come before her, whose traumatic stories rivaled that of the Ojibwe mother who'd lost her baby to the waters of Red Lake River.

Ralph Cadotte met the students at Greenwood Cemetery shortly before dawn—at this time of the year, the sun didn't rise around here until almost 8 a.m. Jeff greeted the finger weaver warmly when they found him. Ralph knew how to dress for the frigid weather. His long, dark hair was tucked beneath the insulated hood of his black winter coat, and his alpine boots looked like they'd seen many a rock-strewn trail.

Jeff wanted his video to serve as an exploration and celebration of Native culture and lore, and Ralph's willingness to accompany them as they followed the haunted trail aroused his gratitude. He would engage in finger weaving while Jeff knit, and everyone would listen for signs of the grieving mother's ghost—some with more enthusiasm than others. Fortunately, the snow wasn't too deep. They were unlikely to lose their way anyhow, given Ralph's detailed knowledge of the site. He'd grown up here, after all.

As the group made their way toward the river, a few birds defied the cold with their songs. Ralph knew nearly all the species that called this area home. He identified the calls of horned larks, Bohemian waxwings, and even the hoots of a snowy owl, whose sounds struck Laurel as fully interchangeable with the moans of a mother desperately searching for her child.

They entered the trail just as the sun was struggling to the horizon, obscured by the haggard shrubs and trees surrounding them. Jeff was knitting a cowl for this video, with colorwork patterns he'd designed to complement the sash Ralph was weaving. Colin counted them down, then Jeff introduced their guest and their projects for the viewers. Laurel had no desire to appear on film, so she tagged along behind Colin. Freeman, on the other hand, milked his role for all it was worth. He asked the fiber crafters questions from a list he'd prepared with Jeff, and Ralph and Jeff took turns answering, while the two of them wove and knit as fast as their freezing fingers allowed.

The sun gradually rose as they slogged their way down the snow-quilted trail, stopping occasionally to check whether they'd heard a moan or a sigh. But in spite of their efforts to welcome the mourning mother's spirit among them, she refused to grace them with anything beyond a persistent feeling of sadness. And that could just as well have been a symptom brought on by their knowledge of the sobering fate affecting the Native in-habitants of this land. Would it have made a difference, Jeff asked into the camera, if the child chief the grieving mother had left at the trail's edge, wrongly thinking he would be safe, had escaped his untimely death and grown to manhood to alter his tribe's destiny? They would never know.

As they headed back to the cemetery, Laurel freely admitted how glad she was that no actual ghost had crossed their path. Getting haunted was the last thing she needed, given all the other trials she had to put up with in life.

Once they reached their vehicles, Jeff thanked Ralph profusely for supporting their project. He would let him know the minute the video was posted. With any luck, it would be as well received as he contended it deserved to be. They parted ways in the hope that this would not be the last time they met in person.

The drive to Red Wing would eat up a good six hours. They would break up the trip with the stop in St. Paul, where they'd gather any details they could regarding the journey north of Laurel's four-times great-grandmother.

Jeff and Laurel had done enough research of their own to flesh out the genealogist's account regarding the barber, William Taylor, and his nephew, Joseph Farr, who'd used Taylor's barbershop and home as safehouses for enslaved people fleeing their vacationing masters as these last had sought refuge from the southern heat along the northern reaches of the Mississippi. They had strong evidence that Hattie Bennett had been one such fugitive, having fled, along with her child, from the vacationing family who'd brought them to St. Paul.

When they got there, Jeff parked at the lot next to Kellogg Mall Park. The foursome spent a good while wandering in the cold along the Mississippi River. They tried to discern traces of the landing area where Hattie and her daughter could possibly have entered the town, and hiked up and down the radically altered streets from Hattie's brief stay at this site in the early 1850s—Kellogg, Cedar, Minnesota, and Third Street—where the house and shop of the now celebrated Black barber and musician, William Taylor, had once stood.

Getting their bearings in relation to the historical map they'd cobbled together from multiple sources in this urban maze of modern structures proved daunting. Laurel conveyed her struggle to intuit the traces of her great-great grandmother's passage through this place, and ferret out any remnants available even mentally from the ground beneath and around them. It was a frustrating challenge. They circled the neighborhood two or three times, each time returning to the intersection at Third and Minnesota, where Taylor's house had reportedly stood a century and a half ago. Colin engaged his camera intermittently. With any luck, the record they made of this visit would be of some meager use as Jeff and Laurel worked on their Hattie Bennett video project.

Overhead the sun shone bright. Until it didn't. Suddenly, a cloud came out of nowhere and passed above them. It cast a sullen, foreboding shadow as they stood along Third Street. Laurel wrinkled her brow and held her hands to her head. "I can almost picture it. It has to have been here!"

Jeff held her by the shoulder. "The house?"

"Yes! They were here, I swear! Her daughter was with her!"

A wind came up—no, not a wind, a *force*. It shoved its way among them and directly into Laurel, who lurched, then cried out. A coarse whisper met Jeff's ears—it sounded like the word "hush," followed by a name. The sound pierced him like a jagged knife. He covered his ears, wincing in pain. Colin continued filming mechanically, his face as white as a sheet, and the darkness around them deepened. The few passing cars barely registered in their perception, while the raspily whispered phrase stabbed Jeff's ears again: "Hush, Tabitha!" Laurel started shaking as Freeman looked on, his brow creased with dread.

Laurel all but screamed. "She was *terrified!*" Tears fell from her eyes as Jeff wrapped his arm around her shoulders. "*Terrified!*"

"It's all right, Laurel." Jeff looked up as the clouds above them parted. "I think she's gone."

Colin lowered his camera. "That was crazy!"

The sun came back, the modern surroundings returned to the fore, and Laurel took several heavy breaths as tears ran down her cheeks. "They were trying to find her." She choked on the words. "They were after her!"

"Did you hear the name it said?" Colin asked.

"Tabitha," Jeff replied. "It's her mother's name."

Laurel wiped the tears from her face. "It's a family name. My mom isn't exactly sure how she ended up with it. It's been recycled a few times across the generations."

Freeman looked her in the eye. "Do you think that could have been Hattie's daughter?"

Laurel nodded as her tears kept coming. "I think so. She didn't want her child to give them away."

Jeff had had enough. "Maybe we should get out of here."

Laurel clung to his arm for dear life. "Good idea. I *never* want to feel her terror again, *ever*. It's *too much!*"

A passer-by asked if they were all right. "We're OK," Jeff told the man. "My girlfriend sort of had a flashback."

He walked on, leaving them to themselves.

"Flashback is right," Freeman exclaimed. "All the way back to the 1850s!"

The color had yet to return to Colin's face. "I didn't think ghosts existed. We went all morning along Dead Man's Trail without so much as a whimper. And now this..."

Jeff nodded deliberately. "Let's go." He held his arm around Laurel as they made their way back across Kellogg Boulevard to the parking lot. Her shivers subsided as dusk descended, lowering the temperature along with it. "We should be able to make it to Red Wing in less than an hour."

Colin released a breath. "I could eat a horse."

"Me, too," Freeman agreed.

"See if you can find us a nice place to eat, Freeman."

They hit the road. Laurel fell asleep in the passenger seat, while Jeff pondered what had happened as he drove down Highway 10. Colin kept replaying the moment on his camera. The recording matched their memory of the incident so precisely, it made Jeff's hair stand on end. He asked Colin to give it a rest. If Hattie Bennett was trying to send them a message, she'd succeeded. When he thought about it, having the name "Tabitha" hurled at them by Bennett's ghost served Jeff as evidence that she was hard at work not only saving Laurel, but possibly her mother, too.

15

Red Wing

As soon as the well-kept buildings lining Red Wing's main drag met their eyes, the foursome perked up. The town deserved its reputation for handsome architecture, inviting shops, and community pride, and Jeff and his friends breathed a collective sigh of relief, now that they were well out of earshot of Hattie Bennett's ghost.

They decided to quell their hunger in the casual atmosphere of a pizza parlor. They gathered around a rustic wooden table and rushed to place their order. All they wanted was some comfort food in front of them—the sooner the better.

Their pizzas arrived, and their mouths watered.

Jeff looked on as Laurel took a big bite out of her slice of Sicilian-style pizza. "You look hungry."

She chewed rapidly. "Starving."

No doubt. Now that they'd put a good fifty miles between themselves and the site of William Taylor's barbershop, Jeff was able to ponder Laurel's perspective on what had transpired from the safety of Red Wing. She'd spent two years trying to fathom what life had been like for the people who'd come before her. But today marked the first time she'd gotten a personal dose of her enslaved ancestors' trauma. How terrified Hattie Bennett must have been that she and her daughter could be found out and dragged back into bondage by the bounty hunters pursuing them. It was one thing to study the abject aspects of enslavement in the safety of a modern classroom, or the comfort of your bedroom, surrounded by your tail-wagging pets. It was another to be assaulted by that *dread*, to share in that spine-chilling knowledge that flight, once attempted, could end in failure, in a return to everything enslavement entailed.

Laurel interrupted her devouring of the anchovy-laced pizza to ask Freeman if he'd given much consideration to these issues. "I'm curious where your people hail from."

Jeff's eyes rested on his friend's corn rows as Freeman responded. He'd learned in Tabitha's class that this hair style had allowed enslaved people to resist their captors, as they could style them in such a way as to embed secret codes. "There were definitely slaves in my family," Freeman replied. "But I'm also a quarter Cherokee. My ancestors lived mainly in Oklahoma."

"Is that where you're from?"

"I was born in St. Louis."

"How did you end up at Great Plains U?" Colin asked.

Freeman snorted. "To be honest, things got a little dicey for me back home." He peeled back his hoodie and T-shirt just far enough to reveal a scar on his shoulder. "See that? Gunshot. My brother got involved in dealing drugs, and let's just say he had some rivals who weren't too thrilled about having their territory invaded."

Laurel swallowed, and it wasn't because her mouth was full of pizza. "That's awful."

"For what it's worth," Jeff put in, "I feel lucky to have you at GPU, Freeman. Our videos wouldn't be the same without you."

Laurel asked whether his brother was OK now.

"Well, considering he's serving a five-year term in prison, who knows? I send him emails with JPay, but he doesn't always respond. I think he wishes he coulda been a better role model."

"It doesn't have to be too late for that," Jeff said.

Freeman shrugged his shoulders. "Well, whatever. I got outa there, and that's all that matters."

Laurel agreed. "That's a good point. You have your future to think about."

Freeman nodded. "I'm not going back home anytime soon. That's for sure."

"What are you studying?"

"Sports and fitness administration. We'll see where I can go with that."

"Sounds interesting. What about you, Colin?" Laurel's pursuit of the topic at hand was a welcome distraction from the aftereffects of what had happened at Third and Minnesota Streets. "Where are your ancestors from?"

Colin set down his glass. "England, Scotland, and France. Nothing too exciting."

"Has your family tried to trace them, or seek out more detailed information?"

"Not like Jeff here. He tells me his paternal grandmother mapped out the entire family tree on his dad's side, then started digging up stories about his mom's side, just because she likes genealogy. Right, Jeff? Is she still trying to chase down those peasants from Southern Italy?"

Jeff smirked. "Yeah, I think so. There's this stereotype about how much the Germans love Italy, so my dad teases Grandma for her obsession with my mom's ancestors, since Mom's Italian through and through."

Laurel managed a smile. "That's sweet. I look forward to meeting your grandmother, Jeff."

"I'd love for you to see her farm. She's got lots of animals for you to dote on."

"I can't wait."

"You know what's cool, though?" Jeff looked first at Laurel, then at Freeman and Colin. "It's thinking about all the drastically different journeys that brought our ancestors here, so that the four of us could gather as Americans around this sticky table at a pizza parlor in Red Wing, Minnesota."

Freeman released a grunt as Laurel laughed. "That's true," she said. "It's pretty damn crazy, when you think about it."

When they finished eating, they walked around downtown Red Wing for an hour and window-shopped. Then Jeff and Laurel drove Freeman and Colin to their motel. As students, they were on a budget, and had booked their room with their finances in mind.

Laurel and Jeff, on the other hand, had decided to invest in something romantic. They'd booked a suite at the historic St. James Hotel. Since moving into her apartment on her father's dime and starting her job at the Humane Society, Laurel had led a remarkably ascetic life. What would it hurt, Jeff had suggested, for her to blow a few hundred bucks on a weekend trip? Not a lot, she'd replied. So here they were. As they entered the gorgeously appointed Victorian space of their suite, with its paneled walls, arched entryways, antique furnishings, and vintage wood flooring, they found themselves in the lap of a luxury neither of them had experienced in a good long while.

Rest and relaxation, that was the ticket. And hopefully, a little romance as well. They set aside the stresses of Friday's grueling drive and their spooky adventures from today. Surrounded by elegant furniture that beckoned them to sit, read, study, or bathe in luxury, they found the bed by far the most appealing option. They shed their boots and winter woolens, and turned down the opulent spread from the king-size four-poster. Laurel grabbed the remote, Jeff grabbed his knitting, and they settled down for an evening of calm.

Jeff unearthed Laurel's sweater project. She immediately gushed over the progress he'd made.

He smiled at her. He had a scheme in mind. "I thought I'd start working on the sleeves this weekend. In fact, if you're game, I could teach you how to help me make those. What do you think?"

She nuzzled his shoulder. "I think you're devious."

"You do?"

"I mean, if my mother never managed to turn me into a knitter, how do you think you're gonna do it?"

He let out a breath. "I see." Laurel snuggled up to him and watched as he added loops of plush lavender yarn onto his short circular needle. "Well, I think I'm gonna do it one," he cast on another loop, "stitch," and another, "at a time," and another. "Now you try." He held the needle and yarn out and hinted that she should take them.

Laurel flashed a helpless smile as she reached for the wooden needle, which was attached by a cord to a second needle and covered with the dozen stitches Jeff had cast on. "How do I hold the yarn?"

"Like this." He grabbed a section a foot or so away from the stitches he'd already made and showed her how to loop the yarn around her left thumb and forefinger, while securing the tail beneath her other fingers.

She followed his lead, catching on quickly as he used the opposite end of the circular needle to demonstrate the next step.

Jeff observed Laurel's hands as they worked, and noticed how similar they were to her mother's nimbly knitting hands. "Nice job. Try to draw the yarn tight, but not too tight." He watched as she pushed the needle in and out of the yarn strung around her fingers. "This'll be great preparation for when you suture up incisions at your veterinary clinic." He laughed.

"Actually, that's true." She met his gaze, then looped another stitch, as the luxurious bedding cradled their tired bodies in its plush warmth. Ten or twelve stitches later, she handed the work back to him. "How many do we have to make?"

"Forty-one should do it." Jeff finished off the row. "Now I'll show you what's called 'joining in the round.'"

"You will?"

"Yup! It's easy. Watch." He flipped the work over, moved one stitch from the left needle to the right, then looped a stitch over that and let it drop below, producing a closed circle of forty stitches. The first row of the sleeve was complete. "Now, I'll show you how to make ribbing." She knew how to make the knit stitches. All he had to do was explain purling, and how to alternate the two to make a squishy, elastic fabric.

Within ten minutes, Laurel had taken over the knitting of her own sweater's sleeve. So Jeff cast on the other sleeve with a second circular needle and skein of lavender yarn—he'd come fully prepared for this moment. And there they lay, nestled on a sumptuous four-poster bed, surrounded by Victorian elegance, knitting together like it was the most natural thing in the world.

It seemed Laurel was finally relaxed enough to discuss the day's events without shuddering. "So do you believe in ghosts, Jeff?"

"I do *now*. That was a first."

"I never encountered one before, either." Laurel watched the stitches accumulate on her needle, while Jeff took in her profile. Hattie Bennett was still on her mind. There was every chance Laurel's four-times great-grandmother had resorted to this craft as a means of setting her own fears and discomforts aside. Tabitha *certainly* did. Her knitting of shawl after exquisite shawl struck Jeff as a way of assimilating her ancestors' experiences.

Laurel seemed to be thinking similar thoughts. "She did this a lot, didn't she?"

"I'm betting she did."

Laurel released a breath. "I think I get it."

Jeff smiled. He thought so, too.

They finished the ribbing for their respective cuffs within minutes of each other. Then Jeff showed her how to switch from the lavender yarn to the purple that would make up the rest of the sleeves before they joined them to the sweater's body.

It was almost too quiet. "Wanna watch a movie?"

Laurel nodded. "Sure. Got any in mind?"

"We could look for *The Princess and the Frog*. Ever seen that?"

She knit her brow. "I don't think so."

"Colin mentioned it to me the other day. Should we give it a try?"

"Sure. Sounds good."

Jeff located the film on the hotel TV, and the thumbnail appeared on the screen.

Laurel released a chuckle. "Aha! A little Black girl magic. I see!"

"You bet."

They lounged there, knitting contentedly as they took in Princess Tiana's adventures.

One thing led to the other. Knitting led to cuddling, cuddling to kissing, kissing to...well, to whatever a romantically inclined couple does when they find themselves under the luxurious comforter on a king-size bed in a posh Victorian hotel room in Red Wing, Minnesota.

The flagship shoe store opened at 11 a.m. on Sunday. Jeff and Laurel could afford to sleep in and breakfast in style. They availed themselves of the hotel's room service. To honor their reason for coming to Red Wing in the first place, they chose the "Big Boot Breakfast" of eggs, bacon, sausage, hashbrowns, and toast, and topped that off with—of course—the St. James' signature Lavender Cake.

Then they put on their Iron Rangers, packed up their things, checked out, and picked up Colin and Freeman.

They arrived at Red Wing Shoes just as the store opened its doors.

The second they got inside, the "Big Boot" acted as a powerful magnet. Laurel immediately looked to her left and stood at attention. "Oh my God, there it is!"

The twenty-foot tall, style 877 moc toe boot was constructed in a size 638 1/2 D, using eighty hides of leather and weighing in at over a ton. It was literally the world's largest boot. Everyone clamored to take selfies in front of this iconic monument to Red Wing footwear craftsmanship, backed by the "Wall of Honor" displaying dozens of work boots previously worn by skilled tradespeople. They all whipped out their phones and took turns posing.

"Just don't be posting my mug on your social media," Laurel admonished them. "I'm not ready for my mom to find out about me and Jeff yet. Got it?"

Colin nodded multiple times. "Got it, Laurel."

The group headed to the right and checked out some old-time shoemaking equipment on exhibit. Then they explored the museum upstairs with its displays of Red Wing shoes and boots since the business had begun in 1905. Laurel agreed with Jeff that wearing heritage boots connected them in a tangible, material way to American history and craftsmanship, while allowing them to take on most any task requiring that they be on their feet. Their boots *empowered* them.

They returned downstairs and ventured into the retail store to check out the latest models on offer. But the real draw was the outlet in the lower level, where stack after stack of leather boots made by Red Wing and sold around the world were available at discounted prices.

The second Laurel reached the bottom step and her eyes found the massive stockpile of footwear housed within this space, her face lit up like a beacon. "I'm in my happy place!" She grabbed Jeff by the arm as they took in the walls lined with kraft brown and red boxes from one end of the outlet store to the other, most all of them harboring boots and shoes manufactured right there in town. The intoxicating smell of leather stuffed with oils and waxes reinforced their excitement.

Everyone picked out boots to try—Beckmans and Blacksmiths, Chelseas and Classic Mocs, Iron Rangers, Roughnecks, even a few pairs of discontinued Merchants. They found boots in all the locally tanned leathers—Ebony Harness, Copper Rough & Tough, Black Prairie, even the rare Hawthorne Abilene. After devoting an hour to trying things on, everyone found an affordable pair to take home. Jeff and Laurel celebrated their couplehood by buying matching footwear, the six-inch Linemans in Black Abilene Roughout. Jeff was amazed they could find such unique boots in their size, which happened to be the same size, another indication of how well they "fit" together.

Their next stop was Welch, where snowboarding was on tap. Jeff found it downright tragic that Laurel had not yet discovered the beauty and wonder of winter sports during her four years in the Northland. "Don't you agree it's time we changed that?"

She cast a glance toward the snow-covered hills as they got out of Jeff's truck. "Probably."

He pumped his fist. "Yes!"

"But if I break my leg, it's on you." She flashed a grin at him.

"Not gonna happen. Let's go!"

They'd secured their rentals of snowboards, boots, and helmets prior to arriving, so everything they needed to indulge in a rewarding afternoon on the slopes was waiting for them.

Jeff coached Laurel on the basic competencies needed to stay on her feet as she maneuvered her way over the snow—gliding, turning, stopping, moving uphill—and admired how she leaned on her dance skills to guide her progress. But even though Jeff was a competent snowboarder, Freeman Brown took the prize. He told them he'd learned snowboarding during his first year at Great Plains U, and embraced the sport as one of the many advantages of his new home. He twisted, jumped, tilted, and pivoted his way over the slopes, stunning Jeff with his expert ollies, grabs, spins, and corks.

"Wow, dude! How in fuck's name do you do that shit?"

Freeman couldn't explain it. He just did what his hip-hop dancer body told him to. He was a natural.

Heading home was the last thing any of them wanted. But given their obligations as students, they did what they had to: stoked themselves full with another meal out, then boarded Jeff's truck for the long, cold drive back to Prairie Plains.

When they got into town, Jeff and Laurel dropped their friends off, picked up the pets from the sitter's, and returned to her abode. After the trip out of state, Prairie Acres Apartments felt more like home than ever.

As they slipped beneath the covers of Laurel's bed, their thoughts inevitably turned to Hattie Bennett. What exactly had she been trying to tell them when she'd haunted them back in St. Paul? They would never really rest until they figured that out.

16

The Wrinkle

JEFF HAD BECOME SO well integrated into the Flatlands Fiber Guild that his attendance at their monthly meetings was practically imperative. If he didn't show up, he'd hear about it. Brenda Wurth would worry herself sick and contact him. Professor Karlsen would give him the third degree during their next spinning lesson. Dr. Howell would subject him to endless gazes of concern during class. Heck, even Sigrun might text him, demanding he explain himself. So not attending the February meeting, in spite of the risks surrounding his clandestine relationship with Tabitha's estranged daughter, was out of the question.

Going there like he always did wasn't without risk, however. What would he say when they asked him about the sweater he was knitting? Well, he could always bring something else to work on, despite the importance of finishing the project in time for Laurel's birthday. What if they asked about his new boots? Maybe he should avoid wearing those this time around. What if the rumor that he was gay surfaced? Hopefully he could set them straight without bringing up the fact that he was seeing someone who happened to be one of their offspring. What if they asked Tabitha how Laurel was doing? He would just have to shut up and writhe as he listened to his history professor's lament that she had no idea.

Laurel agreed that Jeff should attend. It wouldn't help her any if he rocked the boat by disappointing her mom's friends' expectations. People were unlikely to ask questions if he showed up like always and kept a low profile. So Jeff arrived at Dee's Yarn & Fiber Emporium just in time for the February guild meeting, amid flurries of snow floating from an overcast sky.

But the minute he parked on College Ave., he had doubts. He got out of his pickup and walked toward the shop entrance, where he found Astrid and Tabitha engaged in contentious discussion just outside the door. They'd noticed him—turning back now was out of the question. Heatedly whispered words met his ears as Astrid signaled that he should ignore them and go on inside: *grant proposal, Laurel, Bob Lefkowicz, FERPA, not ready either, Laurel, I'm sorry, Laurel, let us help you, for God's sake, nine o'clock, clean up, trust me please.*

Jeff almost regretted having dragged Astrid into his messy involvement with Laurel Howell. She now had as much to hide from Tabitha as he did, and it seemed she wasn't exactly succeeding. This was not the development he'd wished for. It spelled confrontation, assigning blame, and returning Laurel to a state of anger, depression, and self-doubt.

As he entered the shop, the fear mounted inside him that a wrinkle was emerging with the potential to bring down the cardcastle that was their Hattie Bennett video project. Dr. Lefkowicz was a history professor, thus in the same department as Dr. Howell. And Jeff knew that "FER-PA" referred to a law regarding student privacy. *Laurel's* privacy. That's as far as he dared let his thoughts meander as he unzipped his coat and searched for a spot to sit and engage his trembling hands in knitting her sweater, because yes, that's what he'd brought to work on today. Darn it!

Valerie Dittendorf greeted him as he walked past her portable spinning wheel. Brenda Wurth interrupted her knitting and offered to get him some tea. Dannie Novak suggested he help himself to her zucchini bread as she shifted a progress keeper up a few rows on her sweater sleeve.

He returned their greetings distractedly as he removed his coat, then noticed Astrid's felted project bag on the other side of the oak table. No sign of Sigrun anywhere—a good thing. If Jeff sat beside Astrid, maybe she would shelter him from the coming storm. For a storm there would be, if his instincts were right. Jeff claimed the chair next to hers, unpacked the unfinished pieces of Laurel's sweater, and began knitting the sleeves onto the body.

An eternity passed before the two professors finally entered the gathering space. The streaks going down Tabitha's cheeks suggested she'd been crying. Was she angry at Astrid? Relieved that Laurel had shown up in her friend's life? *Perhaps even angry at Jeff?* He breathed a sigh of relief when Tabitha headed for the restroom, without looking his way.

Astrid, on the other hand, walked towards her seat with purpose, sat down beside Jeff, glanced at him with surprising nonchalance, and unearthed the socks she'd brought to knit on. She calmly surveyed the group. Then she leaned in toward Jeff's ear, cupping her hand. "Keep your cool. She got wind of something. Follow my lead."

Jeff swallowed the lump in his throat and nodded, avoiding her gaze. The two of them resumed their knitting. Astrid crossed her legs and settled back in her chair—she seemed as cool as a cucumber. Meanwhile, Jeff's heart pounded and his sweaty hands refused not to shake. The collective conversation got into gear, and although Jeff was too nervous to open his mouth, the women's banter actually did comfort him.

Tabitha finally approached the table, sending his blood pressure soaring again. "I apologize ladies—and Jeff. Don't mind me." She sat unceremoniously between Valerie and Fran.

"Is everything all right?" Valerie asked her.

Tabitha knit her brow as she unfurled her current shawl project. "More or less. It turns out, my colleague in the art department is guiding my daughter in an independent study course without my knowledge. But you're right, Astrid. It is up to Laurel to share that information with me. So again, I apologize."

Jeff twitched nervously. Astrid laid her hand on his thigh and shot him a calming glance.

Brenda eyed the two profs. "Is your daughter resuming her studies, Tabitha?"

Tabitha immediately turned toward Astrid.

"We don't know that yet," Astrid responded. "Everything is in Laurel's hands at this point. One step at a time."

Brenda nodded. "That sounds like a good approach."

It was dawning on Jeff that all the women in this circle had heard stories about Tabitha and her daughter, and knew far more than he ever had about their family drama.

Suddenly, Tabitha's gaze seized on the purple fabric growing in his hands. "Jeff, I am so drawn to that sweater you're knitting. As I mentioned earlier, purple is my daughter's favorite color. You told me you were knitting it for a member of your family—is that right?"

"He's knitting it for his grandmother, "Astrid lied. "Isn't that what you said, Jeff? For her birthday?"

He nodded mechanically. "That's right."

"What a beautiful gift!" Dannie Novak exclaimed. "She's the one who taught you how to knit in the first place, isn't she?"

Jeff's mouth was like a desert wasteland. "That's right." He took a big sip of tea and kept knitting, focusing hard so as to avoid allowing his agitation to cause a mistake.

Brenda followed his fingers with raised brow. "Look at him go. Are you actually joining the sleeves to the body?"

"Right." His hand suddenly spasmed and he nearly dropped several stitches, but he caught himself just in time to avert disaster.

"I could never do that in a group like this. How do you remember all the steps without referring to a pattern?"

Jeff shifted in his seat. Thank goodness they had their knitting to talk about. It wasn't a cure-all, but it definitely helped. "I've already made a dozen sweaters like this. It's sort of automatic."

Astrid encouraged him. "Very impressive. And they said knitting was 'women's work.'" Her laugh sounded forced, but credible.

Jeff reciprocated it—he was grateful for the distraction. His mind was doing its utmost to frighten him into thinking Tabitha knew everything about his relationship with Laurel and would blow their cover right there in the middle of the guild meeting.

But that didn't happen, thank God. The women's chitchat resumed its familiar innocuous character, Tabitha's mood went from sullen to merely subdued, Astrid worked her smile like she was in training for a good cheer competition, and the quiet clatter of Bonnie's vintage spinning wheel calmed Jeff's nerves.

An hour in, and he felt relaxed enough to act on his instinct to flee, however temporarily, from the gathering of matronly hawks circling in on his secret. He got up to look for yarn to give Laurel so she could practice knitting whatever she desired. Their weekend in Minnesota had magically transformed her into an enthusiastic practitioner of the craft.

As he considered what yarn might suit his purpose, he wandered all the way to the front of the shop. He took a few calming breaths. A rack full of Icelandic lettlopi stared him in the face. He pondered the colors of Laurel's spartan wardrobe and the furnishings in her apartment. Earthtones—that was her vibe. Purple on the one hand, earthtones on the other.

Someone's clothes rustled behind him. He turned his head with a start. To his relief, it was Astrid.

"Looking for a gift?"

Jeff met her gaze. They'd discussed their upcoming birthdays during their latest spinning lesson. He nodded.

Astrid reached for a skein and held it out. "I'd try the yellow. If she likes purple, she's bound to like yellow. It's the complementary opposite on the color wheel. It's bright and sunny, too."

Jeff liked the idea—Bonnie had pushed him in that same direction a few weeks ago, and it had worked out well.

He decided now was as good a time as any to learn where things stood regarding what Tabitha had gotten wind of. "How much does she know?"

"Only that Laurel wrote a grant proposal with me," Astrid replied in a low voice. "Apparently Bob Lefkowicz, the Soviet history professor whose office is next to hers, sits on the board that decides which undergraduate grant proposals get funded. He must have mentioned it to her."

In other words, there was a very efficient rumor mill at the university that Jeff had been completely unaware of. "Got it." He hesitated to ask if there was more he should know. As in, had Tabitha learned he was partnering on the project with Laurel.

But Astrid had good news to share. "By the way, your funding was approved. You'll probably get an email on Monday."

"Really?" This lifted his spirits considerably.

"Yes. They were very impressed. The two of you did an incredible job of making your case." Astrid fingered some nearby sock yarn. She must knit those nonstop for her family—Jeff couldn't imagine a Karlsen walking around in anything but handknit wool socks. "Tabitha was pretty pissed that I didn't say anything to her about it. But I reminded her it was up to Laurel to discuss her studies with her parents or not. She seemed to accept that." She took a skein of self-striping yarn as she weighed her options.

Jeff held two skeins of yellow lettlopi and compared their hues as he considered things. "Does she know anything else?"

"Not yet. But keep in mind, Tabitha is no slouch when it comes to ferreting out information. We simply can't assume she won't find out what you and Laurel are up to."

Hesitant to acknowledge the potential fallout of this threat, Jeff marveled instead over Astrid's ability to express herself in idiomatic English, a skill she ascribed to having spent seventeen years in the US, making it inevitable in her words that she would "rival the natives" in her facility with English idioms. Even her accent was barely noticeable. Nonetheless, he acknowledged: "I guess we should be prepared."

"You also have to remember, Jeff: this whole thing is a two-way process. Laurel isn't ready to confront her mother yet, and Tabitha isn't ready to confront Laurel, either. Until they get a few more things worked out on their own, it would only perpetuate their hurt, in my view. I won't go into a lot of details just now. But suffice it to say, we have a sort of two-pronged effort going on that's equally challenging on both ends. You keep working on Laurel, and I'll keep working on Tabitha. What do you think?"

That sounded as good as any plan. "Thanks, Astrid. I think maybe you're the one who's riding around on that white horse now, saving everyone. You're a regular Joan of Arc."

She smirked. "We'll see. Our little house of cards could still easily tumble down in a heap. So we'd better hold onto our shirts, or whatever it is you say."

"Hold onto our hats."

"Yes, that one." Astrid laughed, calming Jeff's butterflies. "Oh, and one last thing. I told Tabitha to buy Laurel a spinning wheel for her birthday."

He arched his brow. "You did?"

"Yes. Last year she had no idea what to get her—she just sent her some houseplants. But she's accepting my suggestion, so you might want to consider buying Laurel some of this." She pointed to where the fiber for spinning was displayed, and indicated a braid of purple merino top.

"Actually, that's a great idea. I'll get that for her, too."

"Perfect."

They brought their finds to the cash register, where Tabitha was discussing precisely what Astrid had said with Bonnie Dittendorf: what spinning wheels did she have on hand, and which did she recommend for Laurel?

"Need some advice?" Astrid asked the women.

"Sure!" Tabitha did nothing to hide her sarcasm. "This was your idea, Professor Karlsen. So yes, please. Do give us some guidance."

Astrid did as her friend asked, while Jeff made his purchase and returned to his seat. Things weren't going quite as he expected, but they were going. A feeling of reassurance washed over him.

Astrid's prediction that more information would get ferreted out proved all too true, however. Only not by Professor Howell—not just yet, at least. But by her own newsmonger daughter.

When Jeff and Laurel arrived at the Karlsen home for their biweekly spinning lesson on Monday, their instructor blocked the way into her house. She greeted them warmly as always, then asked an unexpected question: "Do you trust me?"

To which Jeff responded: "Of course."

Whereas Laurel said: "Yeee...wait a minute. Why are you asking?"

Astrid took a breath. "I'm asking, because knowing that you trust me would be enormously helpful just now."

Laurel wrinkled her brow, took a look at Jeff, and looked back at Astrid. "All right then." She inhaled, then exhaled. "I trust you, Astrid."

"That's good. OK, you can come inside." She opened the door.

Jeff and Laurel's eyes immediately fell on—Sigrun.

She stood beside her mother, wearing an olive-green sweater with a patterned yoke over skinny jeans, her blue eyes and wavy blonde locks virtual carbon copies of Astrid's, and returned their stares with an expression that was part smile, part gape, like she was excited to be in on their secret, but also cognizant of their trepidations.

All the blood had gone out of Laurel's face. She grabbed Jeff's arm and gave him a look that was equal parts "Oh hell, no!" and "God help us!" He returned her gaze, then Freyja had the gall to saunter up and demand to be petted.

Laurel eyed the dog sternly. "Sit, girl!" Jeff almost thought she was talking to Sigrun. Then she reached out to Freyja apologetically and started petting her head.

Astrid put her arm around her daughter's shoulder. "Before you jump to any conclusions, I want you to know that Sigrun, Anders, and I spent six hours yesterday helping your mother clean out her house, while Lars was at work flipping burgers or frying potatoes or whatever it is he does over there at that fast food joint."

Laurel arched her brow. "Seriously?"

Astrid nodded. That was one heck of a revelation. "Sigrun also has something she wants to tell you, Laurel." She flashed a gaze of encouragement her daughter's way. "Go ahead."

Sigrun took a breath, then stood tall. "Laurel, I want you to know I feel really bad about how I treated you back in school. It wasn't fair and you didn't deserve it. I hope you can forgive me."

Laurel stared at her. She exchanged looks with Jeff, who limited his reaction to raising his brow. Then she looked back at Sigrun, her shoulders relaxing. "Thank you. I appreciate it." She said it like she meant it. "And thank you for helping my mother. You all seriously went over there and did all that? Because, I mean, her house was fucking *trashed.*"

Astrid smirked. "Believe me, we know."

"What exactly happened?" Jeff asked. Laurel had mentioned the state of Tabitha's house in passing, but never gone into detail about it.

She unzipped her hoodie and treated Freyja to some more pets. "It all started when my dad left the country. She went on a rampage and flung all his things around the house. She threw stuff, broke stuff—if it was his, she trashed it. I mean, his stuff just ended up *every-where.* Then it was like she just gave up on looking after the place. She stopped cleaning, stopped taking out the trash, stopped caring. Her study is the only livable room in the entire house. When she's not in her office or her carrel on campus, she just stays in that one room. It's filled to the brim with yarn and books."

"All that's changed now," Astrid reported. "I'd say we got it back about ninety percent. Wouldn't you say, Sigrun?"

Sigrun nodded. "That sounds right."

Laurel released a breath. "I can't believe you did that. Every time I went over there, it was worse. No one should have to live like that."

"I think she's figured that out," Astrid said. "We really pushed her. But by the time we left, she was confident she could take over and finish the rest."

Laurel shifted onto her other leg. "Maybe it's time I reach out and help her myself."

"There's no need to unless you feel ready, Laurel. I honestly think your mother recognizes she's handled things badly and she needs to turn over a new leaf. She was so reluctant to let us help her. She hates being dependent on other people. She was grumbling and complaining, yet grateful at the same time. So I think our hard work, which was beyond necessary—it was honestly essential—allowed her to see that, if she doesn't want to rely on others, she'd better damn well help herself. Otherwise, guess what: they'll come knocking at her door and force themselves on her until she shapes up."

Sigrun was practically grinning as her mother talked about the cleanup. The whole event seemed like a huge yet rewarding chore.

"But I have a little advice for the two of you," Astrid said then. "You should know this whole thing blew up when Sigrun found your photo on social media."

Laurel bristled a little. "Wait, what?" She looked at Jeff. "Who could have...?"

He returned her gaze. "It wasn't Colin."

"Then it must have been Freeman."

Sigrun reached for her phone and started tapping around. She held it up to them with a photo she'd found on Instagram. "Actually, you two look great!" It was an image of Laurel and Jeff standing arm in arm in front of the Big Boot at the shoe store in Red Wing.

Jeff recognized Freeman Brown's account. "I'm gonna have to get after that dude. Your mom doesn't use Instagram, does she, Laurel?"

Laurel looked at the photo and scowled. "It would be news to me if she did." She released a breath, shaking her head. "Freeman, Freeman, Freeman."

Jeff laughed. "I guess it's time for me to apologize as well, Sigrun. I'm sorry I misled you when we had coffee together last month."

She shrugged her shoulders and smiled. "I understand. I admit, I was mad at first. But my mom and I had a long talk. A *very* long talk."

"A *very, very* long talk," Astrid agreed.

"You're right, Jeff. I *am* too independent. And my mom made me realize I *like* being that way. I'm glad you found Laurel. You guys seem really happy together."

A welcome sense of relief washed over Jeff. "Thanks." He reached for Laurel's hand, which prompted Freyja to stand and nuzzle Laurel's other hand, her tail waving madly.

Astrid returned to the reason for their visit. "Would it be all right if Sigrun joins us for your lesson today? I thought we'd start learning how to use the spinning wheel, and she's interested in that as well. I feel like she's earned the chance."

Laurel smiled. "Sure. After all that work you did, helping my mom, I'm just really grateful. Thank you."

Astrid patted her shoulder. "And I'll keep checking on her to make sure she keeps the house up. No backsliding."

"Sounds good. I really appreciate it." Laurel reached out to her mom's best friend for a hug.

Jeff decided he might as well join in that effort. He extended his arms toward Sigrun, and they cemented their friendship with a fond embrace.

Freyja accompanied the four of them to Astrid's studio, and they honored Laurel's four-times great-grandmother by exploring how she'd likely used a spinning wheel.

As Astrid had forecast, an email reached Jeff and Laurel on Monday, informing them their grant proposal had been approved. Another missive followed to the entire campus—*including Professor Howell*. Their project entitled: "Spinning Her Own Agency: An Enslaved Woman's Journey from Bondage to Freedom," with primary researchers Jeffrey Nietmann and Laurel Howell, advised by Professor Astrid Karlsen of the Art Department and funded in full for $3,000, received formal announcement.

Jeff and Laurel later learned from Astrid that congratulatory messages began trickling in to Laurel's mother, accompanied by endless questions regarding her daughter's return to college, why no one in the history department was overseeing Laurel's research, and the nature of the relationship between the business school student and the—well, what school was Laurel attached to, anyhow? She was no longer in science. So was she study-ing...*art*?

When Jeff saw this very public announcement of their successful grant application, he knew it would be a matter of time before Tabitha figured out the two of them were more than just fellow researchers. They had to prepare accordingly.

Little did he know he and Laurel would be the ones to give away their relationship.

They'd run into a serious research-related roadblock. How could they prove the Hattie Bennett who'd escaped her enslavers as they'd vacationed in St. Paul had ended up employed at the woolen mill in Ontario as theorized by the genealogist from South Carolina? The grant recipients searched feverishly for any and all possible records shedding light on Bennett's life after she'd escaped the United States.

The working assumption was that Hattie had ended up in a mill town along the Mississippi River—the one in Ontario, not the US—between 1850 and 1870. But Laurel and Jeff were determined to learn more about this stage of Hattie's life, the stage marked by her freedom, prosperity and, they hoped, a substantial measure of happiness. Even more importantly, they wanted to identify the daughter Bennett had rescued. The internet had failed to yield anything useful. Thus their search led down the trail of old-school microfiche records housed in certain Canadian libraries and available via the interlibrary loan system.

Word came that the materials they'd ordered had arrived at the GPU library. But their access privileges were limited—the records would not be allowed out of the building. Neither Jeff nor Laurel had ever used microfiche before. Fortunately, the reference librarian on duty in the reserved resources area was eager to assist them. Once they understood how to search for the information they were after, the couple immersed themselves in the images, consisting primarily of newspapers from Ontario from the latter half of the nineteenth century.

They were peering together at the microfiche reader from the chair they happened to be sharing. Jeff enjoyed the sensation of Laurel's thigh against his as they pored over the pages flipping past them on the gray screen.

Laurel seemed to share his sentiments. "This is actually kind of fun." She smiled as their heads touched when anything remotely revelatory popped up. They were looking for every possible clue—advertisements relating to the textile industry, information on new or established woolen (or woollen) mills, economic reports, Underground Railroad immigrants—basically *anything* that could connect Hattie Bennett to her presumed life of freedom in Ontario.

They considered the mill town the genealogist had conjectured as the one where Bennett might have ended up, and gleaned useful evidence regarding how she and her daughter might have fared there—that was a start. New revelations pointed the way toward further avenues and additional sources for their research. For now, that's as far as they got.

Their eyes having glazed over after two hours of staring at the screen, they returned the microfiche cards to the librarian. They put on their jackets and made their way out to the elevator, trading notes on their progress, and agreed they had reason for optimism that they could unravel at least the essence of Hattie Bennett's life after enslavement.

Laurel dug her hands in her pockets. Jeff expected her to fish out her car keys. But that wasn't what she was looking for. "Where's my phone at?"

"Did you leave it in there?"

She looked at him with knitted brow. "I must've."

"I'll get it. Be right back."

He returned to the microfiche reader, and there on the table lay Laurel's phone. He grabbed it. But as he turned around, he noticed his Black Women's History professor observing him from a carrel across the way. Jeff's heart jumped into his throat. *How long had she been there?* Tabitha was standing as though she were ready to leave. Had she been there the entire time? Like, taking him and Laurel in? Watching them? Pondering their close collaboration, their physical connection, their...*mutual affection?*

Jeff met his professor's gaze. She just stood there—contemplating. Or calculating. Or...Regardless, the jig was up. He knew it was. His heart beat wildly. He started sweating in his Icelandic sweater. He looked over toward Laurel as she stood waiting for him by the elevators. Then he looked back at her mother.

Tabitha nodded at him. *Nodded.* She didn't frown, she didn't swallow, she didn't even furrow her brow. She just nodded.

So Jeff nodded back. Maybe he had less to fear than he imagined. Maybe the evidence that he and Laurel were involved, and had been involved now for weeks, would not be so unwelcome. He took a breath, then tested the waters. "She forgot her phone."

Tabitha quirked a subtle smile—Jeff was certain of it. "She has a habit of that."

Jeff ventured a smile of his own. "I'd better get it back to her."

"I'm sure she'd appreciate it."

He clutched Laurel's phone to his chest, nodded once more, then made his way out.

The elevator had come. He gave Laurel her phone, and they left the building.

Jeff climbed into the passenger seat of Laurel's Equinox. "Did you realize your mother was in there?"

She drilled him with her eyes. "Oh God—you have to be kidding me!"

"She was standing at the entrance to one of the carrels when I grabbed your phone."

Laurel heaved a sigh. "I should have known. That's where she does like half her research."

"Seems like she was there for a good while."

"Did she talk to you?"

Jeff nodded.

Laurel looked into the night through the windshield. "What'd she say?"

He shrugged his shoulders. "Nothing much. I actually think she's OK with it."

She looked back at him. "With us? Being together?"

Jeff nodded. "Could be."

Laurel started the engine. "That's good, then. That's good." Her next breath sounded easier. "Maybe things are startin' to fall into place." She backed out of the parking space and they headed to her apartment.

Jeff hadn't darkened the door of his dorm room in over a week.

The next morning, he was on pins and needles as he entered Dr. Howell's classroom. Tabitha knew more or less everything. But he had no idea what was on her mind. Was she relieved? Upset? Happy? Disappointed? He had every reason to believe she liked him. But it was one thing to like him as a student, a fellow knitter, and guild member. It was another thing to like him as her daughter's love interest.

When the professor began today's session with the announcement: "Class, I'd like to congratulate Mr. Nietmann here on his successful application for an undergraduate research grant on a theme related to this course. Congratulations, Jeff! Well deserved!", he sat up in his desk and was so invested in gauging Tabitha's emotions that he nearly forgot to smile, to say nothing of thanking her for the recognition.

Randall Cobb reached over and smacked him on the shoulder. "That's cool, dude!"

And Angela Curtis's scowl was like a little badge of honor.

Tabitha was actually beaming. Jeff read pride in her expression. Respect. Satisfaction. Even after learning there was more between him and Laurel than a shared interest in American history, she still liked him.

Today's discussion centered on Black existentialism and Black nihilism. Jeff had prepared pretty thoroughly for the topic, and was grateful for his background in philosophy. His performance was unlikely to undermine his girlfriend's mother's positive opinion of him. He even managed to complete a few rows of Laurel's sweater during the class.

When the hour ended, Tabitha signaled her interest in having a word with him. Jeff packed up his things as she fielded a few students' questions. He knew in his heart he had nothing to worry about.

The last student left, and Jeff approached his professor.

Tabitha smiled as she wrinkled her brow, like she was searching for the right words to match her feelings. "I just wanted to say, Jeff...just...look after her... That's it. Look after her."

That was precisely what he had in mind. "I will."

Tabitha studied his face. "It's for her, isn't it? The sweater?"

He smiled. "It is."

She nodded. "Thank you, Jeff."

"My pleasure."

She put one last book in her bag, and they left the room together. Laurel wasn't back in her mother's life. Not yet. But Tabitha had some idea what she was up to now, and she was fine with it. Jeff had to wonder if she had any inkling that the enslaved woman he and Laurel were researching was her own three-times great-grandmother, and how she would react when she found out.

One thing was certain: they still hadn't solved the riddle of how Bennett had managed to rescue her daughter from their enslavers, or who exactly that daughter was. Jeff knew without a doubt that Laurel wouldn't rest until she learned how Hattie's daughter had fared once they'd gotten North. It was like that girl's fate and her own were intertwined. As though the measure of Hattie Bennett's success in assuring her daughter's access to a good life reflected somehow on her own mother's efforts to do the same for her.

17

The Birthday Weekend

Tabitha's efforts to resume her role in Laurel's life took a concrete turn. Because of their grant funding, Jeff and Laurel hung on their university email accounts like a financial lifeline. More often than not, they received the exact same missives, addressed to them both.

But shortly after that "outing" of their relationship in the library, Laurel shared a message she got on her student account to which Jeff was not a party. "Oh, shit!"

He looked up from the business law text he was studying at Laurel's kitchen table. "What is it?"

"She sent me an email!"

Jeff thought for a second, and wrinkled his brow. "You mean your mom?"

Laurel nodded vigorously. "Yes!"

A nervous twitch tightened his gut. "Is it about the grant? Congratulating you?"

She shook her head and turned her laptop so Jeff could see it. The message was from Tabitha.Howell@gpu.edu. The subject read: "Birthday Plans." Jeff followed Laurel's cue to scroll to the body:

Dear Laurel,

I would like very much to visit you for your 21st birthday. While I will be attending my usual Black Studies conference and will be away in Florida on the 15th, perhaps we could get together on Sunday the 16th?
Let me know. I would love to see you and Jeff.

Love, Mom

Laurel huffed a little. "Did you know, she misses my birthday almost every year because of that same damn conference?"

When Jeff thought about it, that was beyond frustrating. No wonder Laurel had a love-hate relationship with Tabitha's career. "That's sad. But one way to look at it is, this would just add an extra day to our birthday weekend."

Laurel sighed. "I don't know. Maybe. My fear is, we'd ask her over here and it'd end up being a huge sob-fest. I haven't seen my mother in almost two years!"

He gave her a hug of encouragement as Teddy ran past them, chasing a fuzzy ball in his usual ungainly manner. His antics induced Laurel to laughter, in spite of her distress.

Jeff looked at the kitten, then back at his girlfriend. "With Teddy around, who needs to sob?"

She laughed into his shoulder, then heaved another sigh. "So you think I should do it?"

"Sure! I think it's high time the two of you mended fences. Don't you?"

It took her a few moments, but she ended up nodding. "I do."

"That's good. 'Cause it looks from her email like your mom is ready. But let's not spoil our video project. First off, we're still missing some essential puzzle pieces. The last thing we need is to share half-baked ideas about the wrong Hattie. Plus, I'd like the final product to be a nice surprise for her. Kind of like a gift, a formalized invitation to restore your relationship. What do you think?"

Another nod. "You're right. We still have a lot to learn about Hattie Bennett. That whole discussion could get really messy. Talk about sobbing..."

"So let's just keep it simple. Focus on the fiber."

She scoffed. "Well, don't go expecting me to whip out my knitting needles in front of *Madam Knits Alot*. I'm certainly not lookin' to humiliate myself in front of her."

Jeff laughed. "OK. I'll knit. You just watch me adoringly."

"Sounds a little more like it." She kissed him on the cheek. "Hmm...you taste a bit like that ball Teddy's been chasin' around." They both laughed. Then Laurel's expression grew serious again. "But what the heck should I say to her?"

That was a good question. "You could try to keep things on your terms. When do you want to meet, where, to do what for how long?"

"Well, it's probably a good idea to invite her over here. Then she'll be on my turf, so to speak. That'll give me more control."

"Sounds good."

"I'd also like it if you could help steer the conversation. If you see that emotional train of mine running off the tracks, get me back in line. I'm not up for any confrontations at this point. They only do harm."

Jeff nodded with confidence. "I can do that. Speaking of running off the tracks, what in the heck is Teddy doing over there?" Whatever it was, it wasn't on his list of prescribed activities.

"Oh shit—he's trying to dig up my plants! Come here, Teddy." Laurel rose to remove the kitten from her umbrella tree plant. She scooped him up, while Pearl looked on jealously, and returned to the table with the curious explorer. "Should we make my mom something to eat?"

That was a good idea. "What does she like?"

"She's not a big eater. She eats a lot of salad."

"So we should invite her over here to eat salad?"

"It sounds really dumb when you say it like that." Laurel laughed as she elicited loud purrs from Teddy with her caresses. "Do you know any other German-Russian dishes she might like?"

Jeff flashed a crooked smile. "I heat up a mean sauerkraut."

"Uh...no."

"All right then, how about borscht?"

"Say what?"

"Borscht. It's a soup with beets, beef, and cabbage. I could ask my grandma for the recipe."

Laurel gave Teddy a few more pets. "You know what? That sounds like a great conversation piece. I'll tell Mom we're inviting her over to eat borscht with us. She won't have any idea what that is, so we can eat up at least a quarter hour explaining it to her. Sounds perfect!"

"So, we have a plan?"

"Yes, we do. I'll go ahead and email her back." She asked him to help put the finishing touches on her reply:

It's good to hear from you, Mom. Jeff and I would love to have you over here at the apartment on Sunday. We'll make some borscht for you. Let us know if 2 o'clock will work. We look forward to seeing you!

Love, Laurel

She hit send, and within ten minutes she got an answer: *Could we make it 4 p.m.? My plane doesn't land until 2. I hope that works for you.*

Let's plan on it, Laurel typed back as Jeff looked over her shoulder. *4 p.m. Sunday at my place.*

See you there! Tabitha replied.

Laurel took a breath as Teddy actually jumped down off the table. He was like a walking miracle. "Did you know, Jeff, that's the first time in two years that I've communicated with her?"

He rubbed her gently on the back. "How does it feel?"

She returned his gaze. "Actually, it feels good!"

That prompted a smile.

Jeff had at least a vague idea of how underwhelming Laurel's past couple of birthdays had been. He was determined to make this one memorable. There was no reason to go stupidly overboard—he'd finished knitting her sweater, and she'd told him repeatedly she would enjoy wearing it day in and day out until summer arrived.

But romance demanded that Jeff add some icing to this substantial cake. And given how he meant business with this chance to finally end his years of navigating life's trials in lonely celibacy, nothing less than a dozen red roses would do the job. He presented these to Laurel the minute she stepped inside the door after arriving home from work Friday.

She literally dropped her keys on the floor. "Oh my God! I love you so much!" She threw off her hoodie, gave Pearl a few quick pets, and took the roses from Jeff with an excited gasp. She rewarded him with a kiss. "Let's put these in some water." She dumped the wooden spoons from their plastic container, filled it at the sink, and placed the roses in it. "Just the right height," she said with a laugh. Then she opened the packet of plant food and sprinkled a little around the stems. She looked sternly at the kitten, who was eyeing the counter with eagerness from the floor below. "You'd better not get into these roses, Teddster, or I'll have your little heinie!"

Jeff laughed. "You know he's doing well when we have to call him out for his mischief. Happy birthday, Laurel!" They surrounded each other in a warm embrace.

They started the weekend off with dinner at a Thai restaurant, where the cuisine was just hot and spicy enough to help them forget the cold night outside. Jeff added a little sunshine by presenting Laurel with the yellow yarn Astrid had helped him pick out. "Make something special. And be sure it's for you."

She smiled. "Challenge accepted." That led to another kiss.

Of course, to do full justice to their romantic yearnings, they had to follow dinner up with a stint under the covers at home. They even passed on dancing tonight. Time was at a premium, given how early they had to get to the Humane Society in the morning. There was no sense doing anything but what gave them maximum pleasure.

There was every chance Jeff's parents would arrive on Saturday while Laurel was still at work. In spite of their reassurances concerning how happy they were to know Jeff had ditched his loner life and finally gotten involved, his brain insisted on worrying Mom and Dad would fail to hit it off with the girl he regarded as his one and only, the love of his life, who was destined to stay by his side, come hell or high water. If they had any reservations about her—she was just a wage earner, had no college degree, wasn't girly enough, took herself too seriously, whatever—it could be a long weekend.

So he was overcome with the jitters the moment his mom texted him that they'd made it into town and were on their way to Prairie Acres, twenty minutes before Laurel got off work.

When they pulled up in Dad's Jeep Wagoneer, Jeff stood outside waiting for them. A concerted round of hugs set his mind at ease. He reminded himself of how neat and clean Laurel kept her apartment, and decided her pets would distract his folks from any flaws they might encounter. They both loved animals, after all. And to his relief, they voiced their approval of the modern apartment he'd come to call home the moment he led them inside, where Pearl greeted them like long-lost relations.

"Looks like you've more or less moved out of the dorm," his father remarked as he surveyed the contents of the living area. Jeff's jackets hung on a coat rack near the door, his snow boots sat on the floor below it, a project bag huddled beneath the coffee table, and some of his favorite snacks were stashed between the coffee maker and the air fryer.

Jeff had to nod. "It's tricky to maintain two living spaces. So yeah, I moved most everything over here." He hoped his parents would greet this admission with acceptance.

They found no reason to object—a victory. After they took off their coats, he went so far as to invite them to accompany him to Laurel's bedroom, where he let Teddy out of his crate and recounted highlights from the kitten's tragic start in life.

His mother took the initiative to sit down on Laurel's neatly-made bed and allow Teddy to limp over her burgundy slacks while she encouraged his purrs by running her slender hand from his head to his tail, over and over again. "What a sweetheart!" she crooned.

By this time, Dad was already taking in Laurel's ancestry board. He towered over it, peering down at the pictures and text through his wire-rimmed specs. "This is quite the research project!"

Jeff moved next to him and pointed out a photo of the plantation where Hattie Bennett had spent her formative years. "That's one of the places we're planning to film next month."

Dad acknowledged that with a nod. "Congratulations on winning the grant. We're really proud of you, Jeff. You know, I've been doing a little behind-the-scenes research on marketing yarn, and it strikes me that this work will provide you with useful background for reaching a diverse audience with any product lines you decide to develop."

That made a great deal of sense. John Nietmann had no shortage of good paternal advice—for that, Jeff was grateful.

As they chatted, he got a text from Laurel. She was out in the parking lot, hesitant to come inside her own apartment. *I'm a little nervous. What if I rub them the wrong way?*

Jeff was no stranger to his girlfriend's self-doubt. It was crucial to send the right message. Keeping things casual struck him as optimal. *We're just in here gabbing. My parents can't wait to see you.*

You're sure?

Jeff suppressed a smirk. *Sure I'm sure.* That oughta sell 'er.

He invited his folks back into the living room. A minute or so later, Laurel entered her own abode, where Jeff and his parents had more or less taken over the space on the occasion of her birthday, no less. He led the way in keeping things warm and encouraging.

Laurel smiled as she set her tote down on her own kitchen counter. That was one big smile—she was definitely working to make it happen. But she did, and it was effective.

Mom and Dad went to greet her, going so far as to offer hugs to Jeff's girlfriend of a mere month. He looked on as Laurel wrapped her arms, clad in her favorite ranch-hand hoodie, complete with the usual Humane Society smells, around his mom in her charcoal-gray cardigan, a product of his grandmother's hands. And when his dad hugged her, she looked almost cute, resting her head against his chest as he looked down over her fro from his six-foot three-inch frame.

"Welcome to my humble abode!" Laurel took off her hoodie and gave Pearl a few pets. It only took a minute or two for her good humor to come out, as Rose and John made themselves comfortable on the sofa.

Laurel offered them all something to drink and joined them. Before long, they were filling her space with spirited conversation. Jeff's dad answered her questions regarding his work, sharing about his brief career as a mountain bike racer, and his adventures with Jeff in everything from snowshoeing to partridge hunting to hiking to kayaking. He related how he'd met Rose in college while earning a business degree in Colorado, then opened a sporting goods store at a location chosen based on a marketing analysis project he'd done for his senior thesis.

Laurel took equally active interest in getting to know Jeff's mom. "I'm curious what it's like to work for your husband." She accompanied the comment with a chuckle. Her own mother was such a go-getter—Laurel's curiosity concerning the career goals of a woman who helped her husband run his store was understandable.

Mom's response made Jeff proud. "It's not exactly what I had planned when I was pursuing my teaching degree, Laurel. But financially speaking, deciding to work with John was the right move. I'd always wanted to work with children. But I'm not sure I would have had the energy to focus my attention on Amy and Jeff, if I'd had to devote it all as a teacher to other people's children."

Laurel greeted that with a nod. "I get it. My mom was definitely stretched thin when it came to raising me. And I'm only one child!" This time, her chuckle was nervous.

Jeff liked thinking his parents' revelations painted the kind of picture that forecast his own success as a father. He wasn't about to call Laurel's parents out, but he couldn't suppress his smile as his mind dared to compare his future father self with what little he knew about Laurel's dad, and he decided he could definitely take Jerome Howell to the mat.

But this was a birthday celebration, and they had gifts to open. John ran out to his SUV and returned with a few packages wrapped in colorful paper, two for Jeff and two for Laurel. Since Laurel's birthday came first, she was first to do the honors.

Jeff had helped his mom pick out her gift of circular knitting needles, and was pleased to see how well they went over. When Laurel turned her attention to the gift from his dad, her smile was irrepressible. The shape of the package alone gave away that she was dealing with LPs, and when she discovered five rare jazz recordings inside, she was beside herself. "Oh my God, thank you! You're so kind! I *love* these!" She shooed Olive from her record player and put on the album from 1967 featuring Mel Lewis and Thad Jones. Their big band swing filled the room, and had everyone grooving to the beats.

Then it was Jeff's turn. His face lit up when he discovered a squishy hank of qiviut yarn inside the package from his father. He could never afford to buy this stuff for himself, and immediately conjured up ideas for how to put the luxurious fiber to use. Gloves—that would be an awesome challenge. And qiviut lent itself perfectly to those.

Then came the gift from his mom. The box felt heavy and substantial. Jeff removed the silver paper, tossed that on the floor for Teddy to play with, then was confronted with an authentic pasta maker, direct from Italy.

Rose followed his movements with a smile. "I thought the two of you might enjoy trying your hand at making pasta. If you need advice, I'm more than happy to share my tips and tricks."

But Jeff knew almost all his mom's tips and tricks. He'd helped her make fettuccini and linguini on repeated occasions, and looked forward to doing the same with Laurel. "This will be so much fun, Mom. I can't wait to use it!"

Between the yarn, the pasta machine, the needles, and the records, Jeff's life with Laurel would be that much homier, cozier, and tastier. His parents had done their job well.

The foursome shifted gears—they had hunger to still. Prairie Plains had a nicer restaurant that billed itself as "European." When Jeff suggested they could indulge in some German cuisine to celebrate his turning twenty-one, they all agreed. *Sauerbraten* and *Rindsrouladen*, those numbered among the eatery's offerings, as well as *Apfelstrudel* and *Kaiserschmarrn*, shreds of caramelized pancake soaked in rum. But the place offered French and Italian dishes as well, so something for each of them. Plus, the "birthday kids," as John Nietmann insisted on calling them, could now drink wine and beer without having to resort to a fake ID, a privilege they took full advantage of this evening.

The parents had to return home the next day. But first, they took Laurel and Jeff out for breakfast at the Cowpoke Café, the site of their first meal together. As Jeff contemplated all that had transpired between his impassioned tryst here with Laurel, and their family gathering today, a feeling of accomplishment washed over him. What he learned next only amplified his conviction that big developments were on the horizon for him and his partner.

Dad interrupted his work of indulging in the cheddar cheese omelet whose scent wafted across the table. "Jeff, there's one thing I wanted to leave you with before we go today." He looked him in the eye. "Your grandmother has made a decision with regard to her will. She just needs to know whether it would meet with your approval."

Jeff set down his knife and took a breath. "What did she decide?"

"She wants to leave you her sheep farm."

A wave of excitement coursed through Jeff. "Really?"

"Yes. Obviously, she's not going anywhere anytime soon. But she wants to have all these things ironed out now, so she doesn't have to worry about them later. After all, she's seventy-five years old. She's not getting any younger."

"Of course." Jeff wiped his beard with his napkin, then cast a quick glance at Laurel. The news wasn't a total shock. After all, his grandmother had been doing the work of two since losing her husband, and her energy reserves were limited. But she could just as easily put the property up for sale as pass it down to him, so this was a big deal.

"Now that's not to say you couldn't get your hands on the ranch earlier," Dad said. "But the tax picture would look different depending on when you take it over. We'll have to consult an accountant to look into the options. She's more or less retired now, so the renters are running the operation. That might be another option for you. Whenever you're ready, you could rent the land from her, then inherit it down the road. But in any case, she wants to know if she can write that into her will, that you would receive her ranch in Montana."

Laurel's eyes were huge. "Montana? That's insane!"

Jeff met her gaze. "What do you think?"

"What do I think?" She gaped and arched her brow. "I think you'd be crazy to say no!"

He wasn't going to say yes, though, unless he knew she'd be game to move even farther away than Prairie Plains from the warmth of her southern homeland. "But how do you feel about Montana?"

"Will Montana have *you* in it?"

Jeff flashed a smile as his parents looked on. Then he nodded.

"Well, let's go! Have they got a vet school there?"

"I think there's one in Washington," John replied. "And Colorado has one for sure. Is that what you plan to study?"

"I'm trying. I had a lousy freshman year because of depression. My parents had more or less separated, and my father moved abroad. But I have a psychologist now, and we're petitioning the university to let me drop some courses from my record. That seems to be moving ahead, so I plan on resuming college come fall."

John greeted her explanation with a nod. "Excellent. You clearly have a wonderful rapport with animals. And from what Jeff tells us, you're also extremely bright."

Laurel drilled Jeff with her eyes. "You said that about me?"

"Of course!" Jeff knew for a fact that Laurel was smarter than he was.

His dad smiled as he observed their exchange. "In any case, there's no rush. Plenty of time to complete your educations. As I said, Grandma's not going anywhere anytime soon. She just wants to get her ducks in a row. So am I hearing you say yes, Jeff? That you'd like to be included in the will that way?"

A no-brainer if ever there was one. "Yes!"

"Awesome. I'll tell her. She'll definitely be pleased."

Jeff and Laurel were pleased, too. He suddenly stood to inherit his grandmother's sheep ranch. What a boon to his future! And to Laurel's future as well. She could hone her veterinary skills as she helped him look after the sheep, maybe even train some border collies to help with the shepherding. And after earning her bachelor's degree, which she was bound to do, she could shoot for a DVM from a school within striking distance of the ranch. Their future together was looking mighty bright.

Preparing borscht proved surprisingly entertaining. Laurel had never cooked with beets before. It showed. But she was fascinated to see how red their juices were.

"Didn't I tell you about that?" Jeff quipped.

She laughed. "No."

He laughed, too. "Now you know."

Thanks to his careless antics, Teddy got splashed with beet juice, and was now running around with pink polka dots across his back. What a clown.

The preparation entailed the chopping and cutting of beets, onions, cabbage, and beef. And as these ingredients simmered with all the herbs and spices, they filled the apartment with savoriness. The aroma calmed the cooks as they waited for Tabitha to arrive.

Laurel's anxiety lurked beneath the surface nonetheless. And when the buzzer rang at four o'clock, she nearly jumped out of her skin, causing Teddy to bristle and hiss. The confrontation with her mother would not happen immediately, though—Tabitha requested help over the speaker to get Laurel's gift out of her car and into the building. Jeff agreed to meet her outside.

He found the professor looking somewhat helpless as she contemplated the best way to extract a large box from her backseat.

"Hello there, Jeff! Thank you for rescuing me."

"It's my pleasure. We're glad you came." They worked the container out from the sedan, and Jeff hoisted it over his shoulder and brought it to the entrance. He shot the breeze to contain his edginess. "I hope your conference went well."

"Very well. I'm just sorry it caused me to miss Laurel's birthday. That's been a regular problem for us, and arguably a thorn in her side. Maybe it's time I stop attending conferences in February." She punctuated the proposal with a smile.

"I honestly think she'd like that." Jeff wrangled the box into the building as Tabitha helped him with the doors. He cast occasional glances her way, trying to assess her mood. Was she nervous? Apprehensive? Excited? Relieved? Then they reached Laurel's welcome mat. "Knock, knock," he said with a laugh.

The door immediately opened. "Welcome, Mom." Laurel's effort to keep her emotions from running away seemed to be working—she sounded genuinely cheerful. Jeff set the box down to give mother and daughter a little space.

Tabitha reached out to hug her long lost sheep. "Oh, Laurel, I can't tell you how wonderful it is to see you!"

When Laurel reciprocated her gesture, Jeff let out a breath. The mother-daughter reunion was starting out well. Then Laurel pointed at the giant box. "What the hell is that?"

Jeff hoisted it again and squeezed his way past them, carefully avoiding stepping on Pearl, whose tail was wagging like a propeller. "There's plenty of time to find that out. First, maybe we should try the borscht."

Tabitha found a spot on the counter for her bag. She took a quick look around, and smiled. "Tell me about this borscht, you two. I've never heard of it."

Jeff took that one. "It's a German-Russian soup that's still popular in Eastern Europe. We thought you might enjoy some home-cooked food."

"Yes I would. Thank you." Tabitha took off her camel-hair coat and spotted a hook on the coat rack, while Jeff set the box beneath the TV.

Laurel introduced her pets to her mother. "This is Pearl. She's no Lady, but she's just as sweet as she can be.

And Olive has been with me a good while now. And this little guy is Teddy." She pointed toward the kitten as he attempted to climb onto the strange box. "We adopted him a month ago. He was injured when he tried to hide inside a car engine."

"Oh my! I bet he's glad he ended up here with you."

Laurel smiled. "I think so."

Tabitha continued to take stock of her daughter's surroundings. "You know, I'm curious. I know Jeff from the fiber guild, but I had no idea you two were dating. How ever did you meet?"

Laurel shot a glance Jeff's way. "He volunteers at the shelter, Mom."

"Is that so?"

Jeff nodded. "I'm sorry I didn't say anything. I wanted Laurel to choose the time. It almost worked."

Tabitha responded with a nod. "I understand completely. You've been through a lot, Laurel. And much of it is my fault. I'm sorry."

"I'm sorry too, Mom. I've been trying to see things from your perspective, and I understand it all a lot better now."

"You do?"

"I do. I've had a few visits with a psychologist. That was Jeff's idea. And actually, it's been really useful."

"I'm so glad to hear that. I like thinking we don't have to just keep avoiding each other."

"Definitely not." Laurel moved in for another hug, this one longer and firmer than the first.

Then Tabitha switched gears. "My goodness, Jeff. How do you find time to volunteer at the animal shelter, alongside all your other enterprises?"

He shrugged. "It's early in the day, just a few days a week. Plus, since I go there with Laurel, I have no trouble being motivated." He reciprocated his girlfriend's smile.

"Most students I teach want to sleep in till ten o'clock. You're much more productive than they are."

He reached for Laurel's hand. "I have a reason to be."

"That's wonderful."

Laurel cocked her head toward the soup on the stove. "Shall we set the table, Jeff?" She'd just come home from work. She had to be hungry.

"I'll grab some bowls."

Although Tabitha's offer to pitch in met with rejection, they got everything ready in no time, and Jeff invited her to sit at the head of the table. Thanks to his grandmother's recipe, the borscht was every bit as good as he'd predicted. He smiled to see how much Tabitha enjoyed it. It inspired them to converse about home-cooked food and ethnic cuisine, and those topics, along with details about Laurel's work and the visit from Jeff's parents, sustained them over the course of the meal. Then it was time for Laurel to open her mother's gift.

They invited Tabitha to sit on the sofa, and Jeff moved the crate into the middle of the living room, where it drew Teddy like a magnet.

"I bought this for you on Astrid's advice," Tabitha reported. "She assured me it would go over well, so here's hoping she was right."

Jeff armed his girlfriend with scissors, and she sliced through the seams around the lid, then put Teddy on the floor and cut through the top seam. As she opened the container, her jaw dropped. "Seriously? A spinning wheel? Oh my God!" Her smile was huge as she had Jeff help her unearth the contents. "This is crazy!"

Tabitha's eyes followed her daughter's every move. "Astrid told me you're a natural, which frankly surprised me. I mean, getting you to so much as lay your hands on a skein of yarn was out of the question when you were younger. I suppose I'm happy to see that's changed somehow, maybe thanks to your boyfriend's influence."

"Sure, Mom." Jeff knew Laurel wasn't yet ready to delve into the details of how her four-times great-grandmother seemed to be guiding her along her unexpected fiber-crafting journey. The two of them were determined to have every possible puzzle piece in place before they shared their work on Hattie Bennett with her scholar-mother. "But honestly, this is an awesome gift. You have no idea how touched I am! These wheels aren't cheap, and I want you to know, this is making me really happy." Tears welled in her eyes.

Tabitha was tearing up, too. In fact, Jeff was close to tears himself. Reuniting Laurel with her mother had been his ambition since he'd first learned of their troubled relationship while discussing her ancestry board, and now it was happening.

But rather than succumb to the urge to bawl, Laurel turned her attention to her deconstructed spinning wheel. "How in the heck do we put this thing together?" There was no clear path to assembling what amounted to a wooden jigsaw puzzle. "What do you think, Jeff?"

"You're asking me? You're the real spinner in this family."

"That's what I hear!" Tabitha agreed.

"YouTube to the rescue!" Jeff pulled out his phone, and quickly found a tutorial that answered their need.

Tabitha raised her brow. "You can just find that sort of thing on YouTube?"

Jeff nodded. "You can find almost anything on YouTube. Even 'Black nihilism.'"

She scowled. "Oh, is that so?"

Jeff laughed. "Absolutely!"

"Huh. I'll have to remember that. Maybe integrating some YouTube videos into my course would benefit the students."

"I'm sure it would. They've helped me out a lot." Jeff conjured up his inner handyman, asked Laurel to fetch any tools she had on hand, and they began setting up the spinning wheel. After a good twenty minutes, they had everything assembled.

Laurel stood and admired it, but soon furrowed her brow. "What am I gonna spin on it? I don't have any fiber over here."

Jeff flashed a smile. "Let's fix that." He retrieved his final gift from its hiding place in the linen closet and handed it to her.

"There's more?"

"Astrid made sure I was prepared. Open it!"

Laurel ripped into the package, unearthing a braid of merino fleece dyed in royal purple. She held it to her face, rubbing it against her cheek with a smile. Then she pulled the spinning wheel up to a kitchen chair and positioned herself to try it out.

Jeff grabbed his project bag from under the coffee table, and cut a length of yarn for her to use as a leader.

He watched as Laurel attached the yarn to the bobbin. "Don't forget to adjust the tension."

"Right. Not too tight, not too loose." She predrafted a small length of fiber, attached it to the leader, and tried her hand at spinning it.

Tabitha watched intently. She'd once made it clear she wasn't a spinner and didn't intend to become one. So Jeff was glad to observe that at least her passive interest in her daughter's spinning skills seemed keen.

"I'm glad Astrid was so very right about this gift," Tabitha exclaimed. "One of these days, Laurel, maybe someone will explain how you metamorphosed into such an enthusiastic spinner."

"All in good time, Mom. All in good time." Laurel's rhythm as she worked the treadles grew steady and swift.

·❤·❤·❤·❤·❤·

18

Final Preparations

JEFF AND LAUREL ARRIVED at Astrid's house for their biweekly spinning lesson. The microfiche records they'd been poring over had failed to yield the details they needed to assert with confidence that Hattie Bennett had thrived as a millworker in Ontario. Nor had they learned her daughter's identity, or anything useful regarding her ultimate fate. They were beginning to wonder whether their research project would dead-end with the ghost's pronouncement of the name "Tabitha" back in St. Paul. They hoped maybe Astrid could help them over the impasse. She was an artist, but she'd proven herself as a scholar, too.

She invited them out of the cold. "Your mother tells me the spinning wheel went over well."

Laurel's face lit up. "I can't believe she went out and got that for me. Thank you for suggesting it to her, Astrid."

"I was happy to do it."

"Jeff looked it up, and he tells me it's a pretty expensive model." They hung up their coats as they entered the Karlsens' living room. Freyja's tail waved madly.

"I told her to get the most expensive wheel Bonnie had," Astrid reported with a chuckle. "I figured she owed it to you. She seemed to agree with that."

Laurel smiled broadly. "You're just as devious as Jeff is."

The professor conducted her students to her studio. "So you had a nice visit?"

"Yes, actually. It went very well. I feel like Mom and I are off to a good start at getting things back on track."

"That makes me really happy." Astrid opened the door to her "inner sanctum" and invited them to partake in some hot cider.

What made Jeff really happy was this incredible fiber studio. As he sat down with his mug of cider, the cinnamony smell wafting up his nose competed with the scents of lanolin and dried herbs. He invited Freyja for some pets and breathed in the delicious air.

Laurel sat down beside him. "Did you know Jeff's parents came out over the weekend to celebrate his birthday? Jeff, you should tell her the news your dad had for you, about your grandmother's will."

Astrid took a seat as well. "Good news, I hope."

"Fabulous news! Tell her, Jeff."

He took a breath and smiled. "I stand to inherit my grandmother's sheep ranch."

Astrid met his gaze. "Are you serious?"

He nodded.

"Jeff, that's huge! When is this all going to happen?"

"Not right away, but basically the farm is mine when I'm ready."

Astrid reached out and shook his hand. "Congratulations! So Laurel, you might have a great place to use those veterinary skills of yours."

"If I make it that far."

"I have complete faith in you. I understand you've been working with your academic advisor to resume your studies."

Laurel confirmed that. "How did you know?"

"Because I spoke with her. She wanted to know how you were doing in our independent study, and I offered to write a letter supporting your petition to have the university withdraw you from those courses you shouldn't have been trying to take in the first place."

"Astrid, I did not know that. That's so kind of you. Thank you!"

"Of course! I was happy to do it. I wrote a strong letter and agreed to speak to them on your behalf. But I don't think it'll be necessary. The fact that you and Jeff got the undergraduate research grant is proving a key justification for reinstating you. In fact, I argued that you should be readmitted to the honors program, so be thinking about that as well. You should develop a plan for an honors thesis with one of the biology professors."

Laurel's chin was quivering. "That's amazing. I'll definitely think about that."

"Well, you two, what's the latest on Hattie Bennett?"

Jeff glanced at Laurel. "We're a little bit stuck."

Laurel corroborated that. "We're having a heck of a time getting information about her, beyond knowing she journeyed from St. Paul, Minnesota, to the Mississippi Valley in Ontario."

Jeff nudged Laurel with his elbow. "Maybe we should tell her what happened to us in St. Paul."

Laurel released a snicker. "She'll probably just think we're a couple of nut jobs."

Maybe so. But what other leads did they have? "Want me to do it?"

Laurel exhaled. "I don't know, Jeff. Maybe I try to think too scientifically. It's just so hard to wrap my head around."

That was certainly true. But still. Jeff eyed Astrid.

"Well, I'm an artist," she pronounced. "Science can be overrated."

He smiled. "Right?" The more he thought about it, the more the haunting seemed to signal a path forward.

Laurel relented. "OK, well...where do you stand on ghosts?"

Astrid raised her brow, then quirked a smile. "I try to avoid standing on them, since they lack substance."

That got Laurel to chuckle. "No—I mean, do you believe in them?"

The professor took a sip of her cider. "You should know I'm a closet Pagan. I don't dare spread that around—people are liable to suspect I'll eat their children or something. But let's just say, I'd be the last person to deny the existence of ghosts."

Laurel took a breath. She looked at Jeff. "Do you wanna show her *that* video?"

Colin had shared his video material from their visit to Third and Minnesota Streets, and Jeff had studied the footage multiple times for any clues it might hold, and failed to get anywhere. Maybe their closet Pagan friend would see something he and Laurel hadn't. He cued up the segment with the haunting that had filled Laurel with dread, then handed his phone to Astrid. "Have a look."

She tapped on play. Laurel went pale the second the video began. Astrid studied it. Not once, but twice.

"What do you make of it?" Jeff asked.

"She's definitely trying to tell you something. Who is this Tabitha she's referring to? That can't be your mother, Laurel."

Jeff shared their theory. "We think Hattie Bennett's daughter might have had the same name."

Laurel elaborated. "That's where we're getting stuck. We can't find any additional records on Hattie's own family, on this girl, or how they managed to escape whoever was coming after them."

Astrid started thinking out loud. "So from what we know at this point, rich white Southerners were vacationing in St. Paul to escape the hot summers down South, and they brought their slaves along to serve them. Right?"

"Right."

"But why would they bring a little girl?" Astrid knit her brow.

Laurel told her what little they knew. "It's clear Hattie was trying to hide her daughter so she could get her to safety."

Astrid sought her gaze. "I hate to even suggest this."

"What?"

"I mean..." Astrid took a deep breath. "He could have been a pedophile."

"The master, you mean?"

The professor nodded. "Obviously, we have no real evidence. But it could explain your great-grandmother's desperation to protect her child."

Laurel stood up abruptly. Her breaths grew shallow and fast. Her enslaved ancestors' struggles affected her deeply—doubtless this new layer of suffering intensified her grief.

"I could be wrong," Astrid said.

Jeff shook his head. "You could be right, too."

"Oh, shit, shit, shit!" Laurel paced back and forth a few times, then dropped heavily back onto her chair.

Astrid leaned forward. "Look. Here's what you need to do. I'm betting Hattie Bennett got married after she arrived in Canada. Have you tried to find any marriage certificates or the like for her?"

Laurel admitted they hadn't. Why hadn't they? Now Jeff was glad they'd shared that disturbing video snippet.

"That should be your next step," Astrid advised. "Perhaps her name changed, and you're just not looking in the right places. She was 'Hattie Bennett' in the United States, but maybe she got a new last name in Canada."

Laurel's expression brightened. "Actually, that's a good idea. We've just been digging around in newspapers and census records. Searching for a marriage certificate might help us really get somewhere."

Astrid looked them both in the eye. "I'll tell you what. You two start searching for any evidence that Hattie Bennett got married in Canada. Meanwhile, I have some contacts at the textile museum up there in the Mississippi Valley. I'll write a few emails, explain the research you're doing, and see if anyone is willing to contribute. I'm certain there'll be a few experts who are eager to help. In Canada, there's great interest in documenting the fate of the Underground Railroad immigrants. Does that sound good?"

Laurel agreed. "It does." Her calm was restored—a source of relief.

"We can start searching ancestry sites this evening," Jeff proposed. His optimism that they would succeed in uncovering the outcome of Hattie Bennett's traumatic journey was well on its way to being restored.

Astrid clapped her hands together. "Great! So Laurel, I kind of hate to put you through this. But today, I thought you two should get a feel for spinning linen and cotton. Wool would generally have been processed for local, everyday use in Hattie's day, while cotton of course was a cash crop. But if we really want to get a picture of your great-grandmother's life, we have to confront the work she was forced to do to make money for the plantation."

Laurel heaved a sigh, then nodded her agreement. "Let's do this."

It was a matter of days before they tracked down a marriage certificate for Hattie Bennett. She'd wedded another fugitive from American slavery, Charles Williams, in Lanark County, Ontario, in 1859. On the heels of this discovery, the dominoes quickly fell.

Later that week, the two of them were immersed in study over their separate laptops. Teddy slept peacefully on the kitchen table where they worked, while Pearl and Olive were sprawled across the floor, Olive treating Pearl like her own personal cat bed. The dark evening outside made the lamp overhead seem bright.

Laurel gave a start and gasped out loud.

Jeff drilled her with his gaze. "What is it?"

"You won't believe this. I found her."

"Her?"

"Her daughter. The one she rescued in St. Paul."

Jeff inhaled abruptly. He looked over at Laurel's computer screen. There it was, in the form of another marriage certificate: *Tabitha Williams*, born in Virginia in 1849, a textile worker in Almonte, Ontario, married Henry Staunton of Lanark County in 1871. Her parents were Hattie Willams née Bennett and Charles Williams, who'd both been born into slavery in the United States and found freedom in Ontario.

Jeff read the document again, assimilating every detail: the years, the names, the occupations, the place. "This is incredible. How are you feeling?" He smiled into Laurel's face.

She released a long, slow breath. "Fantastic. She actually did it! She rescued her daughter by bringing her up North!"

Jeff's smile persisted. "You can relate?"

Laurel nodded deliberately. "I can."

He reached his arms around her. "Congratulations."

She returned his embrace. "I couldn't have done any of this without you. Thank you, Jeff."

"My pleasure."

Their search soon turned up additional family members: two children born to Hattie and Charles, including a son, Joshua, who'd ultimately moved to Winnipeg, that Canadian "Gateway to the West," and established himself there as a rail worker.

The real gold they struck came with the discovery of records from the Black press in Canada. Hattie Bennett Williams had been interviewed for a story in an African-Canadian journal, and Jeff and Laurel succeeded in tracking down her published account. Not only did the memoir confirm everything they'd learned about her life thus far, it added details of enormous consequence for understanding the role played by spinning and knitting in her journey from bondage to freedom.

The discovery was a boon to their preparations for reenacting that journey. The couple consulted with various experts at the sites and museums where traces of Hattie Bennett's odyssey were still to be found, to determine the route their video exploration would follow. Having already visited St. Paul, they decided to focus their efforts on Dinwiddie County in Virginia, and Ontario's Mississippi Valley. The plan was to film any and all revealing places and artifacts, aided by generous experts who were eager to support them in filming this record of Laurel's four-times great-grandmother's eventful life. And they would emulate Hattie's skills as a spinner and knitter all along the way.

19

The Journey

IT WAS A SUNNY morning on a Saturday in March when Astrid knocked on Tabitha's front door. Her two hand-spinning students had returned safe and sound from their trek to Virginia and Canada. To her relief, they'd successfully finished their film project in time for the deadline in Jeff's Black Women's History course. Astrid had considered taking in the video before coming to view it with Laurel's mother, but ultimately decided their watch party would be more fun if she shared in Tabitha's surprise. She'd even brought a treat along. What Astrid didn't know was that even *she* was in for a surprise.

As Tabitha welcomed her inside, Astrid took note of the night and day difference between the state of the Howell home before their cleanup, and its current state. "The house looks beautiful!"

"I've even made some additional improvements," Tabitha revealed. She led Astrid past the living room and into the kitchen to show off her handiwork.

After the sorry sight this room had presented a few weeks ago, it was now fit for featuring in *House Beautiful* magazine. Astrid couldn't stop smiling as she looked around and saw everything in its proper place. The countertop was fully accessible, the stove was available for cooking on, and the kitchen table stood ready to welcome partakers of an enjoyable meal. "This is wonderful. Well done!"

Tabitha pointed out the freshly-painted walls. "Do you like the color?"

Astrid admired the pale orange coating that cast the entire room in its glow. "It looks just like orange sherbet. Absolutely gorgeous. Jerome would be amazed."

"You think so?"

"I really do."

"More importantly, how will Laurel feel about it?"

Astrid thought for a second. "I'm sure she'll love it." She handed her friend a small grocery bag. "I brought a little something. I hope popcorn isn't inappropriate."

Tabitha scoffed. "Popcorn? I haven't had popcorn in ages." But as she took the bag, a laugh escaped her. "I'm not sure it's entirely fitting to the occasion, but what the heck? I could do with a snack."

They quickly microwaved the treat, dumped the buttery-smelling puffs into a bowl, and returned to the living room, where they would take in Jeff and Laurel's YouTube video on the big-screen TV.

Astrid sat down in one of the leather recliners and helped herself to a handful of popcorn. She didn't go to a lot of movies, so the prospect of watching her spinning students' half-hour film seemed like a special occasion she should enjoy to the max. "Are you ready for this?"

Tabitha took a breath. "I think so." She settled into her recliner, filled her bowl with popcorn, grabbed the remote, and went to the YouTube app. "What exactly are we looking for?"

By now, Astrid was familiar with Jeff's channel. "It's called 'Knitmann's Extreme Knitting.' The video should show up at the top of the list."

It cost Tabitha a minute or two, but she succeeded in finding what they were after. "I admit, I'm a little nervous."

"Really? Why?"

Tabitha shrugged her shoulders. "Well, I have to assign Jeff a grade for his work. So it'd better be good."

"Has he ever let you down before?"

"Come to think of it, he's one of my top students."

"See? And we both know how smart Laurel is."

That prompted a smile. "Yes, she is."

"I don't know everything about what they're sharing here. But I do know that much of what Laurel learned about the woman they've been researching helped her gain a genuine appreciation for you as her mother."

Tabitha wrinkled her brow. "How so?"

"Her ancestors are your ancestors."

"My—? I'm confused, Astrid. This project isn't just about some random historical figure?"

Astrid shook her head. "Not at all."

Tabitha stared at her. "You helped them with all this research?"

"I did. But they did all the heavy lifting. I just helped them ask the right questions."

"Huh. I'm beginning to think you know more about my own family history than I do."

Astrid flashed a sly smile. "If we watch their video, we can change that."

"All right. Well, here goes." Tabitha clicked the remote.

The video's title: "Spinning Her Own Agency," appeared over a photo of an enslaved woman standing behind a spinning wheel. Astrid recognized the strains of an African-American work song. Then the film opened at that historic plantation they'd discussed multiple times, where Jeff and Laurel stood, holding a handful each of wool which they spun using the drop spindles she'd provided them with, in front of a rustic slave dwelling. An unkempt lawn backed by greening trees surrounded them beneath the wan sun.

Tabitha pointed at the screen. "That's the sweater he was making! The purple one!"

Astrid zeroed in on Laurel, who was in fact wearing the colorwork sweater Jeff had been knitting on at the recent meetings of the Flatlands Fiber Guild. "So it is! Laurel looks beautiful in it."

"He certainly is a talented knitter."

Welcome, fiber lovers! Jeff began his narration as he worked his spindle.

Laurel took over. *We're here in Dinwiddie County, Virginia, to share with you the journey of Hattie Bennett, my four-times great-grandmother, whose unique abilities as a spinner and knitter of wool allowed her to escape enslavement in the United States and find freedom in Ontario, Canada.*

Tabitha turned toward Astrid abruptly. "Is that true?"

"That's what their research revealed, yes."

"Huh." Tabitha looked back at the screen with furrowed brow.

The presenters then introduced a third person, an expert they'd connected with on the history of slavery in Virginia, who taught and researched in Charlottesville.

"Who's filming them?" Tabitha asked as she munched on some popcorn.

"A teaching assistant from the University of Virginia. The funding they received from GPU gave them access to a number of useful resources for pulling the project together."

"Impressive. And they learned how to spin like that from you?"

Astrid smiled. Her students were doing her proud. "They did."

"I have to say, they certainly get an A for effort. They drove out all that way? By themselves?"

Astrid nodded. "The university is paying their mileage."

"Wow."

The camera followed as the researchers took their viewers inside the slave quarters. The building was rustic to a fault. The brick walls lacked windows, and the floor was of rough-hewn stone. The students revealed what details they knew regarding the work typically performed by the inhabitants, as well as forms of resistance they'd employed to minimize the theft of their labor, building ably on the discussions they'd had together in Astrid's art studio.

Hattie Bennett shared her life story with an African-Canadian newspaper in Ontario, Jeff reported. We learn from her account that her first attempt to flee this plantation ended in failure. She was captured and returned, and it was several years before she attempted to escape again.

Laurel took over as Jeff continued spinning. *In the meantime, the teenage girl gave birth to a daughter.* She shared how Bennett had learned not only how to spin well beneath her abilities to avoid having to work any harder for her enslavers than necessary, but had also found ways to spin on the sly using her drop spindle, a skill she'd mastered to a high level.

As they explored the areas of the plantation where Hattie and her fellow enslaved had labored, their expert informant celebrated the laborers' efforts to undertake small acts of resistance, allowing them to exercise their agency in the face of severe limitations. While their lives had been extremely hard, things would have been even harder, had they not managed to foil their masters' efforts to dismantle their authority over their own daily existence, a point Laurel made clear as she drafted more and more wool onto her spindle.

The pair closed the Virginia portion of their video with footage from their tour of St. Paul, where Bennett and her daughter had gone into hiding. The information they presented from Bennett's own oral history as recorded in the 1873 news article surprised even Astrid.

My four-times great-grandmother gave birth to two children before fleeing along the Underground Railroad, Laurel reported as the film showed St. Paul's Mississippi riverfront: *Elijah, whom she tragically had to leave behind, and Tabitha. She found a way to spin and stash wool in secret, on top of all the labor demanded of her by her enslavers. When she ran away for the second time, now with her young daughter in tow, she was determined that nothing should go wrong. She records that the man who regarded himself as her "master" had been molesting her child, and that was all the motivation she needed to get the girl out of there and flee up North.*

"Nothing too shocking there," Tabitha remarked with a scowl.

Astrid sized up her expression. She wondered how Tabitha's understanding of this traumatic history differed from Laurel's own assessment. She was glad Laurel had taken it upon herself to pry into her ancestors' lives in a way her history professor mother had not yet managed.

Laurel explained how Bennett had taken advantage of having to travel with young Tabitha up the Mississippi to St. Paul, where their enslavers had vacationed in the cool Minnesota summers. Then Jeff took over: *Bennett used the yarn she'd spun in secret to knit a sling with. The sling allowed her to strap her little girl to her body beneath her clothes. She disguised herself with her child bound against her as a portly Black man, instead of the slender mother and child her enslavers were frantically searching for at Taylor's barbershop on Third Street. In her account, Hattie recalls vividly how she often had to tell Tabitha to hush and be quiet, so they wouldn't be discovered.*

Astrid recalled her students' eerie video of the haunting in St. Paul. She looked over and found Tabitha in tears as they heard these unsettling details from her ancestor's life. It was obvious she had no knowledge of this distant namesake from her own familial past. Laurel and Jeff had gone to extraordinary lengths to uncover the story of this other Tabitha Bennett from a century and a half ago. "What are you thinking?"

Tabitha wiped a few tears from her cheek. "It's overwhelming!"

"It kind of is, isn't it?"

"I had no idea Laurel was so interested in our family history. She's dug up details even I never knew about. It's extraordinary!"

The two spinners paused to share their progress. Astrid smiled as she noted that nothing had changed in the competition raging between them to see who could spin the most wool. Against the backdrop of the primitive Virginia slave house, they produced a digital scale and weighed their output.

One point two ounces for me, Laurel bragged. *How about you, Knitmann?*

With a look of good-natured disappointment, Jeff said: *Only three quarters of an ounce.*

Laurel egged him on. *Gotta do better than that, chump. Next stop, Ontario!*

In an instant that utterly obscured the videographers' twelve-hour drive from Dinwiddie, Virginia, to Almonte, Ontario, the filming shifted to the exterior of a historic woolen mill that now housed the Canadian museum Astrid had connected them with. Here Laurel and Jeff stood bundled against the cold, accompanied by a curator with expertise in the history of the Mississippi Valley textile industry and the Underground Railroad immigrants who'd found refuge in the region. The trio shared lore regarding the growth of the woolen mills along Ontario's Mississippi River, and details they'd learned about Hattie Bennett's life in Canada.

My four-times great-grandmother found work as a spinner in a local woolen mill, Laurel reported, *and married another fugitive from slavery here named Charles Williams, a weaver in the same mill.* A yellowed photo of the Williams couple posing in what was likely a photographer's studio showed up on the screen. *Along with Hattie's daughter, Tabitha, they had two other children we know of.*

Jeff added details regarding what they'd learned about Hattie Bennett Williams' progeny as they entered the textile museum, the two of them still pursuing their dogged efforts to hand-spin wool along the way. Astrid shook her head in awe. She'd knit her way through many a department meeting over the years, but this was multitasking at its best.

The young scholars explored relevant exhibits in the vintage space, particularly as related to the technology Hattie and Charles had mastered in carrying out the work they'd performed so they could feed their family. They informed their viewers about the spinning jenny Hattie would most likely have spun on, as well as the looms operated by Charles, and even showed off an industrial carding machine.

The couple's daughter, Tabitha Williams, married a local man named Henry Staunton in 1871, Jeff reported next. They moved into a house just east of here, which has since been torn down. Another historic photo showed the Staunton couple in front of their 1870s home.

As the researchers wrapped up their tour of the textile museum, Laurel suddenly announced they would reveal the identity of their cameraperson, who also worked as a historian where they were filming. Jeff took over the camera and aimed it toward the young woman, and Astrid sat bolt upright: she bore uncanny resemblance to Laurel.

My name is Annie Staunton, the museum worker shared. She traded notes with Laurel on how much they resembled each other. It turned out they were distant cousins who shared one and the same four-times great-grandmother, Hattie Bennett Williams.

Astrid raised her hand to her mouth. She had not been expecting this.

"Oh good word!" Tabitha exclaimed. "This is all so incredible!"

"It's certainly news to me. It's astonishing how they took off with their research once they found Hattie Bennett's marriage certificate."

"How in God's name did they come up with that?"

"Canadian ancestry sites, I think. Laurel clearly inherited your research skills, *Professor Howell*." Astrid managed to laugh.

The smile illuminating Tabitha's face was infused with pride. "I guess she did at that."

Laurel then prompted her distant cousin to do the honors and weigh their spindles so they could determine who'd spun the most yarn. Of course, it was Laurel. *Sorry, Jeff, beat you again. Seems like I'm a natural!* She beamed into the camera, conveying her pride in her ability to emulate her ancestor as a proficient spinner of wool, whose skills had rescued both herself and her daughter and secured their freedom in the northern refuge of Ontario.

As Jeff returned the camera to Annie, Laurel wrapped things up. *Well, fiber lovers, that concludes—*

Wait, just a moment, Annie said suddenly.

Tabitha wrinkled her brow. "There's more?"

Astrid shrugged. "Not that I know of." She watched intently, wondering what could possibly happen next.

Annie trained the camera on Jeff, who began to take off his sweater. Astrid asked herself if she'd seen him wear this one before, and concluded she had not. The striped pullover must be a freshly-finished project.

Jeff talked into the camera as he fidgeted with his sweater. *I've learned a lot from Hattie Bennett Williams over the course of our research project, and I've knit up a garment of my own with inspiration from her.* He flipped the sweater inside out and revealed a hidden pocket he'd knit inside. *I added this secret compartment, and I also knit a little pouch with fingering weight yarn. I had to do it on the sly, just like Hattie, because it's frankly a surprise.* He removed a purple sack that was smaller than a pin cushion from the inner pocket. *This is for you, Laurel.*

Laurel arched her brow as she took the pouch from him. *What's this?*

Jeff got down on one knee. Astrid gasped out loud, while Tabitha sat up in her recliner. *Open it,* he said.

Laurel's expression in the film resembled her mother's as she sat beside Astrid to a tee. *I should open it?*

Jeff nodded. *Yes.*

The camera zeroed in on the pouch as Laurel pulled the miniature drawstring open. She withdrew a ring. The band was a luminescent shade of purple, and it was crowned with a gem that had to be amethyst. Her hands were shaking.

Laurel Howell, will you marry me?

The camera panned out and the two of them were both in the frame. Laurel raised her hands to her face and squirmed. *Really?*

Yes. Jeff's chin trembled as he knelt on the wooden floor. *I want to be your husband.*

Astrid looked at Tabitha to see if her reaction was as emotional as her own. Tears were welling in her eyes.

Laurel exclaimed over and over again that, yes, she would marry him. A *hundred times yes!*

Astrid thought back to that first fraught meeting in her office with Jeff, when he'd revealed he'd fallen in love with Tabitha's estranged daughter. It would never have occurred to her that this would be the outcome of their raw and impetuous relationship. Something told her their ancestors' spirits had guided them on this improbable journey, and she beamed.

Jeff placed the purple ring on Laurel's finger. *Yay, it fits!* He flashed a smile of relief into the camera. He got up and wrapped his arms around his fiancée. They began to kiss, and the image faded, evolving into a photo of their drop spindles filled with the yarn they'd spun during their trek.

"You didn't know about this?" Tabitha piped up. Tears fell down her cheeks.

"No! I'm just as shocked as you are!"

They sat there in silence. Tabitha turned off the TV, almost spilling her popcorn.

Astrid summed up her reaction to what they'd just witnessed. "Wow!"

Tabitha released a long, slow breath. "Well, Jeff is a very nice boy. Did you know he taught that girl how to knit?"

"Actually, she did share that. She knit one of the sleeves on the sweater he gave her."

"Seriously?"

"She really did."

"Well I never."

"Congratulations, Tabitha. I couldn't be happier for you."

"Thank you. And thank you for helping them put all this together, Astrid. It means a great deal to me."

"My pleasure."

They sat there a little longer, indulging in more pop-corn.

Then Tabitha looked over at her. "I think Jeff has earned an A for his project."

Astrid laughed. "I think so, too."

Tabitha was determined to visit with Laurel over her research. Astrid suggested she should invite the couple for dinner in her once again presentable home. That was bound to go over well after their grueling spring break trip to Virginia, Canada, and back.

Laurel and Jeff welcomed Tabitha's invitation. When they arrived on Sunday afternoon, Astrid was there to help usher them into the house as the scent of made-from-scratch lasagna issued from the oven. A round of hugs ensued, accompanied by heartfelt expressions of congratulations and praise. Tabitha was still amazed when she considered the magnitude of her daughter's ancestry research, and Jeff's determination to help her realize her information-gathering goals. It was hard to imagine a more suitable partner for Laurel.

As the young people entered the living room, Laurel looked around with a crooked smile. She'd paid this place an occasional visit as Tabitha had let it go downhill, and must have been mortified to see the state it had fallen into. Now, it looked much like it had when they'd first moved in: neat, grand, and inviting.

Laurel met Tabitha's gaze. "Impressive. Nice work, Mom. It looks really good in here!"

"I honestly couldn't have done it without the help of Astrid and her family. I promise, I'll never let things go again like I did."

Laurel rewarded her with a kiss on the cheek. "I'm proud of you."

"So that's the sweater Jeff knit for you?" Tabitha ran her hand over the lush purple garment, with its yoke adorned by kittens and puppies.

"It is. He made it for my birthday."

"And you knit one of the sleeves?"

Laurel nodded. "How did you know?"

"Astrid told me."

"Oh." Laurel flashed a smile at her spinning instructor. "Try to guess which sleeve." She held out her arms.

Tabitha studied the evenly-stitched fabric covering each arm and smiled. "I don't see any difference. Remarkable! You're clearly a very good knitter, Laurel. And Jeff, I recognize your sweater from the video as well." She admired the striped crewneck knit in a neat stockinette stitch.

Jeff turned beet red as he glanced down at his pullover. "Do you like it?"

"Very much. But how in heaven's name did you manage to knit that without anyone knowing?"

He released a chuckle. "I'll admit it wasn't easy. But I figured if Hattie Bennett could spin on the sly, then I could knit on the sly. I just tried to channel her energy."

"I still can't figure it out," Laurel admitted. "It's like he's got some kind of magic."

Jeff just stood and smiled. It seemed he wasn't about to explain how he'd managed to knit an entire sweater in a couple weeks' time without anyone noticing, just so he could surprise Laurel while they were filming their research project.

Astrid emulated his smile. "That he does. But Laurel, I have *got* to see that ring he gave you."

Laurel held out her hand. "Have a look."

Tabitha looked on as Astrid inspected the stone. "Jeff, where on earth did you come up with such a gorgeous purple ring?"

"My dad helped with that. I'd called him for some advice, 'cause you know, things with Laurel and me were moving pretty fast. But he was totally supportive, and he put me in touch with a jeweler who could do something special for us. The band is heat-treated titanium."

"Absolutely gorgeous. It looks stunning on you, Laurel."

Laurel greeted Astrid's compliment with a sunny smile.

Tabitha invited them to sit in the dining room over beverages as they completed preparations for their meal. Astrid told her to relax and continue their exchange, offering to get everything on the table herself—she refused to take no for an answer. So Tabitha did as she said, grateful for such a good friend, and asked Laurel all about her exploration of the people who'd come before them.

Laurel was like a fountain of knowledge. Astrid was right, her research skills were second to none. And she was so excited to know what she did about the accomplishments of all the Howells, Bennetts, Moores, Duvals, and others whose bloodlines she shared. She vowed to continue following the paths down which her findings were guiding her toward additional relations, present as well as past.

Having gotten to know a few distant cousins in Canada, Laurel suggested a trip to Ontario might make for a nice summer vacation.

Tabitha agreed. "I should have known we had relations up there. That's a very good idea."

"And I want you to know, Mom, it never dawned on me before how all those shawls you knit connect you with our heritage. Since I discovered Hattie Bennett, I feel like I really understand now why knitting is so important to you. And to Jeff, too—its a part of your history, your past, who you are. And it turns out, it's a part of who I am, too."

Tabitha reached for her hand. "I'm so glad you found that out. And say, if you brought along something to work on, we can knit together after dinner."

Laurel greeted that with a smile. "We did, and I'd like that."

The four of them savored their meal around the dining room table, its surface adorned by an embroidered table-cloth made by Tabitha's mother, along with china dishes inherited on the Howell side of the family. The lasagna proved a delicious complement to their conversation, as did the Caesar salad and bold red wine.

Afterwards, the foursome ensconced themselves in Tabitha's study, home to her library of books on Black studies, as well as her extravagant yarn stash, and settled down for a rewarding gathering of knitting and conversation. As they looped their soft woolen yarns stitch by stitch over their needles in shared rhythm, the ancestral spirit of Hattie Bennett Williams lingered among them, her life and those of the others who'd come before them manifested in the work of their hands.

20

The Fête

THE APRIL MEETING OF the Flatlands Fiber Guild took place amid melting snow from a recent storm, the sun shining brilliantly overhead as it heralded the inevitable arrival of spring. Jeff climbed out of his truck and went around to help his fiancée. His pulse raced as he contemplated his first time being accompanied by his partner at a guild meeting. He'd first descended on the group to combat his lonely ways. And now his lone wolf existence was over. "Let me help you with your spinning wheel."

Laurel smiled. "Knock yourself out. Do I have to pay dues or something to join the guild?"

"Twenty bucks. A bargain."

Laurel reached into her jeans pocket. "It's a good thing I have a little cash on hand."

Jeff chuckled. He lifted her spinning wheel from the back seat and they made their way into Dee's Yarn & Fiber Emporium.

As Jeff opened the door and prompted Laurel to go inside, they were greeted by the sound of applause.

Laurel walked past the cubbies and baskets overflowing with yarn, then turned to look back at Jeff. "What's going on?"

He shook his head. "No clue."

Then he heard Brenda Wurth's voice. "Congratulations!"

And Valerie explained: "We're celebrating your engagement."

"You are?"

Laurel's smile was huge.

Jeff found Astrid Karlsen. "Set your things down and help yourselves to some cake, you two." She directed their gaze to a mouthwatering confection. It was topped with sliced almonds and sprinkled with sugar.

Jeff took in the warm smiles of the guild members as he set Laurel's spinning wheel down. "Wow. This is crazy! Thanks, everyone!" They put their project bags on the table near Laurel's mother, then followed the women's invitation to be the first to cut into the beautiful cake and help themselves to punch.

The celebration got into gear as everyone armed themselves with cake, fruit salad, fragrant tea, and sparkling beverages. The conversation bubbled along with their drinks as the crafters got out their projects and spun their yarns, both real and figurative. Dannie Novak had started knitting a summer top of fine turquoise cotton, while Fran Zumbaum continued spinning a luxurious alpaca blend. Astrid was stitching up yet another self-striping sock, and Tabitha was working the lace on a new shawl in soft green bamboo, while Jeff cast on a sweater for Laurel's eternally happy dog, Pearl.

They were just about to embark on their round of show-and-tell, when the bell signaled another arrival. A young man peered into the shop, armed with a drop spindle and a small bag of fiber. He approached the circle of spinners, knitters, and revelers with tentative steps.

After a few awkward moments, Astrid invited him to join them.

The young man heeded her invitation with a nod. "*Bonjour. Euh*, I may sit here too?" His powerful French accent raised more than a few eyebrows.

"*Bien sûr*," Astrid replied in flawless French. "*Asseyez-vous ici*." She found a chair for the newcomer as Fran scooched over to make room.

The youth sat down across from Jeff and glanced at him. Imagine that, another male joining this matronly circle of fiber crafters. Jeff smiled at him. Then the guest opened his careworn canvas bag, withdrew a handful of gray carded wool, and began working his spindle as though it were an everyday affair.

"Welcome," Fran told him.

"We're glad you came," Brenda said with a smile.

Within moments, the guild returned to the comforting rhythm of their spinning, knitting, and chatting, surrounding the newcomer in the warmth of their welcome.

Acknowledgments

Many people have provided encouragement and support for the writing of this book. Thanks to my sister, Nancy Ballew, my first beta reader who provided excellent feedback along the way. Thanks also to Sydney Law Gillespie, whose perspective as a Black woman was invaluable in ensuring I wrote Laurel's story well. Culver Lewis listened to every chapter of the finished novel and helped me with important details. Deryn Lewis has been a steady source of inspiration and information in my quest to portray the lives of twenty-somethings without betraying my age.

I'm deeply grateful to the members of the Minneapolis Writers' Workshop, who helped me up my fiction-writing game, especially Mary Boyd, whose detailed feedback was extremely useful. Thanks as well to Angie Cleberg, who gave the novel one last read and assisted me with final tweaks.

Rhonda May provided the cover art. Her vision expresses the protagonists' journey incredibly well. Thanks to all of my beta readers and writing group friends, for your encouragement and endorsement of *The Ancestor's message*.

I owe a great deal to the students I've taught over the decades, and the professors I've interacted with during my academic career. Their stories have informed the stories of the students and professors throughout the *Romance at the Fiber Guild* series.

The same goes for the many pets who have embellished my life. The cats and dogs who have shared my home have made my life better, and I've tried to portray that same advantage persuasively in my novels.

I wouldn't be where I am today without my fabulous family. Thank you from the bottom of my heart.

And thank you, readers, for spending some of your valuable time with the members of the Flatlands Fiber Guild. You're welcome to join us anytime!

About the author

Virginia L. Lewis is a literary scholar, translator, and retired German professor, who has been writing fiction for more than thirty years. A needlepointer for all her adult life, Lewis discovered the wonders of knitting when her son learned the craft in his high school fashion class. She has since taken up spinning as well. Lewis lives in South Dakota with her six cats and three dogs and is the mother of three adult children who teach her new lessons about life and its rewards with each passing day.

www.ingramcontent.com/pod-product-compliance
Lightning Source LLC
Chambersburg PA
CBHW031250120726
47906CB00003B/670